D1529034

VEILED INNOCENCE

ELLA FRANK

ELLA FRANK, LLC

Copyright © 2014 by Ella Frank

Edited by Candace Wood

No part of this book may be reproduced or transmitted in any form or by any means, electronic or mechanical, including photocopying, recording, or by any information storage and retrieval system without the written permission of the author, except for the use of brief quotations in a book review.

This book is a work of fiction. Names, characters, places, and incidents either are products of the author's imagination or are used fictitiously. Any resemblance to actual persons, living or dead, events, or locales is entirely coincidental.

Dedication

Veiled Innocence is dedicated to someone who is brutally honest, hard-working, and dedicated to the craft of writing. She constantly reminds me of why I love to do what I do, and this book would not have seen the light of day without her.

Candace Wood, you're irreplaceable.

Thank you from the bottom of my heart.

Xx Ella

There is always some madness in love. But there is also always some reason in madness.

- Friedrich Nietzsche

You are free to choose, but you are not free from the consequence of your choice.

- Anonymous

The heart wants what it wants—age be damned.
I love you, Francesco.

- Ella Frank

PROLOGUE

Drifting out into the field, a sense of familiarity hits me. Every time, the dream is the same. It never changes, never deviates. Not even once—ever.

Clasping Daniel's small hand in my own, I cautiously regard the path we will take, knowing this is the only way. Ahead of us, as far as the eye can see, are miles and miles of fields, blanketed in flowers of the deepest blues and purples.

The colors, vibrant and loud, call to me, beckoning me closer—though I know what fate they hold, I cannot change our course. We are bound to this path, as I am forever trapped by my decision that led us here.

Squeezing his warm fingers in my palm, I manage a small smile at the trusting face turned up to me.

I know this dream. I don't want to be here.

Turning my back on such trust, I desperately seek a way out—a way to escape the world I have been sucked back into, but I know it's no use.

"You're late again, Addy."

His voice is exactly as I remember—cheerful, sweet, and a little high-pitched. Looking down, I find the same blue eyes I possess peering back at me.

"Dad's gonna be so mad at you."

"Shh, we won't be late," I promise, pulling Daniel's arm up so I can see his watch. As always, it has stopped at 3:17 p.m. "Damn it."

"Oooo, you cussed."

"Daniel…" I warn, knowing we have no time.

I can hear it as it's chasing me.

Tick, tick, tock.

The watch I was given for my fifteenth birthday methodically keeps time as the second hand ticks around the face.

Tick, tick, tock.

I hear it. I memorize it.

"Come on. If we hurry we'll make it. We still have time."

As I step forward, a breeze brushes my cheek, making the hair on my arms rise as though someone has stepped on my grave.

"No, Addy," he tells me and tugs his hand from mine. "Time's up."

It only takes a second for our connection to be severed. I turn to him, and I know he's right. His time has stopped. It's not my grave that has been stepped on.

Before I can reach him, the flowers around us wilt, shriveling into the ground, and as he disappears with them, everything before me fades to black.

All I'm left with is darkness, a car horn's insistent blast, the counting of the crosswalk—and the ticking of a clock…

Present…

Tick, tick, tock. Tick, tick…

"Addison?"

Tock.

Pulled from one nightmare and thrust firmly into another, I try to focus on the man sitting across from me in the stark temporary office.

Jesus, I know these sessions are tedious, but this is the first time I've fallen asleep. I've known Doc ever since Daniel—well, for three years, and now he's been brought here. To help me, save me—heal me.

Tick, tick, tock.

"Addison? I'm going to ask you again."

He's concerned. They're all concerned by what happened, but it's too late.

Tick, tick…

"Remember, anything you say in here, stays right here."

Tock.

They think that I'm sick, that I'm…damaged.

"When did you last see Mr. McKendrick?"

I tell him nothing. I never will. Not about this.

"It's okay to talk about it, Addison. No one is here to judge."

That's not true.

Ever since I was admitted, Doc's changed. He doesn't see me like he used to. So he would probably be surprised to know that I'm judging him.

"We just need to know. Where did you last see Mr. McKendrick?"

Tick, tick—"You don't have anything to be ashamed of"—*fuck!*

I hate interruptions. He knows that. Plus, I wouldn't be sitting here if he didn't think I should be ashamed.

"Okay, Addison."

I wish he'd stop saying my name like that. It reminds me of…

"We'll try this again tomorrow."

And we will. *That* he's not lying about. But I no longer care. What do I have left? Nothing.

He's gone. I'm alone, and all I can hear is…*tick, tick…*

CHAPTER 1

 ast...

Tock.

I looked at the watch strapped to my wrist before turning my head to Brandon.

"Hurry," I urged as he pulled me down hard on his lap. With a groan, I craned my neck back, gasping into the tight interior of my car.

"What the hell, Addy? I just got inside you."

Straddling his legs, I ceased grinding against him.

"Well if you hadn't been late—" I started, but he cut me off by sitting up in the passenger seat and connecting his mouth to mine.

"Quit bitching, would you?"

I pulled my head back, twisting my fingers tightly through his brown hair.

"Fuck! That hurts."

"You know how I am about this kind of stuff," I reminded him.

"It's the first day back. No one's gonna care if you're five minutes late."

"*I'll* care. I hate being late."

With a rough flex of his hips, he shoved himself deeper inside me.

I guess he was right…I was *poor little Addy, after all*. Plus, I hadn't had sex in months since my mother had planned my entire summer vacation down to the very last detail.

Brandon grunted as he moved once again, and I glanced at my watch, nasty habit that—*Tick, tick, tock.*

I was late…*great*, as if I wasn't anxious enough. This was just what I needed on the first day of my senior year. Then again, it wasn't like any of my teachers would mention it. They wouldn't dare.

Inspecting myself in the restroom mirror, I was careful to make sure that my lip-gloss was perfect. My hair fell in soft waves I had painstakingly curled that morning, and after my earlier activities with Brandon, my clothes were all back where they should be.

Raising my chin, I studied my reflection.

Narrowing my gaze, I pouted my lips. Doc was always spouting something or other about inner beauty being impor-tant, but I'd once heard a quote from Marilyn Monroe that said, *Boys think girls are like books. If the cover doesn't catch their eye, they won't bother to read what's inside.* In my opinion, she had a much more accurate take on these kinds of things. So, as usual, I was careful to make sure that this cover was extra eye-catching.

I peeked at my timekeeper faithfully guarding me and followed the second hand as it made its rounds. I wished it would hurry up and get to the twelve, because then I'd feel right about leaving. Instead, I was held in place in front of the mirror —by invisible chains.

Tick, tick, tock.

First day on the job, and already I wanted out.

I scrawled my name across the chalkboard like the responsible teacher I was expected to be. Unfortunately, the smell of the chalk and the scrape of it along the board did nothing to make me feel responsible; it just made me want to leave.

The clock hanging on the wall of my world history classroom was driving me crazy. I hadn't been any place recently where I needed a clock or a watch, and the reminder that I was back on somebody else's schedule was irritating as hell.

I'd just returned from a six-month trip traveling throughout Europe where I'd gotten to visit some of my favorite historical sites, so to be restricted to four walls and a door made me… antsy. The tie I wore felt as though it was about to choke the life from me, and right then, I would have welcomed it.

Not coming home hadn't been an option. The minute I'd been told about my father's deteriorating health, I knew I had to go to him. So thirteen hours and fifty minutes later, I was back in Denver, Colorado—that was a little over a month ago.

The door to my right crashed open, alleviating the suffocating stillness of the classroom, and the first student stepped into the empty space.

Boy, girl. Boy, boy, girl.

One after another they trickled in, and as the seats filled, I remained in the far corner, leaning up against the bookcase.

I always did this whenever I started a new class, especially at a new school. I observed. It was interesting to see how the students interacted before they knew I was there. *Before* they put on a good show and behaved as they were expected to.

Talking, giggling, and flirting, the students on the first day were always excited to see one another. It was the perfect opportunity to catch them in that snapshot of their true selves. That moment of unobserved freedom.

As everyone took their seats and the second bell peeled through the halls, I pushed away from the shelves and moved to stand in front of the old wooden desk at the front of my classroom.

One by one, heads lifted, and when they found me waiting on them, and realized I'd been standing there all along, they immediately settled. The talking subsided and slipped into whispers and then finally, *silence.*

I remained steady and still until I had every last person's attention. Then the door opened for the final time that morning and *she* stepped into my classroom. Late.

I looked at her—she looked at me.

My ending, staring right at me from the very beginning.

Hating that I was late, I rushed through the classroom door and was shocked to be faced with a man instead of Mrs. Ross.

This was a stranger. A stranger who knew nothing of Addison Lancaster, and right now he was regarding me with annoyance.

That was the moment I first saw Mr. McKendrick.

He was the teacher every girl dreamed about. The one that we all had a crush on the second we saw him. With brown hair streaked gold by the sun and pulled back into a short, messy ponytail at the nape of his neck, he was unlike any teacher I'd ever seen before—and my reaction to him was immediate and potent.

"And who might you be?"

That voice. I swear it touched me—I was that affected.

"Miss?"

Blinking once, I tried to clear my mind and realized that, for one brief moment, the ticking had stopped. My body had overpowered my mind, something that *never* happened with me.

"Miss? I'm talking to you."

Laughter erupted from the class, and suddenly it was back—*tick, tick, tock.*

The new teacher turned on my loud classmates, and as their mouths closed, the room plunged back into tense silence.

Wow, that was some kind of authority right there. One glance from him, and my unruly peers shut down...became respectful—and we weren't even ten minutes into the period.

Again, his eyes came back to mine and even as they conveyed his irritation, they also held something else. Something I instantly craved.

This cover that I had so carefully constructed had caught his eye.

Like a lion, his stare was fierce as he appraised me. All men did—they couldn't seem to help it. No matter how inappropriate they knew it was, I always drew their attention.

With my wide, bowed lips, innocent blue eyes, and a figure that belonged on a twenty-something—I knew what I had and I was never afraid to use it. Unlike most men, whose expression betrayed their unwanted interest, I pictured this one stalking me from across the room and *me* allowing it.

"Miss? I asked you a question."

I'd forgotten what he'd asked the minute I saw him. I was too busy imagining him touching me, tasting me. It took four long strides for him to be close enough that I could see the dark stubble dotting his jawline.

"You're late," he stated, his tone impenetrable as he opted for a different route. "On your first day. Not a fantastic way to start the school year, wouldn't you agree?"

Aiming a coy look at him from beneath my lashes, I finally found my voice and assured myself a firm place on his shit list.

"Maybe you could keep me after school and teach me to tell time."

What a joke that was, considering my obsession when it came to time management. Not that he knew that.

"Since it's the first day, I don't think that will be necessary. But from now on, be on time. Your name, please."

"Addison. Addison Lancaster."

"Thank you. Now go and take a seat."

Shrugging my bag farther up on my shoulder, I spun on my toes and made my way down the second aisle of desks with a little more sway to my hips than usual. Glancing at Brandon, I noticed him wink, reminding me of exactly why I'd been running late. Returning the sexy gesture, I owned the sensual smile I aimed his way as it spread across my mouth.

Flirting to me was like breathing to everyone else, and I always made sure I had their attention when I put on a show. As the school's track champion, I strived for perfection, and I liked seeing the results of my efforts. I was their role model, their person to admire—*and* to hate.

Everyone, including the teachers, knew me, and everyone loved me. Except for the man standing at the front of my world history class. He definitely did not love me, but I'd always liked a challenge. It was in my nature to win.

I took my seat and let my bag slide slowly down my shoulder and onto the floor. I crossed one leg over the other and returned my attention to my new teacher whose eyes were moving methodically over each and every one of us, before finally coming back to rest on mine.

He studied me for a moment in a way that felt calculated before moving on to Jessica, who was seated in the aisle to my right. Just like that—I was dismissed.

"My name is Mr. McKendrick. I'm going to be your world history teacher this year, *not* Mrs. Ross. I have very few rules, but one of them is to be on time," he stated in a perfunctory tone as he paced the front of the room. "The other is a little unorthodox. I want you to be curious…but respectful. Ask questions. Challenge one another. I want you looking outside the box, so to speak, because that is where you'll find some of the most fascinating discoveries."

Mr. McKendrick.

He was intriguing and *definitely* outside the box.

I was, without a doubt, fascinated.

She watched me from her seat—third row from the back, two aisles in—with eyes so blue I could see them from where I was standing. They locked on mine the second she settled, and she continued to scrutinize me.

As I stood at the front of the class introducing the course, I waited for my morals and drummed-in ethics to assert themselves. To remind me that I wasn't supposed to be affected by a student's inspection.

Thirty minutes later, and I was still waiting.

I sat at my desk and observed the students quietly working on their first assignment, but I continued to be drawn back to the young lady who had shown up late.

She was positively alluring. From her porcelain skin to the curls of chestnut hair that bounced against the curve of her high, full breasts—Addison Lancaster was more woman than girl, and she was dangerous.

The other males in the room knew it too if the way they acted around her was any indication. They seemed caught on every lick of her plump, red lips—and yes, I had caught those too.

So there I sat, trying to work out what it was that was making her impossible to ignore and then she glanced up, and I knew.

It was those eyes. They held secrets they shouldn't have.

Dark, sad, and inviting all rolled into one, and yet, she was far too young to possibly understand any of those emotions in their absolute form.

Breaking the searing connection, I focused back on my textbook, but all I continued to feel was Addison Lancaster watching me.

～

The first day of school went by faster than I expected and everything was exactly how it should be. Except for Mr. McKendrick. I had not expected him.

Lying between the white sheets of my bed, I enjoyed the coolness of them as I parted my bare thighs and slipped my fingers down between to touch.

Nighttime was *my* time, a time where I could imagine whatever I wanted, and that night, I imagined my teacher. The man who had dismissed me in the blink of an eye. The man who was making my body weep as I lay in my bed. Why I found his rejection so appealing, I was unable to pinpoint, but it was. Almost... challenging.

Biting my top lip, I slid two fingers along the edge of my panties. I wiggled them in under the pink cotton and flexed my toned thighs. As I parted my legs farther and arched my back, I pushed my body into the weight of the sheet, enjoying the feel of it over me—imagining it was him. I teased myself, flirting my fingers over my bare mound. My mouth parted, his name on my lips as my fingertips grazed my clit and then dipped below to slide inside.

I'd been doing this from an early age, learning my body and exactly the way I needed to be touched. Brandon never got it right. He was always in a rush, and it was over before it began. Didn't that apply to most boys?

But Mr. McKendrick...

I knew he'd be different.

He'd touch me the way I desired, and he'd take me the way I craved.

Not like a boy—but like a man.

CHAPTER 2

 resent...

Tick, tick, tock.

"Would you say that you consciously try to push people's boundaries, Addison?"

Tick, tick—what?

Seated again in the tiny, white office, I glance around at the bare walls, then back to the desk placed in here for my "stay" and I think—*what?*

My face must convey my thoughts because he starts over.

"Or do you think it's more"—he pauses, I'm sure for dramatic effect—"subconscious?"

He knows I'm aware that I don't have to answer, so what does he get from me? Silence. Complete and utter silence.

"Okay, let's go back to Mr. McKendrick."

Let's not, I think as I study my nails.

"You aren't in trouble."

Aren't I? Being locked away sure doesn't help his case in convincing me.

"We just need more information."

Don't we all.

Tick, tick, tock.

"Why don't you tell me a little bit about how things began?"

I feel my anger start to rise. This man knows me better than anyone but about *this*, he knows nothing.

They're all grasping. Grasping for a reason to make this *his* fault.

To somehow make him the devil and me the angel in this salacious little tale of sin.

They want to know who approached whom.

None of your fucking business, that's who.

If he thinks this is going to be easy like it use to be, he best reevaluate.

I only have me to think of now. Me in this place, with nothing but time. Time to remember or, as they are all hoping, time to forget.

Tick, tick, tock—the mouse ran up the clock.

Is my hour up yet? It has to be close.

I glance at the only thing on the wall, a wooden clock, and then turn back to Doc and lick my lips.

Do I like to push boundaries? *Yes.*

I raise my thumb and bite my nail, noticing his eyes drop to it before he shakes his head.

Do I do it consciously? *Yes. Yes, I do.*

∾

Past...

Again, she was late. This was the kind of conduct I could not tolerate. Blatant disrespect for my authority, that's what *this* was. I shut my classroom door with a firm hand and locked it.

She was going to be *that* student. The one I battled all fucking year.

Clenching my teeth, I faced my other students. There was a clear void where she'd sat yesterday and the more I fixated on the empty space, the more annoyed I became.

Everyone sat patiently, waiting to see what would happen when Addison Lancaster decided to grace us with her presence, but she remained a no-show. Knowing I couldn't let a student dictate the way I ran things, I stepped to the front of the room and rested back against the desk.

"Okay, guys. Please open your textbooks to page thirty-seven. As you know, this term we'll be learning all about the reign of King Henry the Eighth. So let's start at the beginning, shall we?"

Straightening from the desk, I slid my hands into my pockets as the kids flipped their books open.

"Did this dude really have six wives?"

I looked down at my roster to check the name of the boy talking. Brandon Williams.

"Yes, he really did, Brandon" I confirmed.

He slouched back in his chair and dropped his arm on the desk. "The dude had game."

"He was a king, you idiot," his friend ribbed. "He was rich and powerful. Women love that shit. Why do you think Addy's with you, your brain?"

"Ahh, Sam? Language, please."

"Sorry, sir," he mumbled, his cheeks turning a ruddy color as if embarrassed, but I'd already moved on and was thinking about…Addy? No, that didn't fit her at all. Not the girl who'd given me that look…that inappropriate look from the day before.

Addy was a little girl's name. It didn't fit, but *Addison?* Addison was a name that belonged to those deceptive eyes.

"It's okay, just don't do it again. So let's read chapter one, then we'll—"

That was when the banging on my classroom door began. I turned toward it and saw her through the narrow pane of glass. The room fell into complete silence as her fellow classmates waited to see what I would do. They had all sat through the same speech she'd been given, so now was the time I'd have to assert my authority over the situation. Something I really didn't want to do on the second day of the school year.

I walked over to the door and saw her looking directly at me. I should have sent her to the principal's office immediately. I *should* have left her standing out in the hall. There were a lot of things I should have done, but instead, I unlocked and opened the door.

"Sorry I'm late. I got...held up. But it was for a good reason," she tried explaining, as she stepped into the room.

Not believing her for a second, I gestured to the hall. "Outside. Now, Miss Lancaster."

I watched her closely as her expression changed, and she gave a cocky grin to the other kids. "But I really *did* get held up."

I ground my teeth in frustration. She was impertinent, she was brazen, and right now, she was pushing every single one of my buttons. Lowering my voice, I once again gestured to the hall.

"Outside. *Now.*"

With an exaggerated sigh, she stepped out into the empty hall and I followed close behind. As the door clicked shut, I noticed the way she dropped the cutesy schoolgirl act and morphed into a much more threatening creature.

I wondered at that moment what I'd done to deserve this. Surely, this was some kind of fucked-up karma because the girl in front of me had the face of a woman that would bring men to their knees.

Men just like me.

~

"I really was held—"

"Stop talking."

The smile that crept onto my lips was sly as Mr. McKendrick cut me off.

I wondered for a brief moment what he thought of the skintight jeans that clung to my hips or the black lace tank that had ridden up over my stomach. I also wore a black vinyl jacket with zippers all over it because my mother had made me.

All the better to keep my secrets covered.

"Listen to me very carefully, Addison, because I only plan to say this once."

He didn't have to worry. I was listening. So much so that I was lip reading as I memorized his mouth. The same mouth that had become a new fascination of mine.

"I will not put up with this kind of behavior from you or anyone else in my class. Do you understand?"

"You don't look like a teacher."

"Excuse me?"

He seemed bewildered, and I liked that, so I continued. "A teacher. You don't look or dress like one."

As if I hadn't spoken at all, he resumed his previous line of conversation.

"I expect you to be in my classroom early or on time. Not one minute after the bell and certainly not ten. It's not only rude, it disrupts the class that's already in session. Do I make myself clear?"

His hair wasn't tied back today but was pushed behind his ears so it hit his shoulders. Dressed in black jeans and a matching long-sleeved, button-down shirt, the picture he made was that of some kind of rocker sex god, *not* a history teacher.

"Do you like what I'm wearing?"

"Addison, stop trying so hard. No one is out here to see."

I pouted, thinking over his statement before I shrugged. I *was* trying hard—to get his attention. "You're here."

"Get inside. If you're late again, I'm not unlocking the door, and you can explain why you are standing out here to Principal Thomas."

"And what do you think he is going to do?" I asked, genuinely curious.

He really didn't know how this school ran yet, *poor delusional man*. I could clearly see just how agitated he was. It was all in his eyes. I daringly stepped closer to him.

"You don't know it yet," I said, deciding to enlighten him. "But you will soon enough. I'm his star. I *make* this school when I step out onto the track, and he won't do anything to jeopardize that."

I'd never been hunted before, usually I liked the chase, but when Mr. McKendrick leaned down and his eyes narrowed, I felt the adrenaline course through me. Instinctively, I stood my ground, all but daring him to attack.

"I don't care who you are, young lady. If you turn up late again, I *will* make sure you are held accountable. Understand? Now get inside, sit down and open your book, and try to remember that *you* are the student."

Moving around him, I caught the scent of his cologne. He smelled just the way I imagined hot sex should smell, and I knew that if I stood there long enough, my panties would do nothing to contain the wetness between my thighs. I paused just before opening the door and ran my gaze down his body a final time.

"I will, when you start to resemble a teacher. Oh, and by the way, *sir*. I like what *you're* wearing, just in case you wanted to know."

～

I silently followed Addison back into the classroom and noticed finger marks on her shoulder as her bag fell. She quickly shrugged the jacket back into place and went to take her seat. As she aimed her eyes my way, I knew I was in big fucking trouble.

The expression in them was definitely not that of a student facing her teacher.

Brandon stretched across the aisle to whisper something in her ear, and as I studied them together, her focus never wavered from me. His lips brushed so close to her hair that I caught a strand of it move with his breath, and I couldn't seem to turn away.

Imagining instead, the unthinkable—me in Brandon's place.

I tried to convince myself that my interest in her was nothing more than annoyance, but after the conversation in the hall, I had to reevaluate my own judgment.

Why was I allowing her to get under my skin? And what did she mean about me not dressing like a teacher? Maybe I needed to change something, present a different front?

Or *maybe*, I needed to stop letting her play me because that was what she was doing...or trying to do. Play me like a fucking game.

A very *dangerous* game.

Present...

Memories are the only thing keeping me sane.

It's surprising how one specific memory is what will make you fight to come out alive. It's what makes you dare to push your way through the darkness, searching for any tiny shard of light.

My darkness comes when you would expect it to...at night.

It's much more than the night closing in. It's the pill I'm given, the way my light is switched off for me and the way I'm told when to *get some rest*. They might as well say *lights out* like they do in prison because that's what this place is like.

Rest is something that eludes me because even in my

dreams, peace is nowhere to be found. It's as elusive as it has always been, except for when...*no*. It's best not to even think it.

Sitting up in bed, I wrap my arms around my knees and tap out a calming beat—*one, two, three*—as a tiny slither of light slips through the crack of my door. It's illuminating a black-and-white picture taped to the wall.

Psyche Revived by Cupid's Kiss.

I reach out and trace my finger along the woman lying back in Cupid's embrace, and I can hear and see him just as clearly as if he's in the room with me...

"Sometimes curiosity should stay just that," he advised as he pushed his chair away from the desk.

"Should it?"

Standing slowly, he made his way behind me, and my entire body shivered with anticipation.

"Yes. There's a reason Psyche was told not to open the flask."

This was wrong. He'd told me that so many times. But I wanted him, and I was going nowhere.

"And that reason was?"

"Because opening it would only bring about the most severe of consequences."

...He'd been right all along.

I lie down and stare into the darkness, searching for answers, but I have none. Our choices tore us apart, and my decision led me here.

My *own* choices and my *own* decisions, I knew that.

Why didn't anyone else?

CHAPTER 3

 ast...

When does an obsession become unhealthy?

I didn't mean to follow him home that first time, but before I knew it, I was doing it every day and had been for the last few weeks.

It was a ritual now to sit in my car at school and wait as the second hand would *tick, tick, tock* its way around to 3:00 p.m.— when he would appear.

Today, he jogged across the field holding his satchel in one hand and his jacket over his head. I'd become addicted to watching him—especially unobserved. I slumped down in my seat, careful not to be spotted, as he exited the track and walked over to his truck.

How many days will I allow myself to do this?

I knew this behavior of mine was insane, but when it came to him, rules didn't seem to apply. Ever since that first day of school, I hadn't been able to think of anything but getting close to him, and every class I sat through only intensified my determination.

I checked to see if he was backing out of the lot, but instead of his truck reversing as usual, I saw him briskly making his way toward me.

No...there was no way he could know I was there. It was raining, and raining hard. My breathing accelerated as his shadow fell across the driver's side, and when his knuckles rapped on the window, I jumped in my seat.

Caught, I'm caught.

I took a deep breath as he motioned for me to lower the rain-streaked glass. Swallowing hard, I pressed the down arrow on the door and heard the slow whir of the window motor as it slid open a crack. He bent down so he was able to peer inside the car, and I could see his lips were now shiny and wet from the rain.

"Are you having car trouble?"

I slouched back in my seat and let out a relieved sigh before I shook my head. He wasn't there to ask why I was following him. He was being what he was—a concerned teacher.

"No, sir."

I could see a frown crease his forehead, and his eyes grew suspicious. "Then why are you out here? School let out thirty minutes ago."

From the dry interior of my Honda, I could see the water hitting his long hair and sliding down the dark strands to pool on his shoulders. The windows were starting to fog up with every breath I took, and my view of him was disappearing.

I twisted in my seat and placed my hand on the glass, swiping off the condensation. When I could once again see through it, I pushed up closer and confessed.

"I was waiting."

"What?" he shouted as the rain fell harder against the car roof. "I can't hear you, Addison. Speak up."

I shifted until my lips were hovering in the open space as I repeated, louder this time, "I was waiting."

"Oh. For the rain to stop or for someone inside?"

I was mesmerized by the way the raindrops clung to his stubble-covered jaw—that was when we slipped into uncharted territory as I admitted, "I was waiting for you."

What is she talking about? I thought as the rain beat down on me and streamed inside my shirt. The water soon went unnoticed as she lowered the window farther, and her perfect face came into view.

Seeing her sitting only inches away had me consciously taking a step back from the car—*away* from temptation. I knew whatever she'd meant by that statement was nothing I could acknowledge, and it was certainly nothing I was allowed to pursue.

Pure calculation swept over her face, and I was jarred back to reality by the popping of the locks. She pushed open the driver's side door and slammed it shut behind her.

I needed to say something to get this back on the right track because the way she was checking me out was *not* helping to remind me who she was—and who I was supposed to be.

"Get back inside the car, Addison. You'll get soaked."

As she stepped closer to me, I surveyed the lot, paranoid that someone would see us. Paranoid that someone would read my mind.

And what exactly would they see?

They'd see me backing a student up against her car and lifting her skirt—the same miniscule scrap of fabric currently plastered to her thighs.

For the past few weeks, Addison had been watching me. I knew it, I felt it, and every time I'd caught her, she'd brazenly held my stare in a way that made my cock hard and my guilt compound.

"I'm already soaked," she explained, and I got the feeling she was not referring to the rain.

"Well, there's no reason to stand out here. You'll catch a cold. Get in your car, drive home, and take a warm shower."

A cunning grin spread over her mouth as she pushed her wet hair back from her face. "Is that what you're going to do?"

Automatically, I answered, "Yes."

"You're going to go home and take a shower?"

"*Addison,*" I warned as the look in her eyes changed.

She scanned the area, much as I had seconds ago, and then moved closer to me. In that moment, I should have stepped away, but fate must have had something else in store for me because I didn't do a damn thing.

"Yes? Sir."

As professionally as I could with the rain continuing to pour down on us, I tried to impress upon her in a voice that invited no question, "You need to stop this."

But question it, she did.

"Stop what?"

"*This,*" I stressed, not wanting to put a name to it but motioning back and forth between us. "Get back in your car."

"I think about you all the time. I can't stop."

Shaking my head, I ran my palm over my wet face. This couldn't be happening to me. I would not allow it. I knew better.

"Addison, it's natural to form attachments to your teachers."

"Is it natural to picture them fucking you?"

I pointed to her car. "Get in, and go home."

With her focus never wavering, she slowly backed up until she hit the car door. She tipped her head back to the sky, parting her lips and poking her tongue out to collect the water.

The youthful gesture tugged at something inside me, and at the same time, it warred with my mind. Her breasts resembled two ripe apples begging to be picked and devoured, and I couldn't tear my eyes away for her.

Surely, if there was a hell, I'd go there for what I wanted in that instant.

She brought her head back up and zeroed in on where I stood. "I'll think of you tonight when I'm in my shower, and Mr. McKendrick?"

I said nothing as she pulled open her car door.

"I'll be thinking of you, in yours."

That night as I climbed into the shower, I did think of my teacher. I pictured him as he'd stood there in the rain, soaked to the bone, with water clinging to his cheeks.

His eyes had roved over my body the second I'd displayed it for him. I wanted him to look at me...to touch me. I turned on the warm water and raised my face to the spray, imagining just that.

He'd wanted me this afternoon and was almost tempted, of that I was certain. It was only a matter of time.

Tick, tick, tock.

Present...

"Good morning, Addison."

I sigh as I make my way into our usual meeting place, choosing again not to answer. These sessions are pointless. I'll never tell him what he wants to hear. I wonder if he already knows that.

"I'd like to talk to you about something different today. Maybe a little bit about Helene."

He's waiting for me to react. Like poking a bear with a short stick.

"You and her...there was something there. A bond, wouldn't you say?"

What does it matter? There's nothing now, is my initial thought, but that isn't the truth. I know that.

"Addison?"

What? I want to scream at him. *What do you fucking want from me?*

But I don't demand that. I stay still, silent.

One, two, three. One, two three.

"Did her actions...hurt you?" he coaxes.

I hate when people ask me questions they already know the answers to.

I hold his gaze and see him nod. He knows he's getting somewhere.

"She was there at an important time in your life, that much I know. Like a sister? Or a mother, perhaps?"

I don't answer, believing it will make all of this go away. I keep hoping that this is all some kind of demented dream, but even in my dreams I can't escape what happened. I'm just reminded by the most unlikely source—*Daniel.*

Studying Doc, I see that he's still patiently waiting.

He's waiting for an answer. I'm waiting to leave.

"Do you miss her, Addison?"

No, is all I can think. I hate her.

~

Past...

The rain had passed by the next morning. I pulled into the parking lot and snuck a quick glimpse of my watch.

Good, I wasn't late for hurdle practice even though it would just be warm-ups due to the damp ground. Making my way across the track, I spotted Brandon showing off.

"Fuck that, Nicholson! There's no way you're gonna beat me at the meet, but you're welcome to try!" I heard him shout from where I was walking to the bleachers.

That was nothing new. Brandon and Luke Nicholson had been competing since they were freshmen. It seemed, however, that in these last two years, Brandon had been getting the edge every single time.

That meant he was the best, the most popular, and therefore, perfect for me.

Well, perfect if you didn't include the new candidate, Mr. McKendrick. He'd stopped to talk to Jessica, who went from friend to rival in the space of a well-timed laugh and a perky little wave.

I kept my eyes on the two of them as I stretched out my calves, and when he responded to something she said with a genuine laugh, my heart sped up.

One, two, three.

It was beyond irritating that Jessica, *plain old Jessica Garner,* had him smiling at her, and I couldn't even get him to talk to me unless he thought I had car issues.

Until yesterday, Mr. McKendrick barely acknowledged me except to answer a question, and even then it was done in a tone that was less than impressed. I knew he did it to keep me in line, but what he didn't realize was that it made him that much more of a challenge—and I thrived on a good challenge.

I balanced on one leg and pulled my right one up behind me to stretch out my quad.

As Jessica ran over to me, she called out, "Addy!"

It's probably a bad thing that I want her to trip and fall.

"Did you see Mr. McKendrick? Oh my god. He's *so* hot."

Pity, she didn't.

"Nope. Missed that. Plus, he's our teacher. Gross."

"Oh, please. He's sexy, like...like...oh, I don't know. But he is and so nice."

"To you, maybe. He's a total asshole to me," I reminded her. She was in our world history class. She had to have noticed the way he treated me.

"Well, yeah, to you he totally is. But *you* pissed him off from the very beginning."

The accusatory comment was completely unlike Jessica, but I couldn't detect any real venom behind it. Maybe it was just in my head.

"How cool is it that he's been to all of those amazing places? I mean, how unreal would it be to stand in the Parthenon? Oh, and the Colosseum? I'd die."

Jesus, this girl needs to shut it.

I was already annoyed that he seemed to think she was worth talking to, and I wasn't. Hearing her moon over him wasn't helping the issue at all.

"Well, I think he's amazing." She paused and turned back to where she'd come from just moments ago. "*Ooh*, and so does Miss Shrieve, apparently."

Spinning around, I spotted my hurdle coach and history teacher shaking hands on the other side of the track. Right then, I knew Jessica wasn't the enemy—*no*—Miss Shrieve had just filled that position.

Stepping away from Jessica, who was still yammering on about European vacations, I observed the way my coach leaned into Mr. McKendrick and laughed. Her face was angled up at him, and her lips were slightly parted as she placed a hand over her chest. Bringing to his attention, *no doubt*, her huge breasts.

Breathe, I told myself—*one, two three*—but it was no use.

My vision blurred, and I could hear nothing but the blood coursing through my veins as he, too, started to laugh.

No, no, no!

Not her, not Miss Shrieve.

Not the one woman who was always in my way somehow. This couldn't be happening.

As their introduction came to a close, she noticed us waiting and waved. She started jogging our way and at the last minute called over her shoulder to him, to *my* teacher.

"My name's Helene—just so you don't have to keep calling me Miss Shrieve."

In that moment, I wanted to hurt her.

The final warning bell for the day rang, and as the students began to shuffle into my classroom, I wrote along the top of the board, *King Henry VIII's wives*. Placing the chalk down, I dusted my hands and was about to face the class when Addison stepped through the door.

Her lips curved as she ran her gaze over me, and any kind of ease I had been feeling disappeared and my guard went up. Addison always added further tension to my class. Her very presence troubled me, and after yesterday in the parking lot, I was even more aware of her audacious behavior.

"Good afternoon, Mr. McKendrick," she greeted, much the same as the other students, but the look and walk that accompanied her words were *unlike* any other.

"Afternoon, Addison."

Instead of sitting down, she made her way over to where I was standing by the board and fingered the strap of her schoolbag—a stark reminder of exactly who she was.

"I see you survived being wet. So did I," she pointed out, her mouth twitching as she regarded me boldly. She was in for disappointment. She would get nothing from me.

"It was just a little water, nothing too bad."

Taking a step back, I crossed my arms, hoping to enforce the boundary I was setting. She was about to respond, but before she had a chance to say a word, her name was called. "Addy!"

She turned her head to Brandon, and I found myself studying the creamy skin of her neck and a stray piece of hair that had escaped her ponytail. It fell down onto her shoulder in a soft curl, and before I realized my actions, I had uncrossed my arms and stepped forward as if to touch.

As she rounded back to me, she caught my movement and whispered under her breath, "Meet me at my car this afternoon."

Choosing not to acknowledge her words, I gestured to the class with my head. "Please take your seat."

"Yes, sir."

She answered as politely as any of my other students, but all I heard was—*meet me*—and all I wanted was to touch her smooth skin.

"Addy, you gonna come back to my place Friday night?" Brandon asked, as I watched Mr. McKendrick take a seat at the front of the room.

Brandon was your typical all-American teen. Popular and full of confidence, he was the *other* star athlete of the school. With his short brown hair and seriously ripped muscles, he was every high school girl's dream, and I had him.

He winked at me, adding arrogantly, "We can celebrate winning."

My eyebrow rose and then I laughed. Hell, he was right. We both *would* win. We were the two to beat when it came to track, so the Friday night meet was something I was anticipating.

It was satisfying and exhilarating to know that you were the best.

"Yeah, I'll be there."

"Perfect! Wear that little red skirt, would ya?"

I knew exactly which one he was talking about. It barely covered my ass and was so tight that it almost cut off my circulation. My mother didn't know I owned it, but what she didn't know wouldn't hurt her. Just like she had no clue that the last time I wore it, Brandon had pushed it up around my hips and fucked me like a raging bull in the front seat of his brand-new Jeep.

"I'll wear it just for you," I promised with a slick slide of my tongue along my bottom lip, loving the thrill I got from the tease.

"Addison?" My name was called from the front of the room.

I swiveled in my chair to face my irritated teacher. "Yes, sir?"

"Do you have something you'd like to share with the rest of the class?"

No, I thought in a silent battle of wills, *but I'd love to know why you didn't single Brandon out.* My eyes held his as I shook my head. *That would be a negative.*

"In that case, how about you keep your mouth shut, and do your work."

"Yes, sir," I replied bitingly and went back to writing down the major facts about Catherine of Aragon.

For the rest of the class, I sat with my mouth closed and my mind whirling. When the bell rang, everyone jumped to their feet and made their way out the door.

Brandon, however, lingered by my desk.

"I have to ask a few questions," I lied.

Nodding, he bent down to kiss my cheek, and I noticed Mr. McKendrick watching us. His attention was on Brandon as his mouth moved to my ear.

"Hurry, my parents won't be home for two hours," he told me, and I couldn't help the smirk I gave when my teacher's attention shifted to me.

I kept my eyes on the man at the front of the room as I replied loud enough for him to hear, "Two hours is a long time to play."

Brandon straightened, unknowing of the private exchange. "Yes, it is. So hurry in here, okay?"

Still focused on my teacher, I agreed. "I'll only be a few minutes, then I'll drive over."

"Sounds good. I'll see ya there," he replied, making his way out of the room and leaving me to face the intimidating silence of Mr. McKendrick.

Reaching down beside my legs, I picked up my backpack and felt him track my movements. He had his hands clasped on the top of his desk as he sat there, silent and alert. I packed my books and pens away and stood from my seat.

When I stopped in front of his desk, he said nothing. But when I dropped my bag on to the floor, and the sound reverberated in the empty room, he pushed his chair back and stood quickly.

"Miss Lancaster."

With one finger, I began to draw circles over the wooden surface of his desk. "Mr. McKendrick."

"Cut the crap, Addison. Did you need something?" he fumed openly.

"Are you married?"

He shook his head, and his mouth pulled into a tense line. "That's none of your business."

"So that's a no."

"That is *not* a no. It is exactly what I said it was, *none* of your business."

Rolling my eyes, I continued to trace my finger on top of his desk, liking the feel of the rough wood under my finger.

"Why did I get in trouble today?"

"You know why," he stated matter-of-factly.

"No. I don't. Why did I get in trouble and Brandon didn't?"

"You were talking."

"So was he," I fired back, unwilling to let him think I was some ignorant child who didn't know what was going on.

He let out a deep, frustrated sigh and pushed his hands into his pockets. "Addison, you need to pay more attention in class."

"I do pay attention."

"Do you? I don't think so. You're so busy talking and flirting that I'd be surprised if you took more than three notes."

Bending down, I snatched up my backpack and unzipped it to pull out my notebook. Opening it to the day's work, I showed him how wrong he was and then raised my eyes to his, as if to say, *see?*

"One day doesn't prove anything. You need to stop disturbing the others around you."

"Like you?" I challenged.

"Like Brandon."

"Jealous?"

Emotions I wasn't familiar with darkened his eyes, giving him away as they singed me. "Don't be ridiculous."

"Is it so ridiculous? I was jealous of you and Miss Shrieve this morning."

"You're out of line, Miss Lancaster. *Way* out of line. You need to leave."

I made my way to the door, but before I walked through it, I looked back to where he was standing.

"Meet me at my car. I'll wait."

As Addison left the classroom, I sat down in my seat and adjusted the erection that was now throbbing like a harsh reminder between my legs.

I felt defeated.

I had come home to be with my father, a man who was slowly fading a little more each day. The same man who'd instilled in me my sense of morality, the difference between right and wrong—yet, here I was, failing him. Just like his heart was.

Addison was a dangerous distraction to a man whose life was in chaos. She was the promise of youth, of being fearless… of being *alive*. She was everything I couldn't have and shouldn't want, but the more she taunted, the more my resolve crumbled.

Temptation had come to visit, and her steely determination would likely destroy us both.

CHAPTER 4

I waited by my car for an hour, and he never came. In the back of my mind, I'd known that he wouldn't, but I held out hope that I'd be wrong. By the time four rolled around, I had several text messages from Brandon.

Brandon – Where are u?

I was still in the parking lot.

Brandon – I'm waiting...

Yeah? So was I.

Brandon – Thought u wanted to fuck?

I did...just not him.

It was now four thirty. I'd been waiting for an hour and a half, and Mr. McKendrick hadn't shown. He was probably watching me, waiting for me to leave.

I liked that idea—that *he* was watching *me*—and at the same time, I was aware that wasn't a normal response. Not that I was surprised because nothing had been normal for me, not since... well, since Daniel.

Deciding it was time to leave, I unlocked my door and got inside. As the engine rumbled to life, a favorite song of mine came over the radio. A smile stretched across my mouth as I cranked the volume up and reversed.

Halfway down the road, I turned off onto a side street. I whipped my car around in an illegal U-turn and pulled alongside the curb.

With the engine still idling, I tapped my fingers on the steering wheel and squeezed my eyes shut—*one, two, three, one, two, three*—and when I opened them, I spotted his black truck as it drove by.

Don't do it. *Don't do it*, I told myself.

How many times could I possibly get away with following him home?

But even as the thoughts echoed in my mind, I put my foot on the accelerator and drove out of the side street.

It takes approximately fifteen minutes to get to Mr. McKendrick's house. I know that because I have timed myself—*every* time. Today, I got there in fewer than thirteen.

My car crawled to a stop at what I believed was a safe distance from his drive. I killed the engine and sat there. He'd likely already gone inside. Usually, he didn't wait around.

He'd park the truck, and make his way to the front door. Once he was inside, I sometimes caught a glimpse of him as he moved through the house, but for today, I was just happy to be close.

Turning up the music so it was pumping through the car, I sat back and undid my seat belt, feeling a sense of calm wash over me—calm at being near.

It was a risk to be parked on his street, but I was willing to take it.

No one knew that I was there, so what would it hurt?

I couldn't believe she'd followed me home.

I was sitting in my truck with my hands wrapped around the steering wheel. I could see her in the rearview mirror, and my heart pounded in my chest as I thought about my next move.

I'd purposely waited to leave until she had gone home. It had been quite the wait, but I couldn't afford to put myself within close quarters of this girl.

She was undisciplined and clearly had never heard the word *no* in her life. She wanted things she couldn't have, and I needed to make that much clearer than in our previous conversations.

I could see the hood of her car peeking out from behind one of the neighbor's hedges and wished I could forget she was there, but this time she had crossed too many lines. She needed to know that this behavior could *not* continue.

Pushing open my truck door, I climbed out and locked it before walking down the drive. I strode purposefully along the sidewalk and tried to think of exactly what I was going to say to this *student* of mine.

Please stop following me? Please stop hitting on me?

They both sounded ridiculous, and I realized that at this point the word *please* needed to be thrown right out the fucking window.

Polite wasn't going to work with Addison Lancaster. It was time to get serious, maybe even mean, because this girl had the ability to destroy me.

I squinted against the sun's reflection on the windshield as I approached her car. She didn't see me since she had her eyes closed and her head resting back on the seat. Her mouth was parted like she was...*fucking hell, her hand...*

I pulled my eyes away from what she was doing and ignored the fact I was certain she was moaning. Instead, I stepped around to the driver's side of the car.

Knocking firmly on the window, I caught her jump as her eyes snapped open, and she removed her palm from between her legs. She frantically sat up, and I knew that she had not expected me to come down here. In fact, she seemed truly panicked.

Good, maybe this would teach her a lesson.

Again, I rapped on the window, harder this time, and when I heard the locks pop, I hauled open the car door.

"Get. Out!" I demanded as she gaped at me wide-eyed.

She visibly swallowed and shook slightly as she climbed out of the car, closing the door behind her. I grabbed her arm and tugged her off the road and up onto the curb.

"What the hell are you doing here?"

"I—"

"Did you follow me?"

Her blue eyes flicked over my face, but this time the move seemed more nervous than flirtatious.

"Did you *fucking* follow me?" I thundered.

"Yes!" she conceded, and I dropped her arm as quickly as I had grabbed it.

"Why would you do that? You know you can't be here!"

She took a step closer, and I backed up like she was contagious.

"Why can't I be here?"

"Because you fucking can't! I don't want you here."

Jesus, what a fucking joke. I felt as though I was about to get struck by lightning over that huge lie. I had just caught this girl masturbating in her car, and all I could think about was watching her do it again, but this time in my bed.

"If I wasn't your student—"

"You *are* my student, Addison. You're my student, and I'm your teacher. This will *never* happen."

"But if I wasn't?"

"Go *home*."

Just like that, I witnessed her nerves disappear before she demanded, "Answer me!"

I felt the headache throbbing behind my eyes and was disgusted by the fact it was keeping time with the blood pumping through my erect cock.

"You're hard."

As soon as her soft observation hit my ears, I told her again, "Go. Home."

"Why are you so worried? No one is here, and I like it."

"I'm not worried. I'm *appalled*. Appalled that someone as bright as you are feels like she has to throw herself at people to get attention. Not only boys, but someone my age."

"How old are you? I'd guess thirty."

"Again, these are all things that are none of your business, Addison. You know that. This behavior of yours needs to stop, or I'll be forced to contact your parents."

She laughed then, a sound so sweet and carefree that I wondered what exactly was going through her head. One minute she was the bright, promising schoolgirl and the next, a bold, reckless imitation of herself who seemed to constantly be pushing boundaries and searching for something...*more*.

"And what would you tell them? Hello, Mrs. Lancaster, I'm calling to let you know that your daughter has been turning up at my house and masturbating in her car. Oh, and can you please keep her away from me because she gives me a hard-on?"

I felt my anger course through me and was annoyed that it heightened my already misplaced arousal. I stepped closer, and she backed up hitting the car. The spark that lit her eyes provoked me even further, so I leaned down over her and did something I'd never done before. I threatened a woman. Worse, I threatened a girl.

"You're trying my patience, Addison. You need to leave me alone. Get in the *fucking* car, and go home. Or you won't like what happens next."

Her eyes fell to my mouth and then came back up to meet mine, but instead of fear, which I'd hoped to instill, all I could sense was excitement.

Excitement and lust. The same emotions that were feeding my own.

"And if I stay?"

Before I could stop myself, I snatched a handful of her

sports jacket in one of my fists and hauled her in close. Close enough that I could feel her breath against my lips.

"This is *very* dangerous, Addison. I'm not another one of your little boys that can be led around by their cock. Now. *Leave.*"

I released her and marched back to my house not even waiting to see if she followed my order.

~

Oh *shit*, I thought as I remained where he'd left me, pressed up against my car door. My legs were barely supporting me as my entire body trembled. My pussy was throbbing so hard I could literally feel each perverted pulse.

One, two, three.

I cupped myself, tightening my thighs around my fingers. *Christ.* He was so fucking intense.

Exactly what I wanted. *Exactly* what I needed.

I replayed his words and bit my bottom lip before removing my hand and walking around to the driver's side.

When I passed by his house, I spotted him through his front window. I zeroed in on him and saw the frustration from seconds earlier still evident on his face.

I continued my secret perusal and witnessed something I knew he wouldn't have wanted me to. Him—unbuckling and unzipping his jeans.

I didn't care what Mr. McKendrick *said*; his body was calling for me, and I couldn't help but respond.

~

Present...

"Addison? Addison. It's time for your meds."

The woman standing in the light blue scrubs is analyzing me as I sit on the old, broken-down couch in the common room.

"Addison?"

I wonder what she thinks of me—Slut? Skank? Whore?

It's ironic. Before coming here, I wouldn't have cared what she thought because I would've known I was perfect.

Not anymore.

According to them, I'm broken and in need of healing—*less* than perfect.

"Your meds. Here." She passes me a small plastic cup with my pills. I take it from her as the TV switches stories.

Tick, tick, tock.

I've been waiting all afternoon for the news to come on just to see if it will be mentioned. Usually, I'm ushered out by now. Either sent back to my room or to see Doc, but someone must have forgotten because I'm still sitting here and it's...

Tick, tick, tock.

Time.

I see the anchorman appear, and a few seconds later, *his* picture flashes across the screen.

Oh God. It feels like forever since I've seen that face.

I drop the pills and slide off the couch to crawl toward the TV. I kneel and place my fingers on the screen. Trying to touch, trying to reach him. Tears are sliding down my cheeks as the man on the TV continues talking about the "missing teacher."

When I'm dragged from the room, all I can hear is, "As of tonight, there's still no word on his whereabouts."

Tick, tick, tock.

CHAPTER 5

 ast...

Unlike most sports, Miss Shrieve scheduled our hurdle practices in the mornings. That way, we avoided the heat, and more likely, the boys.

The morning after being spotted at Mr. McKendrick's house, I made my way across the field to where the other girls were starting to arrive. They all waved as I stopped and dropped my bag onto the ground. Pulling an elastic band from my pocket, I tipped my head back and tied up my hair as Jessica began talking.

"So, I thought you'd want to know, Sam text me last night. He said Brandon was super pissed that you didn't show yesterday."

Resisting the urge to roll my eyes, I faced Jessica and shrugged. "So? He's just pissed he didn't get laid."

"Addy!"

"What? It's the truth. Don't act like you've never done it, Jess."

With an irritating giggle, she replied, "I'm not."

"Ah-huh," was my nonchalant response, not really caring either way what she had or hadn't done. I was too busy thinking about the conversation with my history teacher from the afternoon before. *This is very dangerous, Addison.*

What was very dangerous?

I should have asked him, but I knew, just like he did, and that's why he'd sent me away.

"Good morning, ladies!" Miss Shrieve's voice called out as she jogged over to us. Her blond ponytail swished back and forth as she bounced along the grass.

"I hope you are all warmed up and ready to practice for the big meet tomorrow."

As I bent down to touch my toes, the other girls around me chorused out, "Yes!"

"Good, good! I'm so excited for you all. Addy? How are you feeling this morning?"

I straightened instantly and aimed a guilty look her way. For a moment, I had the insane notion she was referring to something else entirely.

"Legs feeling strong?"

Releasing the breath I was holding, I gave her my brightest, fakest smile. It was the least I could do. Miss Shrieve, after all, was someone who had seen me at my worst, and now, wanted to fuck my history teacher. I could tell because I wanted to as well.

"Yes. I feel very strong," was my reply, and I wasn't lying. Remembering the way Mr. McKendrick had been hard inside his jeans, and his eyes—those intense eyes—both of those things made me feel strong, made me feel *superior.*

"Good! We need you strong to fight for what's yours."

She was referring to beating the overall best time in hurdles, but as I agreed with her and began to remove my track pants, all I could think about was fighting for Mr. McKendrick.

~

This morning I'd requested the first hour of my day free. I wanted to go down and visit my father.

He'd been transferred to a hospice facility a little over a month ago, and watching him become a mere shell of the man he once was had to be one of the cruelest fates I'd witnessed.

Heart disease from years ago is where it had all started, and the road up until this point had been rife with surgeries and setbacks. I'd been given a harsh lesson as a thirty-two-year-old, and that is—live for the moment because miracles don't exist.

Then there was the man himself, always doing what he thought was right. He had lived with this diagnosis for so long without telling me to spare me from the pain. It wasn't until these final months, when everything was failing, that he'd reached out.

Selfish of him or kind? I still hadn't decided.

Getting out of my pickup, I slammed the door shut before making my way through the gated fence surrounding the track.

I was still extremely uncomfortable about what happened yesterday afternoon with Addison and what I'd done after. When she had left my house, I'd been unable to get the image of her sitting in her car pleasuring herself out of my fucking head.

The way her legs had been slightly splayed under the steering wheel and how her hips had moved, giving away exactly what she'd been doing without me even needing to see. As if that hadn't been enough, the way her mouth—that full-lipped mouth—had opened and sighed as she must have touched the very right...*fuck.*

Again, there I was, disgusted with myself and sporting another erection due to my unruly thoughts of a fucking student. At least last night I'd been able to privately take care of the issue and had. I'd gone into my shower and spent a long time jacking off to the image of Addison, which infuriated me because it was exactly what the little tease wanted.

Hurriedly, I made my way into the building. I didn't have a

class scheduled until after lunch, so I wouldn't have to deal with anyone right now. That was until—

"Hey there."

When the door to my classroom shut behind me, I walked over to my desk and found Helene Shrieve, coach of the girls hurdle team.

She was sitting on one of the student's desks with her long legs dangling and an open smile on her face. Helene was a beautiful woman with green eyes and honey-bronzed skin.

"Morning. Did you get lost on your way to the track?"

Laughing good-naturedly, she jumped down off the desk and made her way over to me.

"Nope. I've already been out there this morning. My girls are going to kill it tomorrow…which is why I'm here."

We'd only had one conversation prior to this. Yesterday, when we'd run into each other for the first time, she'd introduced herself, as had I, and then I'd walked away.

I wasn't here to make friends or form relationships. After my contract was up and my father—well, I didn't want to think about that. I would be away from this place as soon as I could.

"And why's that?"

"I heard you like photography."

"Oh, you did, did you?"

Grinning now like she knew a secret, she nodded. "Mhmm. Principal Thomas told me, and I wanted to know if you'd like to come to the track meet tomorrow? Maybe take some snapshots of the students? It'd be great for you to see them in action and show your support."

Somehow, the question sounded a lot like an invitation to a date, disguised as a school function, and if the way she was checking me out was any indication—I was correct.

"I don't know…" I started as the bell sounded.

"Think about it. I'd love to see you there."

With a nod of my head, I watched her walk to the door, and as she pulled it open, she stepped aside.

"Oh, hello, Addison."

~

Jealousy.

That was exactly what I was feeling as Miss Shrieve opened the door to my history class for me. Knowing I had no other option than to be polite, I greeted her and moved into the room.

"Hi, Miss Shrieve. Brushing up on your history?" I asked, turning to face Mr. McKendrick, who was standing behind his desk looking at the both of us.

"Something like that," Coach replied with a soft laugh that grated on my nerves. I wanted to tell her to go and brush up on someone else.

"Well, you better take a seat. Your class will be starting soon," she advised as if I didn't already know that.

She then addressed Mr. McKendrick again. "I hope you'll consider the invitation."

As she left the room, I contemplated the man silently watching me. What was she referring to, and what invitation? My curiosity outweighed my ability to think clearly as I walked over to him.

His focus kept shifting beyond my shoulder to the other students making their way to their seats. When I reached his desk, I stopped and waited.

"Go and take your seat, Addison."

"I need to talk to you after class."

He shook his head and went back to monitoring the door. "No."

I lowered my voice and stepped even closer. "Want me to talk to you now?"

"No," he repeated, but this time he looked down at me.

His eyes conveyed his inner conflict as he pinned me with them, and the combination of heated desire and exasperation made me reckless.

"Making you say *yes* will be fun."

He said nothing, just gave me his back and moved to the chalkboard. Satisfied that I'd won for the moment, I went and took my seat as Brandon walked into the room.

"Where the hell were you yesterday?" he asked loudly, walking down the row.

I snuck a quick look to the front where Mr. McKendrick had stopped writing and was observing. He was more than aware of where I'd been the day before.

"I forgot, okay? Shit, relax, would you? I just went home."

"You forgot?" Brandon sputtered as he slammed his books down on the desk. "How could you fucking forget? We talked about it right before you left."

"*Alright,* Mr. Williams!" Mr. McKendrick's voice cut through the room. "That'll be quite enough out of you."

The entire class hushed as he stared Brandon down, and I felt an irrational sense of joy as if he had said what he did to protect me, or maybe because he *was* jealous.

"Sorry, sir," Brandon mumbled, sinking down in his seat before adding for my ears only, "We're not done, Addy. That's bullshit."

I shrugged like I didn't care and really…I didn't. Brandon could be as pissed off as he wanted. He didn't own me, and he sure as hell didn't have the right to tell me what to do.

All I cared about was the man now asking about Catherine of Aragon and why King Henry VIII annulled their marriage. The answer to that was simple.

Desire, lust, and a woman. They were always the ingredients in man's ultimate betrayal. Whether it was of the heart, mind, or soul.

~

I knew it was coming. The bell rang and the students filed out of the room.

All except for Addison.

"It's time to go," I told her as professionally as I was able.

"I don't understand why you won't talk to me."

"Yes, you do."

The smile that curved her lips should have been…no, it *was* illegal. Not the smile itself but what it made me want to do.

I stayed in my seat and she remained in hers. Thank God she was wearing her track pants today and not some tiny skirt, because as it was, I was finding it hard not to ogle her.

"Will you talk to me if I promise to stay over here?"

Sitting back in my chair, I asked, "Don't you have another class?"

"Yes, but she's not a stickler for time management like you. So? Will you talk to me?"

"I will talk to you about anything to do with your school work. Nothing else."

Her insolence aroused me, and I could feel my cock swell because of the forbidden thoughts running through my mind.

"Where did Miss Shrieve invite you to go?"

"That's not school related."

"Yes, it is. You're both my teachers. Did she asked you on a date?" she persisted.

Even though Helene had not asked me out officially, surely it couldn't hurt to make Addison believe she had, or at least leave it up in the air.

"That's none of your business."

She looked to the door and then back at me. "I want to know what it's like to kiss you."

"Addison."

"Yes?"

"Time to leave," I informed her and sat up in my chair.

"I think you want to know too."

Without meaning to, I muttered, "It doesn't matter," and immediately, I wanted to take it back. I heard her chair scrape and saw her moving my way.

"I knew it."

Standing, so I felt as though I at least had some control over the situation, I disagreed. "I didn't mean it like *that*. Please go, before you do something that will get you in trouble."

Her wide eyes were practically pleading with me, and *fuck*—I wanted her.

"Just tell me. Since you won't touch me, at least tell me that you want to."

The room fell into complete silence, and all I could hear was the—*tick, tick, tock*—of the clock as every shred of common sense I had deserted me.

"I want to."

Time seemed to stand still as her eyes gave permission.

It wasn't permission I needed. It was strength. The strength to resist.

"Now go."

Having gotten what she came for, she silently left my room.

CHAPTER 6

 **resent...**

"Let's talk about the photograph on your wall."

I don't know why Doc insists on saying *let's* at the beginning of our sessions. He's the only one talking.

"*Psyche Revived by Cupid's Kiss*," he tells me, as if I don't already know this. "Do you know the story behind the sculpture?"

This has to be the worst kind of punishment. It's monotonous. It's mind-numbing. It's a waste of my fucking time.

Tick, tick, tock.

"Let's start with Psyche, shall we?"

Questions. Questions. Questions. How long will he go on with no reply? Knowing Doc, forever.

"So, Psyche was the youngest and most beautiful daughter of the king and queen. She was revered as a goddess by the locals in the village she came from. This would make any woman…" He pauses and taps his top lip with his index finger —*one, two, three.* "Feel special. Important."

I know where he's going with this. He's so predictable lately.

"Did *he* make you feel special, Addison?"

And…there it is.

"Come on. You can talk to me."

Tilting my head to the side, I speak for the first time since I have been admitted into the Pine Groves Psychiatric Facility.

"Yes. But I don't want to."

Tick, tick, tock.

~

Past…

Friday afternoon rolled around before I knew it. I thought it would take forever to get here, but it didn't. I'd made myself behave in class today, even though I'd spent the entire time wanting to kiss my teacher.

In his khaki-colored dress pants and black polo shirt, I could see all of his muscles clearly defined. I also noticed for the first time that there was a hint of ink on his left bicep that poked out of his sleeve every time he raised his arm to the board. Mr. McKendrick had a tattoo.

How was I supposed to behave in the face of all that?

The idea that, at eighteen, we were all sweet, little virgins seemed ludicrous to me. Because the last time I checked, all I could think about was sex. Who I could have it with, when, and how often.

Oh, and the popular fallacy that only boys were horny at our age—well, the people who came up with that hadn't had to sit through a class with Mr. McKendrick walking around at the front of it.

"Addison…Addison?"

My name cut through my thoughts as a hand touched my shoulder.

Turning, I found Miss Shrieve standing in front of me with an expectant look on her face. *Ugh*, why did she have to go and jack things up between us?

"You ready for this?"

I kept my face neutral as I nodded at my coach and then jumped up and down, shaking my hands out by my sides. I'd just finished screwing in the new spikes on my shoes and was now finishing my warm-up. I glanced around the track and up into the bleachers, trying to spot my mother in the crowd. She said she would come tonight, and as always, if she said she would be somewhere, she didn't lie. There she was—third row back, sitting in front of Mr. McKendrick.

I didn't have too much time to think about why he was there because my heat was up first, and we were being called to the start-up blocks.

Pushing my thumbs into my track pants, I kept my eyes on my mother—*oh yes, thank you, Mom, for sitting right there*—and then let them shift slightly behind to the man who was...*hmm*, aiming a camera in my direction.

I removed my pants and kicked them aside so I was standing in tight mesh shorts, and out of the corner of my eye, I was sure Mr. McKendrick shifted in his seat.

Feeling a smirk hit my lips, I reached up to my long ponytail and tightened it, knowing that it raised the Lycra tank I wore up over my navel.

"I know you can do this, Addison. Your times have been outstanding in practice," Miss Shrieve told me as we walked to my lane.

Lane four. That was where I was running today. I would have preferred three—*one, two, three*—but I got four. I would make do.

When we reached the starting blocks, Miss Shrieve grabbed my forearm, stopping me and forcing me to turn.

"Are you okay today?"

With a little more force than was necessary, I tugged my arm away from her and gave a swift nod, still remembering the way she had invited Mr....*ahh, this is where she'd invited him.* To photograph the race, not on a date like he'd led me to believe. *Nice try.*

Finding my mother in the bleachers again, she gave the perfunctory wave. I smiled like the good daughter I was, but my eyes were on the man who was waving at the woman beside me.

As Miss Shrieve returned the gesture, she looked back to me with a smile left over from him, and I had a huge desire to scratch it right off her face.

"Okay, you can do this."

I waited for her to take a step back behind the start up blocks, where she could time me. I walked into position and sized up the other girls I'd be competing against.

Competition didn't seem so tough, and as the announcer started to call out our school affiliations, I placed my hands on my waist and started to bounce from foot to foot in a small, flirty dance that loosened my hips and would hopefully lengthen my stride.

As my hair swished back and forth with my little jig, I heard Brandon and the other boys wolf-whistling and calling out my name from the sidelines.

I knew they loved it when I did this. It had become something of an event in itself, and Brandon had once told me it was the sexiest shit he'd ever seen.

I made sure to look up at Mr. McKendrick as I did it for the final time, and his eye, I was pleased to find, was pressed to the viewfinder with the lens directed my way.

He was watching me, and I was about to give him the show of a lifetime.

How the fuck could any red-blooded man look away from that? I thought as Addison—lane four, with school-colored ribbons in her hair —danced up and down from toe to toe.

It would be bad enough if that was all she was doing, but add in the outfit, one pair of short shorts, a tank top that molded to every curve she had, and that sassy smirk she was definitely aiming my way, and yes—I was fucked. With a capital fucking F.

Coming here tonight had been a terrible idea, and now that I was seated in the bleachers tempted by my own personal version of Eve, I knew, if offered, I'd be biting that fucking apple.

Who was I kidding? She'd already offered. All I had to do was bite.

When Addison had waved in my direction, at first I'd thought she was waving at me. Until the woman seated below me raised an arm and her—*mother,* I assumed—waved back.

There I was, thinking about how Addison's long, lean legs would feel wrapped around my waist, while her mother was here to watch her daughter race.

In my mind, there were only two places for people with thoughts like mine.

Prison or the fiery pits of hell.

Still, I zoomed in on the flirty girl through my camera, and I couldn't find it in me to care.

Not one little bit.

With my feet in the starting blocks, I focused on the 100-meter lane ahead of me and blocked out everything else. All of the surrounding noise ceased, and I listened, instead, to the constants.

Tick, tick, tock—my watch—*Tick, tick, tock.*
Tickticktick—BANG!

The gunshot ricocheted through the track, signaling go time —and I was off.

Quick as a flash, I was up and sprinting toward the first

jump while keeping count in my mind, knowing that was essential for this race.

One, two, three—jump. First one down.

Thundering toward the next, I felt confident. I knew how easy I made this seem.

One, two three—jump. Second one down.

Yes! This was what I lived for. I could feel the air hitting my cheeks as I powered on.

One, two, three—jump. Third one down, and I was making this bitch mine.

Nothing felt this good or made me feel so free. As I leaped over the next four, I realized I was over halfway through and by my estimation, nine seconds down the track.

One, two, three—jump. Eight down, two to go.

I loved the feeling of the air rushing in and out, fueling my body as my limbs strived for perfection.

One, two, three—jump. Nine was done, and I had one more.

One more, and I would be the winner. One more, and I would be the best. One more, and…*one, two, three—jump.*

Ten! I was done!

As I slowed my run to a jog and placed my hands on my hips, I pivoted toward the bleachers. There was my mother, perfecting the act of good parenting by standing and clapping. I gave a brisk wave and then I saw *him* step to the side and knew he'd done it so he could see me.

The announcer came over the loudspeaker confirming what I already knew. "The winner…lane four…Addison Lancaster, with a personal best of fifteen seconds."

Yes. I had run my personal best, and now I wanted my prize.

She'd been magnificent. Like a cheetah sprinting into action, Addison had taken off at the starting gun and in fifteen seconds, had torn up the track as if her life depended on it.

I had forgotten all about the photos and was unable to resist getting to my feet when everyone else did. The crowd began chanting her name because *she* was unbelievable. It was clear she was the star of the school and when she finished that race, it was obvious why.

Her mother looked around proudly as Addison crossed the finish line, and when she spotted me, checked me out before jumping to her feet, clapping and waving.

That had been the minute I realized I needed to leave.

I was looking at Addison, and her mother was looking at me. What I was thinking, it was wrong. It was a violation on all levels, and just being there and imagining Addison in such a way made me feel...*guilty*.

As soon as I was able to get around everyone, I moved out onto the steps with my eyes still on the winner at the end of the track. When I got to the bottom of the stairs, Brandon and Sam caught my eye and waved at me.

"Pretty fucking amazing, isn't she?"

I couldn't bring myself to disagree, so I just nodded before making my way into the school.

It was just turning five thirty and I figured I might as well get the class's papers to take home and grade. I needed a distraction to take my mind off its current fixation.

Entering my classroom, I collected up the papers, switched the light back off and made my way out into the hall. I was halfway to the exit when Addison came around the corner and stopped.

I knew that she'd come for me, and if I hadn't been sure, the look on her face clued me in real fucking fast.

"Congratulations on your win," I told her, determined not to let her unnerve me. I was the adult here, not her. I just had to remember that and act like one.

Walking toward her, I was happy to see she had at least added her sports jacket back to the ensemble. Unfortunately, she'd left off the track pants and was still only wearing those short fucking shorts.

"Thanks. I was surprised to see you in the stands." She paused as she walked closer. "Did you come to see me?"

I brought the papers up against my chest and held them there. It was a pathetic excuse for a shield, but anything was better than nothing.

"I didn't come to see you specifically, no. I came to take photographs of the event and support the school."

"But now you're leaving after only one race?"

Refusing to let her walk all over me, I nodded. "Well, I remembered I had papers to grade."

With a knowing look, she bit her bottom lip, and when her top teeth sunk into the pillowy flesh, my cock came to rigid attention.

"Or maybe you already saw what you wanted to see?"

"Addison."

"Yes?"

"I have told you before, this isn't going to happen."

"No? What if you don't touch? There's nothing wrong with…watching, is there?"

My mind raced with the possibilities. She brushed past me so our shoulders met, and I could smell the sweet, sugary body spray she must have used after her race.

She smelled sinful.

I turned as she looked over her shoulder at me and walked into my…no, *our* history classroom.

Closing my eyes, I counted backwards from ten.

This was a bad idea. A really fucking bad idea, but as I made my way back to the classroom door, I knew that I was about to bite the apple.

CHAPTER 7

$\mathcal{T}$he minute he stepped into the room, I knew I had him. He quietly shut and locked the door before walking over behind his desk.

I'd chosen to sit in the first row, middle seat, as opposed to my usual because from here he'd be able to see and hear me that much better.

One, two, three.

He placed the papers down, then pushed all ten of his fingers on the wooden surface so hard they turned white.

"Doesn't your mother need to know where you are?" he asked, and I couldn't help the laugh that escaped my mouth.

"I told her I was waiting on Brandon so we could all go out and celebrate."

Pinning me with an annoyed frown, he accused, "So you lied?"

"Maybe a little. Would you prefer me to call and tell her what I'm really doing?"

He rubbed two of his fingers up the center of his forehead, appearing stressed. "Addison, this cannot happen."

Now things were getting interesting.

One, two three.

"You keep saying that. *What* exactly is it that can't happen?"

I couldn't help the thrill I got at his discomfort.

"You know what I'm talking about. Stop acting naive. It doesn't suit you."

I raised a brow and laughed at the blunt way he called me out. "Okay."

"You have to stop coming on to me. Do you understand how much trouble we would be in if—"

"If?" I pushed when he stopped talking and started shaking his head.

"I'm not allowed to touch you, so stop inviting me to."

"Is that what I'm doing?"

Unflinchingly, he replied, "You know that it is."

"Why don't you sit down?"

"Because I plan to leave."

"Really? I'm pretty sure you locked the door."

"Addison," he said, not in warning this time but more in resignation.

"What's your first name?"

"Oh *no*," he drawled, and for the first time since we'd met, he laughed, and the sound tickled its way up my spine. "I'm not telling you that."

"Well, I can find out by searching the school's web page at home."

One, two, three.

"Then why haven't you?"

Trying for nonchalant, I shrugged. "I wanted you to tell me."

"Why?" he asked, just as I knew he would.

"Because it'll mean more."

"It's not appropriate for me to tell you, especially since you won't be using it."

I lowered my eyes and then peeked at him flirtatiously from beneath my lashes. "But it would be nice to know whose name to call when I touch myself at night."

"*Jesus.*"

"What?" I questioned as I spread my thighs apart under the desk. "It's the truth."

"It doesn't matter. You can't say things like that to me."

"But I can to others?"

He pulled his seat out and sat down. "No. You shouldn't say it to anyone."

"Why? Am I supposed to act ashamed that I like to touch myself? I do, you know, but I promised myself that my next orgasm would be with you, so…wanna help me out?"

His gaze dropped below the desk, and the moment he noticed my legs parted, he brought his eyes back to mine. This time, they were a dark gold and much more volatile—less patient.

"I'm not talking about *this* with you."

"Oh, please. Don't try and tell me you don't think about me."

"Stop. It. Addison," he growled, and the sound of my name reverberating from his throat made my pussy clench in response.

"Don't worry, Mr. M. Can I call you that? It's much easier. I don't want you to touch me. I can do that all on my own. Just watch—watch me."

I pushed my chair away from the desk and leaned back into the seat, lowering my hand down between my thighs. Pressing my fingers against the outside of my shorts, I noticed his eyes skid down to see what I was doing.

"Stop it."

"Make me," I challenged.

His voice was barely audible as he admitted, "I can't."

I couldn't make her because I didn't *want* her to stop.

If anyone could have seen what was going on, it was obvious to me that they would have labeled me a monster and her a victim. However, as I sat there, fighting every instinct to go to her, I really had to wonder which role fit whom in this scenario.

I consciously knew this was *not* supposed to happen. I was supposed to be the one to walk away, but how do you keep saying no in the face of such temptation? If this was a test, was I about to fail?

Addison's smooth legs were spread wide under the desk. Her hand was eagerly massaging between them as she watched me. I remained frozen, fixated on the scene like a deer caught in the headlights.

"Tell me what to do," she invited.

Was she kidding? This was the most demented thing I'd ever done. I wasn't going to compound the situation by giving her instructions to take her pants off so I could see more.

"Tell me," she demanded again as her fingers moved up and slid—*oh fuck*—inside her school shorts.

I squeezed my eyes shut, trying to erase the image as I fought my body's natural instinct. My cock was as hard as a fucking rock as I sat there imagining what she was touching. The only sound I could hear was the—*tick, tick, tock*—of the fucking wall clock. It felt as though it was keeping time with my heart as it pounded inside my chest.

"Mr. M?"

At the breathy sound of her voice, I lifted my head and saw that she'd unzipped her jacket and was focused on me with lustful eyes.

"Addison."

"Don't tell me no."

"I'm not *telling* you anything."

She let out a soft moan, and I figured she'd just touched... *fuck!*

"You don't have to, just your voice makes me wet. Watch me. Watch what you do to me."

Denying myself even that, I stood, determined to put an end to this.

"This is *over*. Stop what you're doing and get up."

"No," she told me as her eyes clouded over, desire starting to take a tight hold of her.

Rounding my desk, I pressed a firm palm against my erection, trying to get it to behave as I moved closer to her.

"Get your fucking hands out of your pants, and go home, Addison. It's called self-control. Try and find some."

"Mhmm, again," she panted, and I could feel my panic closing in on me as her quick breaths were beginning to drown out the ticking of the clock, which was the only thing keeping me sane.

"What?"

"My name, say it again," she pleaded as I stopped in front of her. "*Hurry.*"

Looking down at the way she was sprawled out in her seat, I saw the fingers of her left hand tapping the edge of the desk—*one, two, three*—and her other was underneath it, out of view.

That's when I heard myself say, "Addison."

"*Yes*," she moaned, and I assumed her fingers were now inside her.

"Addison," I repeated again, unable to stop my mouth as she pushed her breasts out for me like a fucking offering.

I felt drawn to her.

With morbid curiosity, I placed my hands on her desk, bringing my face in close to hers. Closer than I'd ever been before. Unable to look away.

Her attention shifted to my mouth in that moment, and the power of my own lust slammed into me, taking full control.

"*Addison*," I rasped out, and as she tipped her face up, I couldn't find the will to back away.

"Yes?" she sighed, so close to my lips I could taste her sweet, warm breath as it entered my mouth.

"It's Grayson," I finally gave over. Her lips curved seductively, and I knew she understood exactly what I'd just given.

Her eyes shut, and the long lashes kissed the top curve of

her rosy cheeks. She sat back and started to raise her hips up under the desk. I rubbed my painfully stiff cock while Addison continued to masturbate less than an arm's length away from me.

I couldn't drag my attention away as her forearm flexed and pushed down every time her body bucked up, no doubt causing her fingers to slide deeper inside herself.

She was stunning.

Provocative, sensual, and so free with her own pleasure that when her eyes opened and locked with mine, I couldn't stop myself from saying, "You're fucking gorgeous."

"Kiss me," she begged.

I stumbled back, shaking my head in denial.

While I wasn't touching her, I could convince myself that I hadn't crossed too many lines. Yet, even as the word, "No," left my mouth, I knew I was a liar.

I'd crossed every fucking line. I reveled in the sound of my name on her lips as those siren eyes closed and she hurled herself to climax.

It was risky, it was decadent, and I knew I'd never be able to step foot into this classroom without envisioning Addison in that moment.

~

Present...

Talking is overrated. I know that now. I just wish I'd known it back then.

Unfortunately, that is all that's on the schedule for me at Pine Groves. Talking about the past. Or should I say, Doc talking and me...just listening.

What a waste of time. Nothing could be undone. It was too late.

"Addison, sooner or later, you need to talk about this."

No I don't, and he can't make me. That's what really kills him.

"Let's talk about Grayson again today."

I want to tell him *not* to use his first name and that I hate when he talks about him as though they know one another—but I don't say anything.

Instead, I sit silently in the corner of this room as I always do. Silent, except for the clock that's keeping track of how many seconds I'm wasting in here.

"It's okay to be angry. What he did was…" His voice tapers off, inviting me to divulge what I know.

Thinking about the past hurts. It's raw, painful, and I can't imagine *ever* wanting to talk about it. But I also can't let a lie continue to be told.

Standing, I move to the center of the room where the good doctor is taking notes.

"I don't want to be pitied because of what I represent to you and every other outraged parent in our community."

Shocked by the fact I've just said more than I have in all the time I've been here, he takes a moment to gather his thoughts before asking, "And what do you think you represent, Addison?"

"The poor little girl who was seduced by the big bad wolf."

I can tell I'm right. He has nothing to say, and once again, neither do I.

What he doesn't understand is that there isn't a poor little *girl*, just a wolf in sheep's clothing, hiding in plain sight— standing right before his very eyes.

Who's afraid of the big bad wolf?

Tick, tick, tock.

CHAPTER 8

 ast...

The weekend.

It represented freedom for most people. Two days to do whatever they wanted—but I'm not like *most* people.

To me, it was two days of forced communication with my parents, who walked around the same house and never once interacted. Virtual strangers.

It hadn't always been like this, and every day in some way, I was reminded it was because of me.

"Addison!"

My mother's shrill voice found its way up our spiral staircase and into my room.

"Addison! Get down here! *Now!*"

Shit. My initial thought was that Mr. McKendrick, *no... Grayson*, had reported me from the day before, but that didn't make sense. If he'd done that, he would also be reporting himself.

I tried to imagine what I had done and felt my heartbeat

accelerating at the thought. It was never good when she was upset, and it was even worse when my father was.

One, two, three. One, two, three.

I looked at the old antique clock sitting on my desk. As the second hand—*tick, tick, tocked*—and penetrated my thoughts, I felt myself begin to relax.

Perfection. It's a goal no one should have to live up to, but after what had happened…how could they love me otherwise?

Pushing off my bed, I made my way over to the oval mirror hanging on my bedroom wall. I studied my reflection and practiced the smile I knew she expected—the one she needed to see. My lips curved and what looked like a smile appeared, but my eyes remained lost.

"Addison!"

Again, her voice found me.

"Coming, Mom!" I finally yelled back.

With a shaky breath, I pulled my hair into a sleek ponytail and headed for the door. Halfway down the stairs I realized several strands had been missed, so I ran back up to my mirror. Knowing she was waiting on me, I yanked the elastic band out with a grimace and once again tied it, this time making sure I caught all of my hair before securing it in place. There, perfect.

Jogging down the stairs, I made my way to the kitchen and found her sipping coffee from her favorite mug. It was one that Daniel had given her for his last mother's day.

It had *I,* huge red heart, *my mom*—and he had.

He'd loved her the most, and she mourned him by pretending it had never happened.

"Addison?" she asked as her eyes ran over me.

It was almost like a spot check.

Hair perfect. Clothes perfect. Behavior perfect.

Check, check, check. *Flawless.*

"Yes, Mom?"

Lowering the mug onto the black granite counter, her face

altered from a frown to a smile so swiftly she would have fooled most, but not me.

"It says here that your time yesterday qualified you to hurdle in the state competition."

"Oh, yeah," I acknowledged, having completely forgotten. That piece of information had been lost somewhere around the time I slipped my fingers into my shorts for Mr—Grayson.

"Oh, *yeah?*" my mother repeated back to me, slowly.

I knew she hated the word *yeah*.

"Sorry. I meant yes. I was told before we left the meet and after we went to dinner. I must have forgotten."

In reality, I'd left the school with Brandon, gone to Cherry Hill and let him put his fingers inside me—where *mine* had been earlier that afternoon for our history teacher.

"Well, young lady, this isn't something you should take lightly. Your father and I are very pleased with your success."

Yes, I'm sure he was. So proud that he hadn't shown up to see me, and so proud he had left early this morning to play golf. The only time my father ever acknowledged me was when I was in his way, so I tried my best to stay out of it.

"We'll go out tonight. To celebrate."

The minute the words left her mouth, I knew the idea was a bad one. Family dinners these days consisted of my mother overreacting, my father over-drinking, and me trying, but always failing, to be the ideal daughter.

"That's okay, Mom."

"We are going out, and that is that. My baby girl, state champion."

This side of her always confused me. She seemed genuinely pleased, but at a moment's notice, her mood could change.

"Mom, I haven't even run it yet."

"I know. But you will, and you'll win."

I didn't look away from the eyes as blue as my own, knowing without a doubt that state champion was what she expected. I also knew in my heart, she'd settle for nothing less.

"Yes, Mom," I agreed and waited, knowing she had not yet dismissed me.

Picking up her coffee mug, she took another sip, and I was reminded again of why I was expected to live up to her high standards—Daniel.

"Tonight. We'll go to Franco's. Be ready at seven."

"But—"

"No buts, young lady. We *will* celebrate this."

I nodded, seeing no way out. "Yes, Mom."

"Good. Good girl." She paused. "What were you doing just now?"

There it was, the question she always asked. The one she didn't really need answered but inserted into every conversation she had with me.

She saw it as good parenting. That question showed she cared, right?

"Nothing, just read—"

"Good, good," she muttered, not really listening at all.

The obligatory words had been spoken. I was now dismissed.

It was Saturday afternoon, and I was standing by my father's bedside. I tried to remember a time when he wasn't suffering, a time when he'd been strong, healthy—*complete.*

I pulled the aqua vinyl recliner next to his bed and sat down facing him. Sometimes, if I was lucky, he'd open his eyes and see—

"Gray," I heard, and I looked into the face of a tired old man.

"Hey, Dad."

I took his hand in mine and squeezed it.

"Hey yourself. What's going on, son?"

Even now, with his world slowly fading, he saw straight through the mask and right into me.

"Nothing's going on. How are you?"

With his usual dry wit intact, a familiar furrow creased his forehead. "How am I? Really, Gray? I woke up this morning, so that's a great start."

"Come on, Dad."

He chuckled softly, which gave way to a cough. "You asked."

"So I did."

"Now, what's going on, son?"

I knew there was no way I could admit the truth. That was *not* the man I wanted to be and certainly not the man I wanted him to remember. *Fuck.*

I couldn't even look him in the eye as I recalled what happened yesterday.

Too close, I had been too fucking close to giving in.

Instead of being the teacher who inspired the desire to learn, I was the teacher inspiring my students—no, one student —to want *me.*

As if that was okay on *any* fucking level.

"Son? What is it? You seem…troubled."

Erasing the revulsion from my face, I tried to assure him. "Nothing, Dad. It's nothing."

He squinted at me and tried a different tactic. "Is it the new school? Are the teachers giving you a hard time?"

I rested my elbows on my knees and clasped my hands between them.

How could I tell him, *no, it's an eighteen-year-old girl giving me trouble.* He couldn't understand because neither could *I.*

"Nope, just the usual. Oh, and my father is sick, you may have heard."

With another congested cough, he shook his head on the stark white pillow. "Don't try and bullshit a bullshitter. I'm sick, not stupid."

"Dad, just leave it alone. It's nothing you need to worry about."

There, if I said it was nothing, then it was—

"You're lying to me. I taught you better than that, son. My students didn't lie to me, and I've never let you either."

Yes, that was the whole fucking problem. He *had* taught me better than that, and I was about to let him down.

"Is it a girl?"

Just that word alone had my palms sweating. *Girl*. Yes, it was definitely a girl.

"What's the problem? You're successful, and you take after me, so we both know you're good-looking. You want my advice?"

For the first time in a long while, my father laughed at what he thought was a lovesick son. He had no idea I was cursing myself on the inside.

"I told you, I'm fine."

I forced myself to keep the connection with him before he closed his eyes and exhaled.

"Life's unexpected, Gray. Hearts come and go. If you want hers, then take it."

I suppose that was easy to say when you didn't know whose heart was up for the taking.

Seven-thirty arrived, and so did we. Three pillars of the community, all immaculately dressed and *all* without a single thing to say.

"Reservation for Lancaster," Mom announced as though we were royalty.

The girl standing behind the hostess table looked around my mother and waved at me. "Hi, Addy."

I had no idea who she was, but manners prevailed when my mom pinned me with her *answer correctly* look.

"Hi."

She beamed at me as if I'd just agreed to be her new BFF and then returned her attention to my mom.

"Okay, Mrs. Lancaster, right this way."

We were ushered inside and about to walk past the bar when I spotted him. He was standing at the counter watching the television that was mounted on the back wall.

I stopped in place, and as my father ran into me, he cursed, "*Shit*, Addison."

That was the moment that Grayson saw us.

It was the first time Mr. McKendrick met my parents.

Present...

Doc snaps my attention back to him with a sharp click of his fingers.

"Addison, as adults we become burdened with different kinds of responsibilities. When do you believe we are ready for that?"

Once again, I find myself sitting opposite Doc as he tries to pull from me the answer he seeks. He does this, as always, by asking questions I don't give a shit about.

Tick, tick, tock.

How am I supposed to know about adult responsibilities when my only examples have been so quick to abandon all of theirs?

That isn't the real question here. *No.*

The real question, disguised so poorly by the *adult* in the room, is age.

There it is.

Only three letters, yet it's a word so big that it can ruin a career, tarnish a reputation and destroy a life. *Forever.*

"He was thirty-two."

His age.

"You were eighteen."

My age.

"That wouldn't be illegal, except..."

Tick, tick, tock.

He'll be waiting a long time for me to finish that statement.

I have time. He doesn't. Doc needs me to talk. To trust him with all of my secrets and all of *his* because without those words, *they* have nothing. I look this adult in the eye, and he knows. He isn't going to get anything from me.

I know where my responsibilities lie, and it's nowhere near him.

CHAPTER 9

 ast...

I could tell by the way he glanced at the door that Grayson's first thought was to run. I guess I couldn't blame him. It was my first thought too. But while he wanted to run to the exit, I felt the irresistible urge to run to him.

He was dressed in dark jeans and a red shirt with his hair pulled back and tied at the nape of his neck. Everything about him appealed to me—including the flash of paranoia that crossed his face, so subtle only I noticed.

Knowing he had no immediate means of escape, I turned to my dad and stated clear enough to penetrate his alcohol-induced mind, "That man over there is my new history teacher. I'm going to go and say hello, if you even care."

My father, I guess I could still call him that even though he'd checked out of our lives a little over two years ago, stared down at me. "Don't talk to me like that, Addison."

"Yeah, whatever." I paused and looked back to where Grayson was paying for a pizza. "I'm going."

"Addison, get back…" he tried, but his words faded as I made my way through the tables. I reached the end of the bar just as Grayson turned to exit.

"Well, tonight just got a whole lot more interesting. Hello, Mr. McKendrick."

~

She appeared untouchable. So immaculately put together that she almost didn't seem real. Her curls hung loosely over her shoulders, and her mouth was painted the same color as the rosy blush tinting her cheeks.

Taking in the rest of her ensemble did nothing to alleviate the heat spreading through my veins. Standing in front of me was a walking contradiction.

Wearing a pink summer dress with short sleeves that cupped her shoulders, Addison should have represented sweet, innocent even. However, the words that left her mouth, and the eyes that found mine, were anything but.

I was losing this battle.

As I stood beside her with her parents making their way over to us, I made sure my focus remained on her face.

"Hello, Addison. I see you're here with your parents. Hi, I'm Mr. McKendrick, Addison's history teacher."

I held the pizza box out in front of me to stay at a distance and angled my body away from hers. Her mother, an attractive lady in her early forties, gave me a much more thorough once-over this time around. When her eyes came up to meet my own, recognition dawned.

"Ahh, yes. Now I remember. You were at the track meet yesterday."

With that wonderful reminder, I became light-headed.

Am I really standing here doing this? Discussing the track meet with Addison's mother as if I hadn't watched her daughter orgasm only inches away from me?

73

I felt like I was going to throw up.

"So you're new to the school?"

The deep, skeptical voice broke through my paranoia. Nodding my head at who I assumed was Addison's father, I confirmed his question without having to speak. *Thank fucking god*.

"He's traveled all over Europe. Greece, Rome…" Addison's voice washed over me, but I blocked it out when cool fingers touched my own where they were holding the pizza box. Addison's mother.

"Have you, really? Where else have you been, Mr. McKendrick?" she asked conversationally, but her regard and touch were beginning to make it more than obvious where Addison's confidence came from.

Usually, I could list the cities in order of each visit, but with Mrs. Lancaster still touching me, I was rendered speechless. I stepped back, more than ready to escape this awkward little run-in, and knocked against the bar as I searched for a way out.

As I did, I caught Addison in my line of sight, and the way she was looking at me had my palms sweating and my cock hardening in a way her mother's touch hadn't.

I needed to leave, right fucking now.

"Well, it was nice to meet you both," I lied and pushed my way past the family. "I hope you have a good night, and I'll see you on Monday, Addison."

I made my way through the restaurant and out the door, knowing my behavior was probably coming off as odd.

Fuck.

Angrily, I kicked a rock that was on the pavement and this time, cursed out loud. "Fuck!"

A couple dashed past me and exchanged nervous looks before rushing inside.

Just great, that's fucking fantastic. Now they think I'm crazy too.

I walked to my truck, pissed off with myself and the entire situation I had gotten into. Tonight needed to be over with.

The sooner the fucking better.

~

"Well, he seems very nice."

Yes, I'd noticed how *nice* my mom thought Grayson was. It'd been obvious as she'd fondled his hand in front of my father.

"How would you know, Sandra? You said all of three things to the man."

They argued their way back to the table, and I made an impromptu decision. "I'll be right back. I need to use the restroom."

My mom looked at me, and for an irrational moment, I thought she could read my mind, until she said, "I'll order chicken for you."

Not caring in the slightest, I made a beeline for the restrooms. At the last minute, I ducked out the side door and saw Grayson climbing into his truck.

Running across the dark parking lot, I called out to him just as he was pulling his door shut. "Mr. McKendrick!"

Will he talk to me? Or just leave?

One, two, three.

When the truck didn't rumble to life, I scanned the area I was in and moved closer. He pushed the door back open and I had to crane my neck to see him.

"What are you *doing* out here?"

He was furious, but at the same time, his eyes betrayed him. They were blazing hot, and it had nothing to do with anger.

Licking my lips, which suddenly felt dry, I placed a hand on the side of the door. "Meet me later."

"Are you fucking insane?"

Good question. Am I? I didn't think so.

"That's not a no."

Gripping the steering wheel tightly, he looked away and said, "Well it's not a fucking yes."

One, two, three. One, two, three.

I waited for him to turn back, but when it was clear he wouldn't, I whispered the one thing I knew would get his attention. His name.

"Grayson?"

Just as I suspected, he responded, speaking so softly I had to strain to hear him.

"Go back inside, sit down with your parents, and eat your dinner. You don't know what you're asking for."

As that last condescending sentence met my ears, the fact that we might get caught disappeared from my mind. I put a foot on the step bar of his truck and held the door, pushing myself up within inches of his face. He moved away so abruptly it was as if I was poison, but that didn't deter me.

"Don't kid yourself. I know exactly what I'm asking for, and you know it. Look at me."

"Go inside," he demanded with a tense jaw.

"I will. *After* you look at me."

Reluctantly, he turned his head, and when our eyes met, I dared him to do something I knew he wanted, but hadn't given in to.

"Look at *all* of me."

Nothing had prepared me for this. Nothing *could*. This was a moment that wasn't supposed to happen. It wasn't allowed to happen.

With my hands wrapped in a death grip, I finally gave myself permission to really admire her.

I started with the chestnut hair that brushed up against the creamy complexion of her skin. It seemed to go on forever as my eyes trailed down her long, elegant neck and took in all that her dress displayed—and it displayed plenty.

The way the material gathered under her breasts framed her

chest almost as well as my hands would. I brought my gaze back up to find her watching me, and the fire I could see burning there convinced me that she was a woman who knew exactly what she wanted.

"Meet me later."

"No." My response was simple and to the point. If I said too much, I'd end up doing something stupid.

"Two-thirty-two Maplewood Drive."

I waited as she stepped down from my truck.

"That's my address."

Shaking my head in disbelief, I asked, "And what? I'm just going to knock on the door and ask if you're home?"

The smile that tipped her lips up at the corners was impish, almost cute. It was the glint in her eye that was pure sex.

"No. But you might want to drive by later tonight and imagine me upstairs in my bedroom, the window to the far left. I'll be thinking about you."

"I'm leaving," I stated, finally saying something fucking sensible. I started up the truck and reached for the door handle.

"Grayson?"

Mentally exhausted, I demanded, "What?"

Stepping away from the truck, she smiled. "Enjoy your pizza."

Good thing she'd reminded me. Within the space of five minutes, I'd forgotten all about the damn to-go box sitting on the back seat of my truck.

Four hours later, I was making my way down Maplewood Drive like the fucking idiot I was.

I hadn't meant to drive over there. I'd gone home, eaten my pizza and downed two bottles of beer. My mind then wandered back to my father—*You want her heart? Go and take it*—and I started to convince myself he was right.

That was before I turned down her street and drove past her parent's large, two-story house. It was close to midnight when I glanced up to the far window on the left side and watched in disbelief as a light illuminated the room.

Shit. I turned off the headlights and then realized how stupid that was since Addison already knew my truck.

While trying to decide what to do next, I felt my heart almost stop when the light shut off. A muted glow then lit up the center arch of the house, and a figure made their way down the interior staircase.

Put your foot on the gas and go, I told myself, but as my car idled just off the side of 232 Maplewood Drive, I saw a side door open. Under the porch light stepped Addison—still wearing her pink dress.

I could hear my breathing as it came quicker in the thick silence of my truck, and just when I thought I knew what to expect, she slipped into a long, white coat and looked at me over her shoulder.

Follow me, she mouthed.

I darted down the side of my house then looked back to the road where his truck remained. He hadn't sat idle. The head-lights were back on.

Got you, I thought and pushed open a small wooden gate that led to an alley between the houses. With a final glance at the man I somehow knew was looking at me, I disappeared to the other side.

As I made my way down the familiar path, I raised my arm and placed my watch to my ear—*tick, tick, tock*—yes, there it was. It would remind me when I needed to be home.

This wasn't something new for me. Sneaking out of the house, making my way down the quiet, shadowed alley. When bright lights lit me up from behind though, I thought, *that is new.*

He was following *me*.

Adding an extra sway to my hips, I made my way to the end of the alley, and when I got there, I spun on my toes and watched the truck pull to a stop. He wasn't too close, so I crooked my finger, inviting him *closer*.

That was when the truck started its slow crawl forward.

Tipping my head back, I laughed into the night sky and practically skipped out to the street. I turned to the left and started to walk faster as the truck pulled out behind me.

After passing the large oak tree on Blackwood Drive, I trailed my fingers along three wooden fence rails until I reached the final mailbox and made a right. Again, I tried to see him through the blinding headlights, focusing on the place I knew he'd be sitting.

With an extra bounce to my step, I crossed the street and walked on the footpath that lined the main road leading out of my subdivision.

I knew exactly where I was going. I'd done it every Saturday night for the last two years. I just hadn't done it quite like this.

Stopping on the side of the main road, I looked across the four lanes of traffic. From where I was standing, I could barely make out the sign that was illuminated by two floodlights, but I knew exactly what it read.

I checked to the right and then to the left where his truck had pulled up beside me. Grayson rolled down a window, and as he peered out at me, I resisted the urge to raise my arm and press my watch to my ear.

He frowned, confused, while I grinned. For the first time, I saw everything clearly.

With him, the ticking had stopped.

CHAPTER 10

 resent...

Tick, tick, tock.

"Do you know what day it is today, Addison?"

Here we go again, but today I can't bring myself to step inside his office. I see Doc sitting in his usual chair and I anxiously smooth my hands down my thighs.

Of course I know what day it is. It's the day Daniel...I can't even think it.

"Why don't you take a seat?"

He seems as uneasy as I am.

"Addison?"

I don't answer, but that's nothing new. I don't want to be here today. I don't want to be anywhere.

"Please, Addison, come inside. Sit with me."

I press my fingers to the outside of my legs but otherwise remain unmoving.

"We don't have to talk, okay? We can just sit."

I wonder if he really means that and if the concern in his eyes is real. It's probably paid for concern.

"It's okay to be sad, Addison," he tries to reassure me.

He raises a hand and beckons me to step inside. Every day, he tries to get me to give something that I no longer have inside me. *Trust.*

"Is that how you feel, Addison? Sad?"

Tick, tick, tock.

With the black shadow looming, always threatening to swallow what little emotion I have left, I finally put an end to today's session.

"I feel nothing."

~

Past...

I peered out at Addison as she watched me from the side of the road and then inclined her head.

Squinting, I tried to make out the words on the sign. I couldn't read it from where I was, and before I could ask, Addison was crossing the street.

Stay or go? Well, *fuck.* I'd come this far, what was a little farther going to do? Lead me down a path straight toward temptation? I think I'd already made that decision when I'd driven over to *temptation's* house.

With the roads deserted, I drove out to the middle lane and then continued into the drive of—Oakland Cemetery.

What the fuck was going on? And where the hell was Addison?

Deciding enough was enough, I turned the truck off and pushed the door open.

A cemetery. I had to admit, this was not what I'd been

expecting when I came to her tonight, and yes, that's what I had done—*come to her.*

I could feel my confusion changing to concern when I realized I hadn't seen Addison since she'd run out into the street.

What if something had happened to her?

Stepping outside, I slammed the door and made my way around the front to the passenger side. There were no floodlights on this side, just a perimeter fence and darkness.

Straining to see, I finally gave in to my apprehension and hissed, *"Addison."*

My heart thumped so hard, I counted each pulse it made while I waited for something—anything. When I got no response, I tried again, feeling the panic start to take ahold of me. *"Addison."*

Sometimes, as I was about to discover, panic of the unknown can be more comforting than panic of the known.

"Yes, Grayson?"

Just like that, with those two words, Addison sealed our fate and I did nothing to change its course.

I'd waited until he got out of the truck before approaching. I didn't want his escape to be as easy as driving away. Standing in the small stone alcove of the gate, I knew it would be best to wait until he stepped away from the lit area. That way, any cars driving by wouldn't be able to see us.

I wanted no excuses, no reason for him to worry, but I could see my silence had caused just as much concern as my presence would have. He turned to me, and I finally took a moment to really look at him the way I wanted to.

His hair was still pulled back but several pieces had now escaped and been pushed behind his ears. The darker stubble lining his square jaw made my fingers tingle with the need to touch.

"Oh, thank God," he whispered, sounding relieved.

I thought he would move away from me once he knew I was safe. Instead, he reached out and squeezed my shoulder.

"I thought something had happened to you."

I don't think he realized that he was slowly massaging me.

"Jesus, don't do that again. Okay?"

Taking another step closer, I agreed quietly. "Okay."

He licked his lips and removed his hands, and I saw in his eyes the minute he decided it was time for some distance.

"What are you doing out here?" he asked. His casual black sports jacket shifted with the breeze, and all of a sudden I couldn't remember why I was there. All I knew was that I wanted to touch him.

"Addison?"

His voice had the ability to make all of the noise inside my head cease.

Blinking up at him, I finally answered, "Yes?"

"What are you doing out here?"

Moving in so my jacket brushed the front of his, I finally reached to touch him, but he grabbed my wrist, holding it away.

"No," he told me, and his voice was so stern I probably should have heeded the warning...but I didn't.

"No?"

His head bent down, and when his face was a hairsbreadth from my own, he repeated, "No. Tell me why you're here."

His breath was warm as it ghosted over my lips, and I couldn't help but part my own, hoping by some miracle I could taste him on my tongue.

"Why are *you* here? That's a better question, don't you think?"

"I know better than this."

I reached up *needing* to touch him, but he took that hand too, holding them both prisoner. Being held in place with nowhere to go elicited a hunger in me that I didn't yet understand. "Know better than what?"

"Than to be *here*."

"Then go," I offered.

That was all it took. He spun me around, backed me up against the truck, and had my arms pinned by my head so fast I lost my breath. Leaning in beside me until his mouth was by my ear, he rasped in an unsteady voice, "I *can't*."

I turned my head to face him and saw all of his turmoil, and finally, the full impact of his desire. "Then don't."

"You're going to be the death of me."

Life is full of ironies, because with him, I'd never felt more alive.

As I stood there, I could feel the pulse in her wrists beating beneath my fingers.

"Kiss me," she pleaded, straining against my hold. "Just once. So I'll know what it's like."

She didn't need to beg; I'd made up my mind. The only question that remained was how I was going to stop once I started. Her lips parted, and as her tongue slipped out to moisten them, the time for waiting was over. I was drawn to her in a way I couldn't describe.

Lowering my head, I slowly tasted her upper lip with the tip of my tongue. She didn't move, not even to breathe, as I did it again. This time, as I was about to pull back, those soft, plump lips of hers closed around my tongue and sucked it inside her mouth.

I couldn't help the groan that escaped me. It was as much from the sweet torture she'd put me through as it was from the searing arousal she was currently igniting.

When her mouth slipped away, I chased it with my own and pushed my tongue inside, taking what I wanted without any thought of the consequences. Slow disappeared as her body shifted, trying to get closer to mine, and I didn't dare release her.

Addison's mouth was sweet, and her body...it was fucking sinful.

I lifted my head, my harsh breathing now matching hers. Her nose brushed against mine as she softly touched *my* lip with her tongue. My hands tightened where they were.

Once is a mistake, I can play that off. But twice...can I really let this happen?

As she whispered, "Again,"—I knew the answer.

Releasing her, I trailed my fingers down her cheek and then cupped the side of her face before kissing her again. This time she was more than ready to reciprocate. She grabbed the side of my jacket and pulled me to her as I wrapped my arms around her waist, hauling her up against my body.

The moan that left her was raw, sexual, and made my cock harder than I thought possible. I cupped her ass and slammed her back against the truck. Her legs wrapped around my hips, and I ground my erection against her.

Heaven or hell? At this stage, it could have been either. I didn't care.

Her fingers found their way into my hair, and she angled her head, pushing her tongue deeper inside my mouth. I felt her pull the tie free, causing my hair to fall down in a curtain around us.

For a moment, our mouths stopped moving, our tongues stopped tasting, and I held her there, trapped against the side of my truck. I took from her each breath she gave and returned it with one of my own.

"This is crazy. We can't...*I* can't be doing this. Not with you."

I knew right then after only one taste, that if I couldn't have her, there would *be* nobody else.

~

Trying to keep the connection, I ran my fingertips over the hard line of his jaw and then pushed his hair back behind his ears.

"You're so sexy."

He let out a self-derisive laugh and shook his head.

"What? You don't think so?"

"I don't think that *you* should think I'm sexy."

I couldn't help the thrill of satisfaction I got when he squeezed my ass and pushed against me. He closed his eyes as if he was trying to get himself under control.

"Well, this doesn't help me to think otherwise."

"*Addison*," he growled. "You're trouble."

"And you're hard. So I'm guessing you either like trouble, or you think I'm sexy too."

Releasing me, Grayson ran his hands around the waist of my coat and then drew one of my long brown curls between his thumb and forefinger.

"I *think*...we shouldn't be doing this."

"But we did."

He took a step back and agreed, "Yes. We did."

Pushing away from the truck, I raised a hand and laid it flat on his jacket, over his heart.

"I want to do it again."

Turning away from me, he shoved his fingers through his hair and scuffed a foot into the ground before asking the question I knew would come.

"Why don't you tell me why we're here?"

I could tell he was trying to move on and push aside what just happened. Maybe even convince himself that it had been a one-time deal.

I let him believe what he would in that moment and told him the truth.

"I'm here to see my brother."

"Your brother?"

"Yes," I confirmed as I made my way past him. "I'm here to see Daniel."

Present...

Open.

Eyes—open.

I lie still amongst the flowers and listen for it, but it's not there—there's no tick, tick, tock. There's nothing.

The dream is familiar. This is where I meet Daniel, but this detail... this silence is not familiar. Like a whisper on the wind, I hear Grayson as clearly as if I'm back in his classroom. "Bukowski once wrote, find what you love and let it kill you."

Whipping my head around, I look for him.

Is he here? Did I somehow pull him into this dream?

I see nothing, and still, there's no ticking of my watch.

Defeated, I lie back down in the fields of purple, and just before my eyes close, I hear, "I found you."

My eyes snap open, and there it is.

It's back, and he's gone—tick, tick, tock.

CHAPTER 11

 ast...

"Your brother?" I asked.

I turned as she walked over to the gates. After she pushed them open, Addison looked back to where I was standing rooted to the same spot.

"I don't understand."

"I know," she simply replied. "You may want to park your truck inside, so no one reports it."

Great, now she's telling me the smart thing to do.

I cursed myself as I got in the truck and followed her down the drive to a small, empty lot. I sat for a minute watching her where she stood bathed in my headlights once more. Dressed as she was in her pure white coat, she resembled an angel. An angel I'd been kissing only minutes earlier. An angel I was thinking of in the most impure way possible.

Cutting the lights and darkening my view, I got out and came around to where she was standing.

"Do your parents know where you are?"

The mischievous smile she aimed my way let me know she was onto me, and there was no way she was going to let me forget what'd just happened. Not when she finally had me where she wanted me.

"Do yours?"

"Addison."

"Grayson," she countered and held out her hand. "Come with me. I want you to know who I am."

"I do know you, a little too well."

Not in the least bit deterred, she wrapped her fingers around mine, and I followed her despite my reservations.

"I want you to know more of me. I want you to understand."

I felt her touch like a live wire as it traveled up my arm, shocking me in its wake.

"Okay. But I'm driving you home after. You're not walking alone at this hour."

With her hand clasped in mine and my cock stiffening at being this close, I thought it completely hypocritical of me to be concerned about her safety—especially with what I was thinking.

"Are you worried something will happen to me?"

I nodded. "You shouldn't be walking around this late. Anything could happen."

"Anything?"

She didn't let up for a second. Always pushing me and leading me down a road I know I shouldn't be on.

"*Okay*," she drawled. "You're no fun."

It was an odd comment to make while standing in a cemetery, but before I could remark on it, she tugged me off the path and onto the grass.

"This way."

I had two choices—let go of her and demand she get back in the truck. Or follow her...*again*. Like the fool that I was, I followed.

She led me through several rows of tombstones with tall flowers sprouted alongside, almost as though the cemetery had been built in a field of—

"What are these flowers?" I asked, pulling on her to stop.

"Monkshood. Have you heard of them?"

I *had* heard of them. They were a cult classic but usually in herb form, not as a flower. "Yes, it's Wolf's Bane. You do know how poisonous these are, right?"

"Yes, I know. There are signs. See?" she replied, as if we were discussing the color of the sky.

"Don't you think you should have mentioned that? This is serious shit, Addison. You shouldn't be here, especially at night. Jesus. Come on, let's go."

She placed a hand on my chest and slid it up my shoulder and into my loose hair as she came up on her tiptoes. With her lips hovering over mine, she whispered, "They are also known as the *queen of poisons*. Did you know that?"

I didn't, but being in a cemetery with poisonous fucking flowers wasn't what I called a good time.

"Stop fucking around. This isn't funny."

"Are you planning to bend down and pick the flowers?" I could feel her lips curving into a grin against my own.

Considering the situation and what we were discussing, she sounded somewhat crazed. I found myself reaching for something to ground me. The fact that it was her waist was of no consequence as I gripped her tight.

"What kind of game are you playing?" I demanded, not realizing until then that was what I was feeling—*played*.

"No game," she breathed out then licked my lip, causing me to yank my head back.

"The *fuck* you're not."

Her fingers massaged my head as she cocked hers to the side. "I told you."

"Your brother?"

Nodding, she answered, "Yes…Daniel."

"What happened to him?" I asked.

Without flinching, she replied, "I killed him."

The hold Grayson had on my waist was so tight I would have a bruise for sure, and the way his mouth fell open at my admission made me wonder what was going through his mind.

I released his hair and touched his hand.

"Come," I invited. "*Don't* touch the flowers."

He didn't answer, but his fingers took mine, and I led him farther across the dewy grass. When we arrived at the far back corner, I stopped in front of the tombstone that had Daniel's name inscribed on it.

Without looking at the man beside me, I explained, "Every Saturday I come here, hoping this is some kind of nightmare. One where I'll walk through those gates, and this won't be here. That all I'll see is a field. A field that's *full* of these poisonous flowers. It would be better than this alternative. Right?"

That was when I faced him.

Grayson was tall. I knew he was, but in that moment, I really took notice. His shoulders were broad and represented strength. To me, he was safe, and the entire time I was with him, I had not heard—I lifted my wrist and brought it to my ear.

"Why do you do that?" he asked gently.

Lowering my arm, happy that the watch was still working, I looked back to where Daniel lay buried beneath the earth.

"Because I was late."

The silence that stretched between us was complicated for so many reasons, and even though I wanted to explain, I wasn't sure I could. I'd never been able to before, not even to Doc, who my mom had been making me visit at least once a week for the past two years.

"What were you late for?" he asked, seeming to understand

that since I couldn't describe my obsession, it was best just to ask why I had it.

"*Who*, not what." I felt a tear slip from my eye and trail down my face. "I was too late for him."

~

Present...

"Tell me, Addison, what does this picture mean to you?"

I look at the photograph Doc is holding in front of me. It's a picture of a beautiful purple flower. A flower shaped like a monk's hood.

I remain silent.

"Nothing?"

My eyes shift to his. *The waiting game? Oh, I can wait.*

Tick, tick, tock.

He turns the picture around and examines it.

"It's a photo of a Monkshood flower," he says, but he knows I'm already aware of that. "It's very pretty, don't you think?"

Bait me. That's what he's trying to do. He *will* fail.

"I didn't know they grew here in Denver, but they do."

I arch my brow, and he knows me well enough that he continues.

"People often do stupid things when it comes to something pretty...even when they know better." He pauses and sits forward, giving me the photograph. As my fingers touch it, he asks, "Did Grayson?"

For a split second, I wish I could tell him everything, but I have no answer. Not the one he wants. He wants me to ask for help, but even if I could, I wouldn't.

I don't need protecting.

Sitting back in my seat, I trace the shape of the flower with the tip of my finger and remind myself that *he* is gone, and nothing will change that. All I have to do is...forget I ever knew him.

Raising my head, I pin Doc with a vacant stare and answer his question.

"No. *Akoviton.*"

Doc's eyes remain on me. "I don't understand."

"Without struggle."

I can see his mind working as he asks, "Who? Grayson went without struggle?"

A sly smile stretches my lips. He thinks I'm giving him something. I'm giving him nothing.

"This flower, *Aconitum,* comes from the Greek word *akoviton,* which means...without struggle."

He says nothing as he leans back in his chair. I can tell he is trying to decide if there is more to my statement than what's on the surface.

Let him wonder. Let him think.

This session's over as far as I'm concerned.

Tick, tick, tock.

~

Past...

"Come on, Addison. Let me take you home."

I could tell she had gone somewhere in her head because she was no longer talking as she stood beside me. She was counting.

One, two, three. One, two, three.

Over and over she repeated the numbers, and the instinct to wrap her in my arms now came from concern. She was visibly upset, and I wasn't sure if my touch would help to calm her or cause further distress.

"Addison?" I coaxed.

Her hair shifted softly in the breeze, and when those blue

eyes of hers found me, I thought she appeared as perfect as the first time I'd met her.

The perfection, however, was marred. Not in a horrible disfigured way but on a deep subconscious level. She searched my face, for what I wasn't sure, and continued to count—*one, two, three*—in a way that I would never stop hearing.

This girl was damaged. Why hadn't I seen that?

She was broken, and some part of me wanted to fix her.

I took her hand, gently squeezing her fingers, and with that small touch, the counting stopped.

"Let's go. You can tell me more on the way," I said, walking us back in the direction we'd come.

She was silent the entire way.

Like someone lost, she let me lead her, and I couldn't stop myself from wondering what would've happened if she'd trusted the wrong person?

Or had she?

I unlocked the doors and shook off the thought. Before she climbed into the cab, into the small space I would soon lock myself into beside her, she said so softly I almost missed it, "You make it go away."

Not understanding, I asked, "I make what go away?"

Dropping all pretense, she replied, "The chaos."

I climbed into his truck and watched him walk around the front.

I wondered how he did it. How did he make it all stop?

He got into the seat beside me and pulled the door shut, sealing us inside.

"I'm sorry," I offered, thinking I needed to say something to make him understand that I didn't mean to be peculiar—I just was.

I was forever trying to hide this side of myself, never wanting to show I was anything other than okay, but with him it was different.

He didn't know the story. He hadn't been there that day.

Not like the rest of them.

Grayson started up the truck, but instead of leaving, he switched on the interior light. For the first time tonight, I felt like I was back in his classroom because the look he was giving me was expectant and concerned.

"Want to tell me what's going on, Addison?"

I began to nibble on my thumbnail, and almost like it was habit, he swatted it away from my mouth. "Bad habit?"

I shrugged, feeling shy.

"A nervous one."

He pulled away, and I knew he'd taken that wrong. I reached across the space between us and brought his hand back to me, placing it on my bare leg.

"*You* don't make me nervous..." I trailed off, concentrating instead on how large his hand was where it rested on my thigh.

"I should."

"Why?"

His fingers flexed, but before he could remove them, I placed mine on top.

"Because you're older than me? Or because you're my teacher?"

"God, Addison," he groaned, sounding tortured. I squeezed my hand, pressing his fingers harder against my naked flesh. "*Both* of those reasons, and..."

Having forgotten all about my moment of weird, I licked my lips and dared to ask, "And?"

I watched as he shifted in his seat so he could face me.

"And because of all the things I'm thinking."

I could feel my breathing coming faster. He pushed his hair behind his ear, and suddenly, I was burning up. It was hot, too hot.

Not ready to release my contact with him, I used my other

hand to unbutton my coat. When I pulled it apart, I heard a strangled sound leave him.

As my pink dress came into view, I knew he could see the swell of my breasts rise with every breath I took. I curled my fingers around his and slowly urged them up my leg.

"Tell me what you're thinking."

"Addison—"

"*Tell* me."

He switched off the interior light. As the cab plunged into darkness, he moved his palm farther up my thigh, and his voice found me.

"I'm thinking about what's under your dress. I have been since I saw you tonight at Franco's."

I laid my head back on the headrest and demanded, "More."

His hand skimmed the inside of my thigh, and his fingers pressed softly into my flesh, parting my legs.

"Even though I shouldn't, I can't stop thinking about how you would taste."

I could feel myself throb as his words reminded me of our kiss. "*More*."

His lips lightly grazed my jaw, and he teased me for the first time. "Greedy. I'll tell you more if you tell me why you count."

"It calms me when I'm…anxious."

His hand slipped even higher under my dress. "You're not counting now…"

"No," I sighed as his mouth moved closer to mine.

"Why?"

His warm breath touched my lips as the tips of his fingers finally brushed my damp panties.

"Because of *you*," I moaned, closing my eyes. "Your voice calms me. When you speak, I feel safe. I have ever since I met you."

"Open your eyes, Addison," he instructed, and I felt my

pussy moisten as I did as he asked. "Do you feel calm right now?"

"*No*," I whimpered, knowing if he stopped I'd beg.

He chuckled softly. "How do you feel?"

"Hot, wet..."

"And?"

"Ready." *So damn ready.*

"If we do this, we can *never* tell anyone. Do you understand?"

"*Yes*," I agreed, pulling him in that final inch. "God, yes."

I pushed my hips up so the full weight of his fingers were against my wet cotton thong and vowed, "I won't tell a soul."

That was when he *moved*.

~

As soon as the words left her mouth, I took her.

With ravenous lips and a forceful tongue, I pushed inside, kissing her fiercely as I stroked the soaked scrap of material between her smooth thighs.

Her legs spread even wider, and I braced myself on the seat beside her shoulder. Lifting my mouth from hers, I kissed the corner as my fingers curled into the leg of her panties. Her lips opened with a cry, and her eyes glazed over when she realized what I was about to do.

"Is this what you thought about? When you were lying awake at night?"

She pumped her hips up, trying to get closer, trying for contact.

"Not yet," I told her and ran my finger up and down the material's edge.

"*Grayson*," she begged, using her hold on my jacket to lever herself up.

"Yes, Addison?"

"*In* me."

ELLA FRANK

With those two words, my cock became so painfully hard I almost lost what little control I had left.

"I thought about them inside me. Fucking me."

That was it. Whatever had been holding me back snapped, and I ripped her panties, pushing them out of my way. My fingers found her, and as her warm juices coated them, I groaned and took her mouth.

As my tongue slid between her lips, my finger pushed inside her body, and the shout that left her made me fucking grateful there was no one around to hear.

With her eyes on mine, she released her hold of my jacket and pulled the stretchy material of her dress under her perky breasts.

Fuck, I was in heaven. I was also aware that I was pretty damn close to being assured a spot in hell.

Her bra...*Jesus*. Her lacy bra was the same pink as the dress.

I traced the flimsy material and tugged it down to reveal her soft, rounded flesh. I lowered my head to take her hard nipple in my mouth, and at the last second, I hesitated—but it was too late. She wove her fingers into my hair, pulling me to her, and in that moment, she owned me. I would have done anything to have her, and I did.

I had a firm hold of his hair when his lips closed around my nipple.

Grayson was driving me crazy.

His fingers filled me, and my pussy tightened and pulsed around them. My whole body bowed off the seat, and I couldn't help the scream that left me as my body tensed and my orgasm hit.

I'd been wrong, I thought as he raised his head.

He didn't have the ability to calm me...

Grayson had the ability to make me forget.

98

CHAPTER 12

 ast...

I drove Addison home that night in complete silence. I didn't know what to say. What the hell had I been thinking, touching her?

Now here it was, Monday morning, and I was standing in my classroom waiting for the fucking police to drag me away. Well, I'd been waiting for that all weekend if I was honest with myself.

The bell had just rung, and I was staring up at the clock on the wall, the loud—*tick, tick, tock*—reminding me of Addison as it signaled the day had begun.

The door slammed opened, jarring me from my thoughts. In walked Brandon, closely followed by the woman...*no*, the *girl* I'd had my fingers inside of this past weekend.

She glanced my way, and I could feel the heat rising up under the collar of my shirt. This was fucking insanity. I was going to either have an anxiety attack *or* a heart attack if she came any closer.

Luckily, Addison seemed to understand that was not going to help in this situation. Instead, she followed her boyfriend down to where they usually sat.

I gripped my tie and loosened it, hoping it would help me breathe easier, but it didn't help at all. All I kept hearing was—*I thought about them inside me. Fucking me*—and all I could see was my whole world spinning out of control.

One night. One hasty decision, and I'd gone to her—just as she'd asked.

What else would I have done had she asked?

Trying to pull myself together, I made my way to the door and closed it after the final student meandered inside. It gave me the perfect excuse to stop looking at her. To cease my inspection of the navy blue skirt she was wearing and the stretchy white tank top that didn't hide anything from curious or, *in my case,* greedy eyes.

Her legs, those long, lean legs that had propelled her over the hurdles just last Friday, were now crossed under her desk—and I hated that all I could think about was getting back between them.

I couldn't stop watching him. I was trying my best to listen to Brandon, but all I could concentrate on was Grayson. He was wearing jeans that reminded me of the ones he'd worn Saturday night...

God, just thinking about that night made me hot. The way he'd kissed me and the way his fingers had moved inside me. I still couldn't believe it'd really happened, but I knew it had. I could tell by the way *he* was acting.

It wasn't obvious in the sense that he was ogling me. In fact, it was just the opposite. He wouldn't look at me at all, and when I did catch him, he always turned away.

When I replayed that night, I kept coming back to the same

conclusion—with Grayson, my mind was at peace. What I'd started to believe was madness had disappeared.

"Okay, guys, let's open your books to chapter five," he told the class from behind his desk.

"Last week, I told you we would be starting the term with King Henry's wives, and we read about Catherine of Aragon. Funny thing is, what most people remember about their marriage is that King Henry divorced her."

"What a great way to go down in history," Jessica spoke up from the seat in front of me.

"Better than being the one whose *head* he chopped off."

My voice cut through the room and Jessica swiveled in her chair to face me, along with the rest of the class and Mr. McKendrick—I suppose that's who he was *in here.*

"Whose head did he chop off?" Jessica asked, horrified.

I didn't move other than to raise my eyes to my teacher.

"Anne Boleyn's."

Jessica spun back around to face the front of the room, as did the rest of the class.

"It's true," he confirmed. "He pursued Anne Boleyn relentlessly. At first, he was with her sister, Mary—"

"You mean he was screwing her," Brandon joked as his friend gave him a high five. "Hell yeah."

Agreeing with the boys, Mr. McKendrick gave a slight nod of his head. "Yes, I guess you would be right. He *was* sleeping with her. She was his mistress."

"I doubt he was doing much sleeping," Sam piped up.

"Okay, settle down, would you? This isn't personal health class."

Unable to help myself, I decided to speak up. "It could be."

As my teacher's eyes found mine, he disagreed. "No, it couldn't. That's next month, and I'm sure it won't be with me."

He wasn't wrong. Usually the class was taught by Miss Shrieve. If I had my way, though, it would be much sooner than that. It would be a one-on-one class, and he'd be giving me a *very* private lesson.

⁓

Moving along so I wouldn't fixate on the way Addison's eyes were undressing me, I went back to the subject.

"So, let's get back on track. King Henry was married to Catherine when he started an affair with Mary Boleyn, Catherine's lady-in-waiting."

"Jerk."

"Ass."

Refusing to be sidetracked, I ignored the comments and continued. "He, however, was drawn to, and became completely enamored with, her sister, Anne."

"Because she refused him."

Addison's voice reached me from the back of the room, but I avoided eye contact.

"Yes, at first. The king was quite persistent, though, and pursued her anyway. Some believe he did this because of Catherine's inability to produce an heir, and the king, desperate to have a son, sought out a young woman of childbearing years. But many believe he chased Anne *because* she resisted his attempts, thus provoking the king into doing everything in his power to annul his marriage to Catherine. It was that act that served as one of the contributing factors leading up to the English Reformation."

The classroom was completely silent until Jessica asked, "So, why'd he chop off her head?"

I laughed. *Of course it's the illicit details that captures the attention. It always is.*

"Well, that's what we're going to learn. It's believed that while Anne's intelligence and independence are what made her so attractive to the king in the first place, it was ultimately her downfall. She refused to be the woman behind the man and play the submissive role expected of her. Her spirited nature was intoxicating as a secret lover, but as a wife to a king? Her outspoken ways were frowned upon and eventually led to her"—stopping for dramatic effect, I drew my index finger across my throat—"execution."

The students began chattering as I moved back to the board and wrote, *Ambition, adultery, and accusations. In the end, do you believe that Anne Boleyn got what she deserved?*

I placed the chalk down on the tray and faced the class. "Well, come on, what are you waiting for? Get writing. We'll be meeting at the library tomorrow for further research, but for now use what you have."

As the students opened their books, I pulled my chair out and sat. I grabbed my own textbook and studied the photograph of Anne Boleyn.

King Henry may have initially wanted her, but it was her *own* ambition that had gotten her everything she desired. Her seduction of him, now made legendary, was one that was forbidden and eventually deadly.

Looking up, our eyes collided.

Addison wasn't unlike Anne.

She was young, beautiful, and ambitious, and ever since I'd met her, she'd gone after exactly what she wanted.

It just so happened to be *me*.

∼

Present...

"You know, you use to talk to me, Addison. When did that change?"

I look at the man sitting beside me on the stone bench. He asked me to meet him outside by the fountain today.

The sun is shining through the trees surrounding the facility, and I can hear birds in the distance. Angling my face toward the sun, I bask in the rays as it warms me. It feels like years instead of days since I've been outside.

Subconsciously, I reach down to the watch strapped to my left wrist. I can't hear it, but I know it's—*tick, tick, ticking*—its way around the face.

"When you stopped listening." My voice is steady. It's emotionless.

"Is that what I did?"

Opening my eyes, I face Doc. I can tell he's waiting for me to say more, and for the first time—I *want* to tell him.

I want to tell him that *everyone* stopped listening.

Instead, I feel a tear, the first in weeks, as it escapes my eye and trails down over my cheek.

"Addison?"

I wipe it away and look back to the trees.

"Addison, tell me."

Tell him what?

That there is no one to care how I feel now that *he* is gone?

No one cares that my dreams will never come true, not the way I want them to.

He'd calmed me when no one else could.

He'd saved me from myself.

If only they knew the truth…

But no one is listening, and *his* time is already up.

Tick, tick, tock.

~

Past…

My first three classes passed by, and as soon as the lunch bell rang, I was making my way back through the halls hoping to catch Mr—*Grayson*—before he left for lunch. I practically jogged toward the door at the very end. It was closed.

I stood in front of it and took a deep breath before reaching out to turn the handle.

Pushing it open, I stepped inside the room I'd been seated in earlier and saw him. He was standing at the back of the class pushing one of the chairs under its table when his eyes found mine, and he straightened.

"Addison, you shouldn't be in here."

He moved to the next chair and corrected it.

"I needed to see you."

"No, you didn't."

I looked at the clock on the wall and noticed the second hand was moving, but instead of following it, I found I could turn away. "Yes, I did."

"Was there something you needed to discuss?" he asked, stopping where he was.

I dropped my bag on the floor and locked the door behind me.

"Unlock the door, Addison."

"I want to talk to you."

"And I want *you* to unlock the door."

He strode up the aisle and was in front of me before I knew it. He grabbed my arm and led me to the far corner of the room before releasing me.

"This is *not* the place."

"Then where is?"

"*Not* here." His agitation was evident as he paced the floor.

"I want to see you again," I told him. "I want you to see me."

"Trust me, I *do* see you," he stressed. "You're all I fucking see, Addison. When I close my eyes, when I open them, when I'm teaching. You're. There. All. The. Fucking. Time." He rubbed his face. "Sometimes I wish I'd never seen you."

My pulse began to hammer, and I whispered, "But you did, didn't you?"

Grayson placed a hand on the bookshelf I was backed up against and shifted until his foot was between both of mine. I said nothing when his fingers stroked over my naked thigh, and when he flirted with the edge of my skirt, I barely managed to breathe.

He raised his leg slightly, and his hand slipped under the fabric to cup my bare ass. As his fingers dug into my flesh, he growled low in his throat, and I had to bite my lip to keep my moan inside.

"I see you," he answered, his words strained. "I see you, and I want to lift your skirt just like this. That's why you wore it, isn't it? To drive me fucking crazy."

My eyes closed as he pulled my hips forward.

"Open your eyes," he demanded.

Obeying, I watched him shift and felt the denim of his jeans abrade the inside of my bare legs. I could feel every pulsing throb of my body, and all I wanted to do was rub against his strong thigh. He leaned in close and licked his top lip, and I was immediately reminded of his mouth on mine.

"Tell me where I can meet you," I pleaded.

"What for?"

I rolled my hips against the ridged muscle under me. He tightened his fingers on my ass, the tips brushing the satin strip of my thong, and yanked my hips closer.

"Oh, *God*," I moaned.

"What for, Addison?" he asked again. "*Why* do you want to meet me?"

I grabbed ahold of his wrist and ground down on his thigh. The only sounds in the classroom were his and my heavy breathing as I continued to use his leg to get myself off. I wanted to come, and I knew I was close.

"I want to see you naked."

My words couldn't have been a shock to him, but when

Grayson lowered his head and admitted, "I want to see you too," I almost lost my mind.

I attempted to kiss him, but he pulled his mouth away from me.

"No, not here. Use me."

I pushed my breasts out and pressed myself against his thigh.

Fine, no kissing. I could do that. The arm around me tensed, holding me in place, and I used him—just as he had told me to.

The friction and heat between Addison's legs was penetrating my jeans. I could feel her fingers squeezing my wrist as her thighs tightened around my own. Her tight, round ass in my hand clenched every time she rocked her hips up my leg. The noises leaving her throat had me so fucking hard, I was positive my cock would be damaged if I didn't do something soon.

She was the sexiest thing I'd ever seen, and as she greedily took her pleasure, I couldn't find it in me to regret what we were doing. I knew it was wrong, but with each blissful sigh from her lips, my control slipped that much further from my grasp.

"You're hard," she whispered, and I couldn't help my smirk.

"Yes. I'm very fucking hard."

"I want to see," she boldly stated.

No one could accuse Addison Lancaster of not going after what she wanted.

"Well, we don't always get what we want."

She licked her juicy lips, and the look on her face would have brought a saint to his knees.

I was only human.

"I'm going to have you," she promised, and the words sent a thrill down my spine.

Promise or threat? Either way, the words made me want to

lift her up against the wall and shove my cock inside her. But not here, not now.

Pulling my hand away from the shelf, I gripped her hair and arched her neck back.

My lips hovered over hers. "You are going to *ruin* me."

That was when she did the unexpected.

She placed her palm over my heart and tapped—*One, two, three. One, two, three*—before whispering, "You're going to *save* me."

All rational thought halted.

"This afternoon," I heard myself say.

"Yes," she panted, squirming against my leg.

"This afternoon, follow me home like you always do."

The incorrigible minx had the audacity to smile, so I tightened my fingers in her hair and shoved my thigh higher against her.

"*Fuck*," she whimpered and clutched the arm I had around her. "Yes. I'll be there."

"Good," I agreed before releasing my grip on her hair.

I smoothed her skirt down and took a step back. Her eyes narrowed on me, and the annoyed flush that hit her cheeks made it impossible not to think about fucking her into next week.

"What are you doing?"

Sliding my hands into my jeans, I pushed the material around, trying to make them slightly more comfortable for the aching hard-on I had trapped inside.

"Waiting, and so are you."

"But…" she sputtered.

"Yes?"

"You're going to leave me like *this*?"

Oh, this is interesting—Miss Perfect has a temper.

"Well I'm like *this*, so it's only fair. Don't you think?"

Her eyes shifted to the erection I had no hope of hiding and then flew back up to my face. "Well, I could…"

"*Not*. Here," I reiterated through clenched teeth.

I stepped forward, and she retreated until her back hit the bookshelf again. This time, however, there was no touching.

"Maybe next time when I tell you to do something, you will listen."

Her mouth pinched into a grimace.

"So this was all some kind of fucked up lesson? Well, thank you, *Mr. McKendrick*."

I checked her out in a way that let her know it was *much* more than a lesson, but I was not going to be convinced to act any further on it. Not right now.

"No, it wasn't, Miss Lancaster," I disagreed and made my way to where her bag had been dumped on the floor.

I picked it up and held it out to her as she marched over to retrieve it. I made sure not to give in to the amusement I was feeling when she snatched it from my fingers and went to unlock the door.

Before she yanked it open, I slapped my palm against the wood and held it shut.

"This afternoon. My place. Be there, and I'll teach you the rest of the lesson."

"Oh yeah?" she snapped at me. "And what's that?"

Her anger didn't leave her as her eyes wandered over me. When they came back to rest on my face, they were a stormy grey—from which emotion I couldn't be sure, but it didn't matter. Nothing could have stopped me.

"I'll teach you how to come with a man inside you." I removed my hand from the door and released the lock. "Not a boy, Addison, a *man*. Now go."

Her eyes widened in shock before she walked out the door, and I had to wonder—how would *I* go down in history.

CHAPTER 13

 ast...

Why I was so nervous, I had no idea. I was sitting in my car near Grayson's house, tapping my fingers on the steering wheel —*one, two, three, one, two three.*

Yes, I was nervous.

All afternoon I'd been thinking about his final words to me. His dismissal had me so worked up, it was all I could do not to alleviate the ache.

I looked into the rearview mirror and checked my hair, making sure it was perfect. Making sure *I* was perfect.

Once I was satisfied and had gotten out of the car, I locked the door and made my way along the sidewalk. The closer I got, the more my heart raced.

I surveyed the area to make sure no one was around before I stepped up to his front door. Luckily, it was hidden in a small alcove.

This was going to change me. I knew that. Yet, as I raised my arm and knocked on the door, I welcomed it.

I knew what I was doing, and when Grayson opened his front door and stood aside, there was nothing anyone could have said to make me change my mind.

~

When I opened the door, I tried to see Addison the way I knew I was supposed to, but all I saw was a young woman.

A woman whose expression screamed—*now*.

I didn't offer her any words. Instead, I stepped aside, leaving the decision up to her. It didn't take longer than a few seconds.

She stepped over my threshold and stopped beside me, placing a palm on my chest.

"I'm ready for my lesson now."

That much was obvious.

If I shut the door, it was over—all of the pretense, all of the self-denial—gone.

I took her wrist, yanking her in close. My will to leave her alone was a thing of the past. No longer was she the student and I the teacher. Right here, in this moment, she was a woman, and I was the man about to have her.

I kicked the front door shut and crowded her back against it. My hands pulled her skirt up and my fingers found the top of her satin thong. Impatiently, I drew it down her thighs.

Caressing her sweet ass, I told her, "I want you out of these."

Swiftly doing as requested, she kicked them aside, and I moved back in against her.

"How the hell did you end up here?" I asked.

She brought one of her hands up to where my tie was knotted and tugged on it.

"You invited me."

Yes, I fucking did. She rolled her hips against me, and I knew I'd abandoned all of my carefully structured rules to do so.

"You are definitely persistent once you set your mind to something."

"I set my mind on you," she said, panting as I rubbed my hardened cock against her.

"I know. I never stood a chance."

Before she could say another word, my mouth took hers in a blazing hot kiss.

Her lips opened, and my tongue entered. Just like that, my control was shot to shit. She pressed her body against my strained jeans, and I wanted to unzip them so I could get inside her. I pulled her hips against me and lifted her against the door, attacking her mouth so fiercely she let go of my tie to wrap her arms around my neck.

I squeezed her breast through the white tank top, and she pulled her lips away to push her chest out to me, squirming all the while against the zipper of my jeans.

"*Yes*," she hissed and brought her hands to my shoulders.

Moving as if she were straddled over a bucking animal, she curved her back and fondled her breasts.

"Fucking hell, Addison."

I knew what she was about to do next because she'd done the same thing in the truck. She pulled the material down over her hard as hell nipples, and I couldn't keep my mouth off her.

I lowered my head to lick one of the hard, pink tips before sucking her into my mouth, and the throaty sound that left her was satisfying. I brought one of my hands between us to where she was rubbing her wet, naked pussy all over my jeans and grazed her clit with my finger.

"Fuck!"

"*Yes*," I encouraged, lifting my head and bringing my mouth back to hers. Fuck was exactly the right word. It was the number one thing inside my head right now.

I want to fuck, and after I have, I'm going to *be* fucked.

Jesus, what a goddamn mess.

I trailed my fingers down to her swollen pussy and began to

tease her. "You're so fucking wet," I said, sucking her bottom lip between mine.

Her hips followed the glide of my hand with an eager thrust as she continued to shock me with every word that fell from her immoral mouth.

"I'm always like this around you."

Oh, God. Did that mean even in—"Always?"

"Yes, always. At home. At school. Someone just has to say your name."

I stroked my finger through her juices and when she trembled in my arms, I pushed it inside her. "Well, I want to hear you scream it."

Her sweet breath seduced me as she dared to ask, "And which name would that be? You have two in my head."

I jerked her higher up against the door and thrust a second finger inside. I tasted her lips with my tongue as she rode my hand. Her core clenched when I grazed my thumb over her clit, and that's when I said, "In this fucking house, I only have one name. What is it, Addison?"

~

As my body shook and my climax hit, I couldn't help screaming "Grayson" into the empty house.

I could still feel myself throbbing around his fingers when he spun me away from the door and walked us through the hall to the living room. My breath was coming fast and I had a hard time catching it as he slowly lowered me to my feet.

He brought his index finger to his mouth and licked it, managing to hypnotize me. Usually, I was the one who held the power, especially with boys like Brandon, but in this equation with him—I held nothing.

He studied me as I stood there, and I wondered what he saw.

"Get undressed, Addison," he ordered, his ragged voice stroking all my sensitive spots.

I didn't hesitate, fearing that the conflict I could see in his eyes would make him change his mind. I removed my jacket and threw it on the floor. My tank top was next to go, and then I wriggled out of my skirt until I was standing in front of him completely naked.

He ran a hand through his hair.

"How could I ever fucking resist you? You're breathtaking."

I felt mischievous in the wake of his comment and went to do a spin for him. That was when I stopped and saw it.

There, right in front of me, was *me*. I was naked and flushed from head to toe in his floor-to-ceiling, wall-to-wall mirror.

Before I could say anything, he stepped behind me and placed his large hands on my hips with his fingers pointing downward.

"See?" he asked, and in the mirror I saw him lower his mouth to my ear. "Breathtaking."

My chest was rapidly rising and falling, and when his palms glided around to my upper thighs, he framed my pelvic bone with his thumb and index fingers—a triangle had never been so perfect.

"A mirror?" I raised my brow at his reflection. "Kinky."

Without breaking our searing connection, he pulled me in close, and I could feel his hard cock nestled up against my ass.

"They came with the house. Up until this moment, I hated them," he replied.

I rested my head back against his shoulder. "And now?" I watched him with languid eyes as he cupped my naked breasts.

"I'm still deciding." He thumbed my nipples and then quietly instructed, "Put your arms back around my neck."

I was still unbelievably aroused as I raised my arms and did what he asked. I curled my hands around his neck and interlocked them under his hair, displaying my body fully to the ravenous man behind me.

He kept his left hand on my breast and brushed the back of his knuckles down my body until he cupped my bare mound. I rocked my hips forward and whimpered.

I wanted more.

"Let me see you."

I want him.

"You *can* see me."

"I want to see you naked. *Please,*" I begged, realizing how out of character that was for me.

"Okay. Let's put your hands where they won't get in trouble," he suggested, taking them from around his neck and placing them low against my back.

He was standing directly behind me, but I could see his collarbone and the top of his chest. I was captivated as he removed his tie, and when he took off his shirt and threw it aside, I couldn't help the instinct to turn around and look.

"No, Addison. Stay just as you are," he instructed, almost daring me to disobey.

"And if I don't?"

I heard the sound of his zipper and then he lowered his head so his chin almost brushed my shoulder. Our eyes met and held in the mirror—stalemate.

"You don't want to find out."

Holy shit.

He disappeared from view to remove his jeans, and I licked my lips in anticipation, waiting for what was next.

As soon as he was finished, he took my wrists and placed my hands back behind his neck. He pushed his hard-on against my ass, and I let out a satisfied sigh.

Finally, there was nothing between us.

"Do you feel that?" he asked, rubbing his cock between my cheeks.

My mouth became dry, and I had no words as he resumed his original position—one hand on my breast and one between my legs.

He pushed his hips against me again, and my eyes began to flutter shut.

"*No*. Remember what I told you?"

"*Yes*," I managed through a shaky breath. "Keep them open."

"Fuck, yes. Watch us, Addison. Because I can't bear to."

His words were passionate and full of torment, and I couldn't have ripped my eyes away if I tried.

He bent his head and kissed my ear as his fingers found my slippery clit. His other hand pinched my nipple as my heart raced and my breathing tripled. I could see him touching me, and I could feel his cock, hot and heavy against my ass, and I wanted...no, *needed* to see his body. I wanted to see it all.

"You," I panted.

"What about me?"

"I want to see you. I *can't* see you," I almost cried, wanting to look at him with everything inside of me.

"Then turn around," he invited.

I turned to face him and for the first time, I got to see Grayson. He was so much better than any fantasy in my head.

He stood there in his natural state, allowing me to take him in. I'd been right—on his left arm there was a tattoo of a snake with the end of its tail curled around his strong bicep. I didn't spend too much time on that, not when all of his muscles were flexed and straining as if he was holding himself in check. He had very little hair on his chest, and from his navel down, that same dark golden hair led a nice trail to his erect cock.

Subconsciously, I hummed as I saw his fists curl at his sides. I probably should have been nervous, but as I waited for the counting, waited for the ticking...I heard nothing. Just our combined breathing.

"Seen enough?"

I wrapped my fingers around his cock and smiled. "Not yet. When you put *this* inside me, I want to watch."

I stroked my palm up his rigid length, and he gripped my

hair so I was forced to look up at him. He looked like a man on the edge. I didn't know what to expect, but I was looking forward to whatever he was going to give me.

Leaning down until his lips brushed mine, he said, "Turn around."

I released my hold on him and did as I was told.

"Get on your knees."

I couldn't help the sensual curve of my lips as I faced the mirror. I knew where this was going, and I was ready.

As he stood behind me rolling a condom into place, I dropped down to my knees and didn't wait to be told to get on my hands too. I moved into position and began to crawl closer to the mirror, swaying my ass, which in turn made my breasts gently move from side to side.

The sound that left Grayson didn't sound human as he got to his knees behind me. He gripped my hips, pulling me to a stop and then his body was over me and his lips were pressed against my shoulder.

"What is it about you I can't fucking shake?"

He lined his hips up with mine, and his cock brushed between my legs. I could feel his thick length sliding between my swollen lips. I looked in the mirror and felt my excitement intensify at how big he was compared to me.

"Nothing. I've done nothing to you."

He raised his head, and his fevered gaze caught mine. "The hell you haven't. Does *this*," he asked, shoving against me harder this time, "feel like nothing to you?"

"It feels exactly how I imagined it."

I pumped my hips back, trying to get him inside me.

"And how's that?"

"Hard and ready to fuck me."

My nipples were beaded tight, and my pussy was soaked as the tip of his cock kissed the opening between my wet lips. Narrowing my gaze on the intense man hovering behind me, I pushed him that final inch.

"I've been thinking about this ever since I got in trouble for being late to your class."

It was a combination of her eyes, her words, and as she rocked back on me—her body, that finally did it. With a firm thrust, I drove my cock deep inside her, reveling in the erotic sound she made as she shoved her round ass back against my hips.

"*Ahh, God,*" she cried out, but I didn't stop.

My hand tangled in her hair and pulled her head up, making her watch.

Someone should get the visual pleasure here, and since I couldn't admit to what I was fucking doing, it may as well be her. I was more than happy to study the creamy curves of her voluptuous body but then I heard her softly say, "Watch us."

Who am I to ignore such a plea?

My eyes caught hers in the mirror, and I pushed deeper inside her. With each forward motion, her eyes stayed locked with mine and blazed—like she couldn't get enough.

Her breasts swung every time our hips connected, and when her shiny lips opened and she told me, *harder,* I almost came.

I wrapped an arm around her waist and pulled her back until I was kneeling so she could sink down over my cock.

"*Christ,*" I cursed as I pushed her hair over her shoulder and ran the back of my hand down her side to where we were joined.

As I watched the two people in the mirror, it was hard to imagine them as anyone other than a man and woman enjoying each other—and that was exactly what I was doing. Enjoying the *fuck* out of her.

"Look at you," I encouraged, now beyond any delusions.

This woman I was with—this gorgeous, sensual woman whose body was made to take mine—was spectacular. As her hands caressed her breasts and she watched us together, nothing could have convinced me that this was wrong.

My fingers found her clit and rubbed it gently, causing her hips to buck and a cry to leave her.

"Look at you sitting here with your legs spread and my cock so fucking deep I don't think I'll ever leave. *Jesus*, Addison. I thought you were perfect before. Now I fucking know it."

I watched her shake her head in denial as she rocked on me. "Not perfect, never perfect. *Again*, do it again."

I held her hip and plunged up into her as she continued murmuring, *"Not perfect, never perfect."*

"Addison," I whispered.

Her eyes met mine in the mirror as she continued to repeat herself, so I thrust inside her again and made her moan instead.

"Perfect for *me*. Look at us, and tell me this is not fucking perfection."

She watched carefully as I moved under her, and when her fingers pinched her nipples, I brushed my thumb over her clit. I could see my cock each time I pulled out of her and then watched as it disappeared again between her folds. That was when I felt her muscles clamp around me.

My own climax hit me, and I shouted out her name. Her eyes squeezed shut, and she bit her lip as her body tensed and she screamed mine. Together, we gave in like two warriors who'd just surrendered to the ultimate fight.

CHAPTER 14

 resent...

Fairy tales don't exist. I don't know why we're told stories about them as girls.

Why set us up for disappointment?

There's a library here at Pine Groves. It's a small room with three rows of books. *Fictional books.*

Books full of made-up characters in their make-believe stories.

That's how I feel right now. *Fictional.*

I finger the spine of one and read the title before pulling it from the shelf. I run my hand over the cover and flip it open, skimming through the pages.

Tick, tick, tock.

There's a clock on the wall in here. Doc had them put one up for me. He knows I like to come here to think. Which leads me to believe that he probably put this book on the shelf too. *The Other Boleyn Girl*—well, who cared about her anyway? No one cares about the *other* child when the most important one is gone.

Annoyed, I put it back on the shelf, searching for something very specific instead. The dictionary.

I open it and turn the pages until I reach the letter *F*.

F, for fairy tales.

As my eyes run over the definition, I'm left with a sense of clarity.

My parents weren't setting me up for disappointment. They just presented the facts wrong.

Fairy tales are stories full of the unimaginable.

Why not tell the truth? That it's *all* a lie.

They are nothing but stories to mislead and deceive us into *thinking* we can have what we want.

I'm not allowed to have what I want.

I can't have the prince…because *I* am the unimaginable.

I'm the catalyst in the destruction of my own happy ending.

If only someone had warned the prince.

Tick, tick, tock.

∾

Past…

I could see Grayson from where I was reclining on his king-sized bed. He was silently observing me from a leather chair in the corner of his room behind a dark wooden desk.

I'd stolen his shirt so he was left only in jeans, and when I nuzzled into the collar, I could smell him. *Yes, I'd been right.* It was the smell of hot sex.

"I like your photographs," I said, inspecting the black-and-white stills on his walls. There were three on the far left, which I recognized right away.

The Pantheon, The Colosseum, and The Sistine Chapel.

"Did you take all of these?"

His eyes moved to the images hanging vertically.

"Yes. Last summer."

I scooted over to the edge of the bed but kept my attention on him as I stood. Pushing my hair behind my ears, I strolled over on bare feet and stopped in front of them.

I ran my finger along the ruins of The Colosseum before turning to him. He had one foot resting on his knee and his fingers steepled over his naked abdomen.

I'd never been in the presence of a man so incredibly sexy.

"What are you thinking about?" I asked, curious about everything when it came to him.

"I was just wondering how you ended up in my bedroom asking questions about my personal photographs."

"You carried me in here," I reminded with a sassy wink.

Arching a brow, he agreed. "That's true. I did. I was also contemplating how sexy you are in *just* my shirt."

I don't know exactly what I'd been expecting, but that hadn't been it. I suppose somewhere in the back of my mind I'd expected regret or rejection, but it seemed like my teacher had finally accepted the unthinkable. *Me.*

Giving him a coy smile, I fingered the material tickling my bare thighs and played with him a little. "Yeah?"

"Yes, Addison. Very much."

"Well, I like wearing your shirt. It makes me *feel* sexy."

He must have pushed off the floor with his foot, because his chair rocked back slightly. "Good. Maybe I'll keep you in it."

I liked that idea and was about to say more when I spotted the opposite wall and a large black-and-white photograph centered on its own.

It was beautiful, and I was drawn to it.

Walking across the plush carpet, I stopped and studied the image. I had no words. It was mesmerizing.

The sculpture was of a nude woman lying on her side with her arms raised back over her head and wrapped around the neck of a winged—

"That's Cupid."

Grayson's voice, that hypnotic, commanding voice, found me and made my body shiver.

"And who is she?"

"That's Psyche."

I traced my index finger along her naked form. I started at her head then moved down over her breast and continued all the way to her toes.

"What's their story?"

The chair behind me creaked, and I looked back to see Grayson sitting up with his arms resting on the desk.

"Well, Venus, Cupid's mother, led Psyche down to the Underworld to retrieve a flask."

Curious, I frowned at...my history teacher.

"Why?"

Grayson's mouth stretched into a slow smile as he checked out my legs. When his eyes came back up and rested on my face, he answered.

"Venus was jealous of the way the villagers revered Psyche. They spoke of her as a goddess because she was so beautiful, and that enraged Venus. She ordered her son Eros, better known as Cupid, to avenge her. But he took one look at Psyche and became enamored with her instead. He believed she was perfect in every way."

I shifted from one foot to another and pushed my right toes down onto the top of my left.

"But no one's perfect."

Grayson shook his head. "No, no one's perfect. Not even Psyche."

I agreed with a swift nod of my head and waited for him to continue.

"Psyche's father was very upset that his daughter wasn't married because she was too beautiful not to be. So, he took her to see the oracle who told them that they would all meet a disastrous fate *unless* she was sacrificed to a monster."

"That's horrible! He got rid of her to save his own ass?"

I shot an annoyed look at Grayson, and I could tell he was enjoying himself. His eyes were lit up, and he was grinning at me in a way that made my heart thump harder. He was enjoying teaching me *this* lesson.

"Well, yes. He left her where he was told to, however, instead of a monster coming and taking her away…"

"Cupid did?"

Grayson chuckled and sat back in his chair. "Yes. But *she* didn't know that. He took her to a palace, one that was covered in sparkling gemstones, where she would live for the rest of her life. Every night when it was dark, he came to her, and they made love, but he forbade her to know who he was…it was a secret."

Grayson's eyes zeroed in on me, warming all of the places he had touched earlier. I was *his* secret, and in that moment, he was conveying it with no more than a look.

"Psyche was curious, though…too curious. She wanted to see her lover. Wanted to *see* who touched her. So one night while he was asleep beside her, she shined a light over his face, and her lamp dripped hot oil on Cupid, waking him."

I brought my thumbnail up to my mouth and began nibbling as I listened. I was enthralled.

Grayson stopped for a moment to ask, "Nervous?"

I nodded. "What did he do? Was he pissed off?"

"He wasn't happy. He felt betrayed, so he left her there."

My mouth dropped open in outrage.

"*What?* That makes him just as bad as her father. He took her to a palace where no one else lives and then just leaves her there? Because she wanted to see him? That's not fair."

"Maybe so. But that's what happened."

"Yeah? Well, that's shit."

Grayson laughed then, a full-bodied belly laugh. His shoulders shook, his chest moved, and his teeth gleamed at me. I wanted him. *Bad.*

"Gee, Addison, tell me how you really feel."

I walked forward, rolling my eyes. "So how did she end up with him in the sculpture if he left her?"

"Well, Psyche went after him. She was distraught and wanted him back. When she fled the palace, Venus saw her and began unleashing horrible events. Eventually, Psyche was led down to the Underworld to retrieve a flask. The only condition...she was not, under any circumstances, allowed to open it."

Almost as if he was calling to me, I moved closer to the desk and raised my hands to the top of his shirt.

"But she did, didn't she? Psyche was too curious not to."

Grayson's eyes shifted to what I was doing as I unbuttoned the top button and moved on to the one between my breasts.

"That's right. It didn't matter that she'd been told not to. Psyche wanted to know..."

His words trailed off as the third button was freed, and I parted the material, leaving a wide strip of skin.

"Wanted to know what?"

"She wanted to know what was in the flask."

I pushed one of the sleeves down my arm and let his shirt fall to the floor, leaving me completely naked.

"The first day we met, you told me to be curious. This is me being curious. What was in the flask, *sir*?"

Grayson's brow rose as he opened his jeans and freed his cock. He was hard, I was wet, and I wanted him all over again.

"Sometimes curiosity should stay just that," he advised as he pushed his chair away from the desk.

"Should it?"

Standing slowly, he made his way behind me, and my entire body shivered with anticipation.

"Yes. There's a reason Psyche was told not to open the flask."

This was wrong. He'd told me that so many times. But I wanted him, and I was going nowhere.

"And that reason was?"

"Because opening it would only bring about the most severe of consequences."

"Which was?"

"Death. Except she was revived by Cupid, who touched her with his arrow. That sculpture depicts the moment he finds her and fears he's too late. He reaches for her as she does for him, and his touch makes her immortal."

I thought his words over as I read the quote hanging above his desk.

"Whoever fights monsters should see to it that in the process he does not become a monster."

Suddenly, I had a different question. "Do you fight monsters?"

I wondered if Grayson and I had more in common than the need to be with one another.

His hands clasped my bare shoulders before he ran them down my arms—then his mouth was by my ear. "Don't we all?"

I turned my head to the side until our mouths were only inches apart and pushed for an answer. "What's your monster?"

"What's yours?" he pushed back, not responding to my feeble attempt to dig.

Instead of telling him the one thing that would make me less than perfect, I looked back at the quote.

"Who wrote that?"

"Nietzsche. Friedrich Nietzsche."

He entwined our fingers and brought our right hands up until we were both caressing my breast before he slid the other down to stroke between my thighs.

"He also stated that, *'The true man wants two things: danger and play. For that reason he wants woman as the most dangerous plaything.'*"

Our fingers found me hot and wet, and I shivered, resting my head back on his shoulder. I felt safe there, wrapped up in his arms with his warm breath against my ear. Everything I feared, everything that made me the person *they* all knew, disappeared.

Here in Grayson's house, I could let go of all the things that made me broken. I could cling to the illusion I was creating. The one where he would complete me, and we'd live happily ever after.

"And you? Are you a true man?"

I sucked in a breath as he pushed two of our fingers inside me.

His mouth found my ear and he sucked my lobe between his lips. He manipulated my fingers until I was brushing them over my nipple and grinding my hips on the hands between my legs. I turned my head, and when our eyes caught, all I could see was the same hunger and need that I was feeling.

"Addison, the time for play stopped when you walked through my front door." He pressed his lips to mine and conceded, "But the other half is true. You are so fucking dangerous that I'm not sure I'll survive you."

Was this where we were supposed to decide?

Every decision comes with a choice. There were two here— bliss or survival—and as the taste of him hit my tongue, I knew my answer.

Naked and aroused, I moved so I was facing him. He stepped closer, causing me to back up against his desk. As my backside hit the edge, he lifted and placed me down on the surface. I spread my thighs for him and braced my hands on the cool wood as he pushed his jeans away from his hips.

"I have no idea why I'm allowing myself to be with you, but I have no clue how to stop."

Moistening my top lip with a flick of my tongue, I asked, "Do you want to stop?"

He grabbed a condom from the desk as he stepped out of his jeans, kicking them to the side. He walked back to me and slid his hands around my thighs until they were under my knees and then tugged me forward so my ass was on the edge of the desk. When his hard cock pressed up against the entrance of my aching heat, his lips found mine and he admitted, "No, I fucking don't."

Present...

"Addison?"

The intrusion of Doc's voice rips me from my past. I must have fallen asleep in here. I glance around at the rows of books and blink several times before I hear it.

Tick, tick, tock.

Yep, I'm back in reality, all right.

"You were supposed to come and see me at four."

The clock on the wall indicates it's now going on five—*shit*, I slept through therapy. Oh well, sleep here or sleep there. Either way, it usually has me wishing I was elsewhere.

"What are you reading?" he asks, walking over to me.

I look down at the dictionary, still flipped open. I move to shut it, but Doc places his fingers on the page and turns it around.

"Fairy tales…"

I look up at him as he eyes me skeptically.

"Why fairy tales?"

I don't plan to answer, but before I know it, I hear myself saying, "Why not? We have all the characters. The prince, the princess, and the monster."

Doc concentrates on me as I push away from the table. "Is that what you think? When you think about what happened?"

I walk around the table until I am shoulder to shoulder with the man who is supposed to be helping me. Really though, he just wants to *solve* me—like some kind of fucked up puzzle.

"I don't know. Why don't *you* tell me, Doc?

I feel him turn, and I know he's confused. "Addison?"

Without looking at him, I whisper, "What happened is...the fairy tale ended."

Just before I walk away, I feel a hand on my arm. "Did it?"

I meet Doc's eyes this time as he studies me, trying to work me out.

"Of course. There's no fairy tale without the prince."

My eyes remain on his until he removes his hand.

"You can talk to me about him, Addison."

I shake my head. "And which *him* would that be?"

"Both. But right now I mean Grayson. Talk to me, let me help you."

"And why would I do that?"

"You need to talk about him."

"No," I murmur. "I need to forget. Forget that I knew him. Forget that he ever existed..." I walk to the door thinking, *forget that I destroyed him.*

"Addison?"

"What?"

"What happened wasn't your fault."

And there it is, the unimaginable—*me.*

What happened *was* my fault, but like all good fairy tales, everyone chose to believe the lie.

Tick, tick, tock.

CHAPTER 15

 ast...

Miss Shrieve.

Mentor? Teacher? Coach? Rival?

As I stood there watching her Tuesday morning, I tried to decide if I needed to be concerned. Did I need to worry about her interest in the man I'd had inside me yesterday afternoon? It was obvious she *was* interested.

I wasn't the only one who'd noticed. That first day when she'd introduced herself, she'd laughed and leaned in as if she wanted him to kiss her. Not that I blamed Miss Shrieve because I'd wanted him to kiss me too. The only difference was, I'd succeeded and he'd kissed every inch of me the day before.

I also couldn't forget her invitation to *my* track meet. That didn't bother me half as much as her hidden intentions. I didn't mind her using me to impress him, especially when he'd left with an extra appreciation of *me*.

I had him, not her. *Rival? I think not.*

"Addison?"

Shit, Jessica had been talking to me for the last five minutes while I'd been busy observing my hurdles coach. I spun around and plastered a confident smile on my face.

"Sorry, I zoned out for a second."

"No shit. What's wrong with you lately? Brandon says you haven't called or text him, and let's face it, we know you hate being at home. So what gives?"

That *was* true. I hated being at home, but I hadn't been there, had I?

I'd been with Grayson on Saturday night, giving him a tour of the not-so-perfect part of me, and on Monday afternoon and into the evening, I'd shown him just how perfect *we* could be together.

The hours in between I'd spent counting—*one, two, three*—and watching the clock. *Tick, tick, tock.*

I looked to where the cars were parked, but he hadn't shown yet—where was he?

"Addison?"

"I don't know. I just haven't felt like dealing with Brandon lately."

"Really? You don't want to 'deal' with the most popular boy in school? I'm pretty sure there are plenty who would."

I was never one to back down from a direct confrontation, and Jessica was all but daring *Addy* to come out and play.

"Oh yeah, Jessica? Like who? You?"

With a dismissive shrug, she denied the accusation. "Nope. Just sayin' is all."

Walking up to stand beside the girl who suddenly implying my status in this school was changing, I asked, "It's *what* you're saying that's so interesting, isn't it?"

Her brown eyes met mine and a mean sneer stretched her lips. "Brandon's bored...he's going to go elsewhere. I just thought you'd like to know."

Let him fucking go was my immediate thought, but when Miss

Shrieve waved in the direction of the parking lot and I saw Mr. McKendrick, my mind shifted.

No, I needed Brandon.

We needed Brandon—he was the perfect cover for our crimes.

～

Present...

"Let's talk about the men in your life."

I nod at Doc and ask, "Including yourself?"

"Oh, good. You're talking to me today."

"I spoke to you yesterday," I point out quickly.

"Yes, but I had to coax the words out of you."

Well it's the only way to make you be quiet...clearly. "That was then."

"Yes, and this is now. So while you're feeling chatty, let's discuss the men in your life."

We're back in his makeshift office. He in his chair and me in mine.

"*You* are the only man in my life." I raise a brow at him. "How does that make you feel?"

Tick, tick, tock.

His eyes narrow on me. Doc has an uncanny way of saying a lot without saying anything at all. "That wasn't my question."

"No, it was mine."

In his right hand he's holding a pen, and for some reason I find myself fascinated with it today. "I'm not here to answer your questions."

"And I'm not here to answer yours." I pause and then cock my head to the side. "I'm here because you all think I should be. Yet, you keep asking."

Choosing to ignore me, Doc continues. "Brandon, Daniel, your father?"

He's left *him* out on purpose. If he's waiting for a reaction, he won't get it.

"These men—"

"*Boys*. They were boys. Except for my father."

"Okay, these *boys* each had a big impact on your life. Wouldn't you say?"

I notice the pen again as he begins to tap it against his tight lips. He's thinking, trying to ask the words in his mind without alienating me.

"Yes, they did."

"And Grayson?"

My eyes connect with Doc's curious ones as he waits for me to finally crack…to ask for forgiveness and spill all of my secrets. All of *our* secrets. That won't happen though, because I don't feel regret.

How can one seek forgiveness when they aren't searching for it?

"Did he have a big impact on your life?"

"*He* wasn't a boy."

"No, he wasn't. So? Did he?"

"Have an impact on my life?" I ask. "He was my teacher. Of course."

"He was more than that."

"Says you."

"Says the state."

I run a hand through my hair, agitated. I don't want to be thinking about what *they* all think, not now—not ever.

"You'd think this would be easy," I grumble.

Doc's pen stops tapping, and he asks, "Why isn't it?"

I don't answer for a minute and bite my nail instead.

Nervous habit? I can still hear Grayson's voice in my head.

"Because nothing I say and nothing *you* say will change a fucking thing."

Tick, tick, tock.

Fuck, can't this be over already? I can tell I've surprised him. Not only am I talking, I'm showing emotion, but then...he hits a little too close to home.

"Addison? Where did all the men go?"

Just like that, the mask slips back in place as I answer his question stoically and without subterfuge.

"Away."

Tick, tick, tock.

∼

Past...

Am I a good actress? When I walked through the library doors for class and saw Mr. McKendrick talking to Brandon by the checkout desk, I thought I deserved an Academy Award.

He was dressed in khaki pants and a white shirt, not unlike the one I'd been wearing yesterday—in his house, in his bed—and my body instantly recalled what it had experienced with this man.

When the door clicked shut, those golden eyes rose over Brandon's shoulder and caught mine. Nothing was conveyed there, nothing given away.

He was a great actor.

"Hey, Addy," Brandon greeted with a smile as he made his way to me. He kissed my temple and hugged me tightly as I continued observing Mr. McKendrick.

What is he thinking?

I didn't have long to wonder because the rest of the class began arriving and he led us through the rows of books to the study section at the back of the library.

"Okay, guys, use your hour today to research Anne Boleyn. I expect your report by the end of the week."

We all dumped our books on the tables as he continued, "Remember, you are in a library. So keep your voices down. I'll be coming around to check on your work as you go, and you better have something. This isn't an hour to play around. Got it?"

Brandon wiggled his brows suggestively. "Wanna play with me?"

I laughed as he expected, but all I was thinking was—*No, I want to play with our teacher.*

"Okay, so get to it," Mr. McKendrick's voice cut through my thoughts.

I took Brandon's hand, letting him lead us through the library. As much as I wanted to, I couldn't really hang back to talk to Mr. McKendrick. I had no excuse that would be convincing enough.

When we got to one of the end rows, Brandon pulled me in and wrapped his arms around my waist.

"Brandon, quit it. You heard him."

He rested back against the books, and his brown eyes twinkled mischievously as he grabbed my jean-clad ass.

"He's not going to check on us for at least twenty minutes."

I could feel Brandon's erection when he rolled his hips against me, so I placed my hands on his shoulders, trying to halt him.

"Come on. You know we both need to pass this class to stay on the track team. I'm already on his shit list. Mom will have a fit if I get kicked off."

He grinned in a way that would melt the panties off any other girl. The problem was, a man had ripped *my* panties off and that was all I could think about.

"Well at least kiss me to keep me happy. I feel like you've been avoiding me."

I rolled my eyes and played with a button on his blue polo shirt. "You seem plenty happy. Your hard-on is digging into me."

He chuckled and squeezed my ass. "That's because I'm fucking horny. Come on, Addy, it's been days."

"Oh you poor thing. Days? You have a hand, don't you?"

"Yeah, but it's not half as good as your pussy."

Deciding to throw my "boyfriend" a bone—other than his own—I ran my fingers through his hair and tightened them, pulling his head toward me. He loved it when I was aggressive—*huh*, just like I loved it when Grayson was.

Maybe that's why I was drawn to him, because he didn't let me get away with anything. *He* was the one calling the shots, not me.

I kissed Brandon's mouth, and when his lips parted and his tongue came out to touch mine, I hesitated.

I wasn't allowed to tell anyone about Grayson. I was supposed to act as if it never happened. So did that mean I was still supposed to date and kiss my boyfriend?

"Quit teasing, Addy."

Deciding that I was right and this *was* the best cover possible, I pushed my tongue inside Brandon's mouth. Unlike Grayson, who was controlled, seductive, and made me throb the second he was near, Brandon was rushing me, and it became awkward.

I pulled my mouth away and noticed that he was still hard and I was...*unaffected*. I couldn't let him know that though.

"We have to stop," I whispered. "I don't want to get carried away." *Total lie.*

"But—"

"But nothing. You heard what he said, he's going to check on us and if he sees we have no work done—"

"I know. We're screwed."

"Exactly."

I pushed away from him and was about to leave when I spotted our history teacher standing at the far end of the row. His legs were slightly spread, and his arms were crossed over his chest. His mouth was pulled tight, and his eyes kept moving back and forth between Brandon and me.

"*Shit*," Brandon cussed. "We are in so much trouble."

He had no idea.

"I thought I made myself clear earlier." Mr. McKendrick's voice traveled the distance separating us.

I could see Brandon stand up straight out of the corner of my eye as our teacher began walking down the row.

Caught. We couldn't go anywhere, but what were we supposed to do now? What was I supposed to say, I'm sorry?

"Sorry, sir," Brandon mumbled behind me.

Apparently, sorry *was* what was called for in this situation.

Instead of following Brandon's lead, since he was losing major points for cowering, I placed my hands on my hips and did nothing to apologize.

"We were looking for a book."

Directing his eyes to mine, Mr. McKendrick didn't stop walking until he was right in front of us. "Really?"

"Yep," Brandon agreed, finally managing to contribute.

Mr. McKendrick—that *was* who was in front of me right now—looked past my shoulder to the boy behind me.

"And did you find it? In Addison's jeans?"

He raised an arm and pointed to the other end of the row, telling Brandon, "Go. Find a textbook, sit down on the opposite side of the library, and write your paper. Do I make myself clear?"

"Yes," Brandon grumbled, and I felt his arm brush against my ass as he walked away.

I listened for the noises surrounding me and waited for my own instructions. When all that met me was silence, I resorted to my other nervous habit and brought my thumbnail to my mouth. *One, two, three.*

The expression on his face conveyed irritation, and it became clear he wasn't going to say anything, so I shrugged and started to walk by. When he grabbed my wrist, I looked down at it and then gazed back up to find Grayson.

Ahh, there he is.

"You do the same, and while you're at it…" he advised, his voice dropping to a hushed pitch, "be very careful, Addison."

"Of?" I dared.

His eyes moved to my mouth as he stepped closer. "*Me.*"

"Why?" I asked, as we stood there, arm-to-arm.

He looked from one end of the row to the other and then back to me. "I don't want his tongue in your mouth."

"Neither do I."

"And yet that's where he had it."

I nodded as my body clenched in response to the index finger circling over my pulse.

"It's a good cover, to hide the truth." I peered up at him batting my lashes. "Don't you think, *sir?*"

The fingers around my wrist tightened, and his voice lowered. "I won't play games, Addison. If you want my fingers, tongue, or cock anywhere inside you, you'll make it very clear to boy wonder that things are over. Got it?"

I swallowed once, feeling my embarrassment and indignation rise as I yanked my arm away.

"You're *jealous,*" I spat out.

Grayson walked forward until I was backed up against the shelves of books. He was no longer touching me in any way, but the fulminating look on his face told me if he could—he would.

"So what do you want me to do? Break up with him?"

I glared up at the man who was affecting me in ways I'd never imagined, and remembered how it felt to be naked underneath him. I wanted him to touch me. I knew I could get him to. All I had to do was provoke the beast, the one I could see barely restrained in his eyes.

Grayson shoved his hands into his pockets before he replied, "I don't care what you do, Addison."

"I think you do."

"Just remember this isn't a game anymore. You wanted me, and you got me. But *don't* fuck around with me."

I knew my smile was bold, almost as bold as the way I slid my palms down my jeans to cup between my legs.

"*Mmm,* but I can't wait to fuck with you."

"Behave yourself."

"I don't want to." I laughed softly as his eyes dropped to where I was rubbing. "You don't want me to either."

"It doesn't matter what I want. Anyone could see, so fucking behave yourself."

I focused on his mouth and noticed his cheeks were a ruddy color under his stubble.

"What would you do right now…if no one could see? Tell me."

"No."

"*Yes,*" I challenged, and for a moment, I thought he was going to give in and touch. Instead, he checked out the aisle.

"I'd unzip your jeans, put you over my knee and redden that sweet ass of yours until you promised to behave."

Turning on his heels, Grayson began walking away and then looked back to where I was standing by the shelves, flushed and aroused.

"Opposite side of the library. Find a textbook, and write your damn paper."

I raised a brow and nodded, so turned on I felt the need to shove my hand down my jeans to finish what he'd started.

"Whatever you say, sir."

His gaze lowered back down below my waist, and my body responded. "*Don't* touch."

I should have been annoyed by the order but I wasn't. It just made me want him even more.

CHAPTER 16

 ast...

As the bell rang for lunch, I made my way through the bustling halls and down to the teacher's lounge.

I was on a mission. I wanted some answers, and the one person who would have them would be in there.

Miss Shrieve, *Helene*—Addison's coach.

It wasn't hard to track her down. In fact, I usually avoided the lounge because she was in there, but today I needed something, and she could give it to me.

Jesus, when did I become such an asshole? Avoiding a woman until I decided to use her? It was so unlike me, but ever since laying eyes on Addison, nothing I'd done made any fucking sense.

I wiped my hands on my pants and took a step into the restricted area. All around me stood my fellow co-workers— some my age, some significantly older. As I walked into our designated "adult" space, I found myself forcing a smile.

This was ridiculous. I'd never lacked confidence or been one to feel uneasy, but now, due to my own reckless actions, I found myself faking it with everyone around me. Lying and hiding behind a careful facade and a nod of my head.

"Hey there, Grayson."

Rodney Fowler. He was one of the English teachers here. He was about late thirties I'd guess and dressed more like he was in his late fifties. He held his hand out, so I took it in a firm handshake and greeted the man.

"Hey, Rodney. How's it going?"

"Good, man. Haven't seen you in here before. How's your morning so far?"

When he released his grip, I looked around the room and spotted Helene sitting down at one of the tables, her blond hair pulled back in its usual ponytail.

"So far, so good. Nothing out of the ordinary."

Except for me wanting to fuck one of my students against the stacks in the library. Oh, and that would be the same student I fucked yesterday afternoon at my house.

"Well, that's great. You let me know if you need anything. Those seniors can be a handful at times, especially for a newbie like yourself."

Outwardly agreeing, I gestured in the direction of the fridge.

"I'm just going to get my lunch and try to relax a little, you know?"

"Sure, sure. Have a good day."

Wishing him the same, I made my way past a few more staff members. I waved, nodded, and smiled—all fake, all contrived, as I got closer to my goal—*Helene.*

Stopping behind the empty seat opposite her, I waited until she looked up at me and then gave her a smile. When her eyes twinkled with pleasure, I hated myself for not feeling one damn thing.

"Well, hello. This is a nice surprise."

I pulled the chair out and sat down, doing my best to make her feel what I wanted her to—*attraction*. Yes, it was official. I was an asshole.

"Is it?" I teased a little.

"Yes," she said, smiling as she sat back. "You never eat in here with the rest of us."

"I like my downtime, that's all."

"*Ahh*, the quiet before the storm."

Unable to help myself, I found the smile on my mouth was finally…genuine. "Yes. Something like that."

"So mysterious, Mr. McKendrick," she flirted. "What do you do in your downtime that is such a secret you can't do it with the rest of us?"

The image that came to mind was Addison on her hands and knees in front of my living room mirror—naked and waiting as I moved behind her, inside her, out of control.

"Oh, you know. The usual."

Helene winked. "Well, normal for some isn't so normal for others."

No shit.

"But I'm glad you're here. For whatever reason it may be."

"About that…"

"Yes?"

"I'm actually here to pick your brain about one of my students."

Sitting on the table in front of her was a shiny red apple, and I had to wonder at the symbolism.

"Oh? Okay, let me see if I can help."

Now…how to ask? How do I ask without sounding like anything other than a concerned teacher? Which was all I was as far as Helene knew.

"It's about Addison Lancaster."

Just saying her name had my mind chanting—*guilty, guilty, guilty.*

Helene picked up the apple and took a bite. As her teeth sank into the crisp skin, I thought for the millionth time—*What the fuck am I doing?*

Was I really willing to throw my whole life away for...

"Addison. She is...*unique.*"

Yes, she was, and right then I had my answer. I *was* willing to do anything to know more about this girl who'd shaken my foundation.

I was changing. I was risking everything, and I needed to know why.

Why was I so—bewitched?

As the flirtation in her eyes disappeared, Helene's voice lowered and in its place was sympathy. Sympathy and pity.

"Let's walk," she suggested and pushed back from the table.

My lunch in the fridge was forgotten as I followed her out into the hall.

"I'm surprised you haven't heard anything about what happened before now."

I was trying to act ignorant, but in the back of my mind, all I could see was the cemetery, and all I could hear were Addison's words—*I killed him.*

I couldn't erase the way she'd referred to all of *them,* as if I wasn't a part of whatever happened to her back then. Is that why she acted the way she did with me? Because I hadn't been there?

I needed to know what happened.

I noticed Helene had walked us to my classroom, so I pushed open the door and waited as she stepped inside. Following her into the empty room, I naturally moved behind my desk as she made her way to the back of the class. She seemed uncomfortable, and I wasn't sure if it was due to what she was about to tell me or because I still hadn't said anything.

"Addy wasn't always the way she is now."

Huh, that was an odd way to start this discussion. I had

nothing to say so I waited, curious as to how Helene would continue.

"She used to be a sweet, happy girl. Bright and so very smart, but quiet, almost introverted. She kept to herself."

I was trying to envision that version of Addison, but all I had to compare her with was the bold temptress that I knew. I couldn't even begin to imagine it.

"A little over two years ago, Addy's brother, Daniel, was killed."

Oh, *fuck*. She hadn't been lying. What had she done?

"It happened here at the school in front of everyone."

Needing more information but really not wanting it, I waited. I stood and made my way around the desk and leaned back against it, bracing my hands on the edge.

"What happened?"

Helene let out a deep sigh as she began walking up to the front of the room.

"The final bell of the day had rung. All of the kids ran for the door and out to the bus lines, nothing unusual at all. Addy would walk down, cross the street, and meet her brother on the sidewalk so they could catch the bus home together."

I sat completely still, unable to find one word to say as Helene continued.

"She was running late that day. I know this because she'd tracked me down after math class to ask how she could join the hurdle team."

The look on Helene's face right then was what I'd been feeling earlier, *guilt*, but unlike me, I knew this lady had no reason to feel it. She looked away, almost as if it were easier to talk when she wasn't being held accountable.

"She was running late and ran down to cross the street. Daniel must have seen her, I don't know." Placing her hands on her hips, Helene stopped, trying to compose herself. "To this day I don't know why he stepped off the sidewalk. There are so many stories from people who witnessed what happened, but what it all comes down to is Daniel stepped out into the road without checking that everything was clear. A couple of seconds later, he was lying on the ground in front of his sister and the entire school—he never stood a chance."

I rubbed my fingers against the stubble on my jaw and down to my mouth.

Addison hadn't done *anything* wrong. She'd been late, that was all.

Why would she ever think anything different?

"Wow...okay. That explains a lot." I paused and looked at the loud, irritating clock on the wall and then thought about the way Addison always checked her watch or brought it up to her ear. She'd told me it was because she'd been late. "The clocks and the watch?"

"Yeah," Helene confirmed. "After that, Addy was never the same. Her mother told me the doctors think she suffered a psychotic break from witnessing what we all saw that day. The clocks help her to stay focused, which explains the constant time check. But honestly, Addison's behavior did a one-eighty. It's as if she's a completely different person."

It was obvious that Helene was upset, so I moved closer to her and reached out. Intending to offer a comforting squeeze to her shoulder, I was shocked when she wrapped her arms around my waist instead.

Shit, this was not what I wanted.

With my hands hovering in the air, I had no other choice but to pat her gently on the back. As I touched her jacket I heard the door to my classroom open. Looking behind me, my eyes collided with cobalt blue and the emotions swirling in them gutted me more effectively than the emotional woman in my arms.

Addison's eyes moved to my lower back and then came back to mine.

Betrayal. Jealousy. Anger.

No words were needed, and no words could be said as Addison turned on her heel and fled.

As I stood in the silence of my classroom with Helene's arms around me, all I could think about was how to comfort her enough to release me from her emotional burden—so I could go and add to my own.

How fucked up was that?

~

I raced down the empty hall and stopped at the end of the lockers, pressing my back against the cool metal. I took several breaths and closed my eyes.

One, two, three. One, two, three.

I didn't want to think about what I'd seen when I walked into the classroom. *Her* with him—the rightness of that moment.

I wasn't stupid. I knew that she was who he was supposed to be with, not me. But it didn't matter. I couldn't let her have him; I needed him. He stopped the chaos.

I pulled my fingers through the long strands of my hair and tightened them as I listened to the watch at my wrist keeping time of my torment.

Tick, tick, tock.

"Addison?"

My eyes snapped open at the deep voice calling out my name.

No! No, I couldn't let him see me like this.

I was strong, confident. I was—

"Addison?"

Found.

Grayson stopped in front of me. His face was troubled, and his eyes held something new, something I hadn't seen before—pity.

What exactly had they been discussing in there?

"It's not what you think."

"Move," I demanded, feeling the need for distance.

Grayson put his hands on his hips as one of his eyebrows rose. "Excuse me?"

"Move out of my way."

Instead of stepping aside, he remained unmoving, his body large and impenetrable. I may as well have been trying to get past a brick wall. "I think you're forgetting who you're talking to."

At that moment, any anxiety I'd been feeling left and in its place was anger. He'd been talking to *her* about *me*. "Oh, I know exactly who I'm talking to. Do you?"

"What's that supposed to mean?"

Pushing off the locker, I walked forward until my shirt brushed his. He should have moved away but he didn't.

"Who do *you* see in front of you right now? Your student or the person you were inside of yesterday?"

He swallowed before he answered, and I was mesmerized by the way his throat moved. I wanted to reach out to him.

"I see both," he admitted. "You're *all* I see."

I silently fumed as I concentrated on the mouth that, despite my anger, I wanted on mine.

"But now you see something else. What did *she* tell you?" I asked.

He looked caught off-guard. "What?"

"She said something to you. You're looking at me like *they* all do."

"And how is that?"

"Like you feel sorry for me," I spat out. "I want you to *fuck* me. Not pity me."

With no warning at all, Grayson seized my shoulders and firmly directed me back against the lockers. He crowded in with no regard to our surroundings as he promised in a voice that sounded distinctly like a threat.

"That's all you want, is it? A quick fuck? You could have

gotten that from Brandon. But you want more from me, just like I want more from you."

His mouth was close, so close that if I leaned in…

"*Don't.*"

"No?" I whispered as his breath floated over my lips.

"No. Not here."

"I need you," I admitted breathlessly. "I ache for you."

Grayson moved away so fast it was as if he'd been electrocuted. "After school," he promised.

"Yes?"

"Follow me…my truck."

His eyes left a scorching trail down my body as he backed away, and I checked my watch to see how much longer I had to wait. I wasn't surprised at all that the second hand was *silently* making its way around to twelve.

Once again, he'd silenced the madness.

Three thirty and the final bell for the day rang. I grabbed my bag and followed the last student out the door, turning the lights off as I exited.

I locked up and made my way out to the parking lot, knowing that what I was about to do was wrong. I had also known it yesterday, but as I made my way to my truck, I spotted Addison leaning back against her car, and I couldn't find it in me to care.

She was laughing at something Brandon must have said. Her head was tipped back, the sun shone on her face, and the smile on her lips made me want to punch him for putting it there.

Nice. Now I was jealous of a fucking teenager.

As I stepped onto the road, Brandon saw me and waved.

"See you tomorrow, Mr. McKendrick."

I returned the gesture and shoved my other hand in my pocket.

"Yes, you will," I replied as my eyes met Addison's, and I couldn't help but add, "Make sure you do your homework tonight. Only a few days left, and I want that report on my desk Friday."

"I know, I know. The Boleyn chick."

"That'd be her."

Brandon grabbed his bag, which was resting by Addison on the hood of her car, and kissed her cheek. My teeth clenched as I unlocked my door and climbed inside.

I started the truck and looked out my windshield to see Brandon driving away. That's when I let my eyes find Addison's.

She was sitting in her car and when I pulled out of my spot, I heard her car turn over.

Yes, I thought as I drove out on to the street.

This time *you* follow *me*.

I made sure to let several other cars leave ahead of me before I turned and followed.

After navigating the streets and weaving through traffic, he entered the highway. I was curious where he was taking us. I knew it had to be somewhere private since there was no way we could be out in public. He exited the off ramp and I followed closer now that we were away from the school.

Around fifteen minutes later, we turned down a dirt road and drove in a mile or so before he stopped at an old gate. Opening the truck door, he jumped down and came for me. Running a hand through his hair, he began striding my way as the wind caught his shirt, molding it to all of his muscles.

The man was hotter than hell, and nowhere in sight was my history teacher.

This was *all* Grayson.

His eyes stayed on me as he braced a hand on the roof of my car and indicated I should wind my window down. Once it was lowered, he rested his forearms on the door so our faces were only inches apart.

"Park the car, Addison."

"Park it?"

"Yes," he replied, his voice velvety and commanding. "Do you remember what I found you doing the first time you parked in front of my house?"

He was driving me crazy, and he knew it.

"Yes."

"I want you do that again, here. Just for me."

It shouldn't have been any different than the time I'd done this in front of him in the classroom, but as he leaned in the window and his tongue tasted my bottom lip, I suddenly felt nervous.

This *was* different.

Unlike those other times, here he held the upper hand, and he knew it.

"Right hand on the steering wheel, left hand inside your panties, and your eyes, those beautiful fucking eyes—keep them on me the entire time."

I pulled the keys from the ignition. Bringing them up between us, I dangled them on my finger and when he took them, the side of my mouth curved.

"I don't want them back until I'm so satisfied I can barely walk."

As I unzipped my jeans and placed my hand on the steering wheel, something primal flashed in his eyes as he promised, "By the time I'm done with you, you'll be lucky if you have the strength to crawl."

Reaching for me, he took my chin and turned my face to him.

"Are you ready for that?"

I brought my left hand to his mouth so he could suck my

fingers, and I felt my core clench and throb as I lowered them down into my jeans.

My lips parted on a sigh as my fingers slipped inside me, and I asked, "Are you?"

He looked to where my hand disappeared into my jeans and uttered two words that signaled the time for talking was over. "Fuck yes."

With that, he opened the driver's side door to my car.

CHAPTER 17

 ast...

As I pulled open the car door, I caught the way Addison's chest heaved with every breath she took, and my cock stiffened. I was sick and tired of worrying about every fucking move I made, and right now I ordered myself to stop.

She was seated in her car with the belt still fastened. Her hand clasped the steering wheel and the other was down her jeans. As she turned her head on the headrest and her eyes found mine, she looked exactly like I pictured she would—a fucking bad girl.

"You like this, don't you? Me watching you?"

"*Yes*," she replied. "You do too."

"I definitely have no complaints."

It was clear she knew exactly how to touch herself as a throaty moan emerged. I couldn't help what I did next any more than I could help the need to breathe.

I unbuttoned and unzipped my pants then shoved my hand inside and wrapped it around my hard cock.

"Show me," she said in a voice laced with arousal.

"A little demanding, aren't we?"

"You want to show me as much as I want to see."

I stroked her chin, needing to touch her in some way. Addison seemed to have a gravitational force surrounding her, and she continued to pull me in with her curvy fucking body and brazenly dirty mouth.

In the back of my mind, I'd known this would happen when I opened her car door, but for her to want it too? *That* I hadn't expected.

Knowing how shaky my resolve was, I firmly told her, "No touching."

Her eyes locked with mine and the question screaming from them was, *why*? Instead of answering, because I didn't have a reason that made sense, I swooped down inside the car, placed my own hand on the wheel and took her mouth with mine. I speared my tongue between her lips, and when she moaned into my mouth, I felt her entire body arch forward.

I tore my lips from hers and reiterated, "No touching."

She continued writhing in her seat. "*Okay*, no touching. Show me."

I brushed my thumb along her wet bottom lip and pushed my pants apart to release my stiff cock. Her eyes focused on my erection and I dipped my index finger into her mouth. As she began to suck me, her hips lifted, and she fucked herself harder.

Her knuckles were white as she held the wheel, and when I pushed a second finger between her lips she took to it as if she knew exactly what I wanted. Finally, when I had to touch myself or fucking die, I pulled my fingers free from her mouth and smeared the pearly drop of pre-come down my impatient cock.

I braced myself against the side of her car as I began to stroke my erection only inches away from her. While she watched me, her fingers slid in and out of her body, and it didn't take me long. I could feel my climax clawing at me as my balls tightened, and my muscles tensed.

However, it wasn't until she whispered, "I want to taste," that I moved like lightning, leaning into the car to unbuckle her.

She was breathtaking. She was beautiful. I was in so fucking deep with her that no one could save me now.

~

I was so close to coming I was shaking, until he moved and took a step back.

"Come on, Addison. Get out of the car."

I couldn't believe he'd *stopped*, but he had and now he wanted me to. His voice was hoarse as I reluctantly zipped my jeans.

What was going on? Had I done something wrong?

Climbing out, I noticed him righting his own clothes and felt my entire body react. He walked to me, cupped my face and took my mouth.

The kiss was full of heat and sex, and as his tongue rubbed over mine, I moaned at the contact. One of his hands wrapped around my waist as his other tightened in my hair, and I reciprocated by brushing my palm over what had to be a painfully hard erection.

"Damn you," he admonished. "*This*, what we're doing? It won't end well, it can't."

I touched his face, running my fingertips over his cheekbones. "It doesn't have to end at all. I'd never hurt you."

With his forehead resting against my own, he shook his head, our noses gently brushing against the other. "*You* are not the person who worries me."

"Then who?"

"Everyone *else!*" he stressed as he released me and turned away. "*Fuck*, Addison! You're not stupid or naive. This is wrong!"

"*No*. This is the only thing that's right," I tried to explain as I stepped behind him, feeling my desperation to get through to him riding me. Touching his back, I confided softly, "You're the first person who sees me."

He let out a scoff and spun around.

"No one will care. Don't you get it? No one will even stop to ask as they haul my ass away. This is *illegal*. Do you understand that?"

"Of course I understand that! I'm not a fucking idiot." Pointing a finger at him, I asked, "Why are you here, then?"

He pushed his fingers through his hair in frustration, and as the words "Sometimes I have no idea" left his mouth, my anger blindsided me.

I felt the sudden urge to get away from him, so I ran.

I had no idea where I was going, but as I sprinted past the gate his truck was parked in front of, all I knew was that I needed to get away.

I ran out into the field and made my way through the waist-length wildflowers. Miles of them spread out and surrounded me as I continued through the meadow. I could feel my muscles kicking in as if I was on the track, and my breathing found a rhythm.

I was in the middle of nowhere, all alone. *Not something new— not by a long shot.*

My feet pounded across the soft grass as I became aware of the sounds around me. The birds chirping in the trees, the wind whistling through the branches, and then...the distant footfalls of someone chasing me down.

Grayson.

Feeling my competitive nature kick in, I pushed harder, my legs picking up the pace as I weaved and zigzagged my way through the open space. The adrenaline that coursed through me was heightened by the irritation I felt from his response.

I dashed to the left and heard the crunch of a branch as he closed in on me. I kept running until a firm hand snagged my arm and pulled me around. It happened so fast I lost my footing, and we tumbled down onto the grass beneath us.

Landing with a thud, I grunted at the weight of him on top of me, and I thrashed around under him until he took my arms and pinned them by my head.

"Addison, calm down."

"Fuck you and your I don't knows!" I shouted back and bucked my hips up under him. Freeing one of my hands, I brought it up to slap him and caught his cheek. With a grimace, he recaptured my wrist and pinned it again, and this time when he put his weight over me, I felt *all* of him.

"Stop fucking hitting me, or I swear you will not like the consequences."

His eyes blazed at me as his hair fell down and concealed our faces from the world.

"Let me go."

Tightening his grip on my wrist, he hissed, "*Not* if you're going to slap me."

"I won't."

With a skeptical look on his face, he asked quietly, "Promise?"

Promising nothing, I told him again, "Let. Me. Go."

He released my arms cautiously, and I pushed my hands into his hair. Pulling him down, I pressed my eager mouth to his, and when his tongue slid passed my lips, I whimpered and bowed up against him.

As I spread my legs, I marveled at the way his body fit naturally with mine. One of his hands slid down my thigh to my knee and hitched it up over his waist, causing me to gasp and rub myself against him.

"Grayson…" I panted as he lifted his mouth.

"*Yes*," was the only word that escaped him as he smoothed my hair away from my face.

"Don't stop this time."

He pulled back to kneel beside me, and the struggle on his face was evident—but so was the desire. He undid his pants and I unzipped my jeans, kicking my way out of them. I peeled my thong down and watched as he slid his wallet from his pocket.

"Thought you'd need one of those?"

He brought the silver packet to his mouth and gave me a look that was almost feral before ripping it open and rolling the condom on. I trembled with need as he crawled between my naked thighs and lined up the head of his cock with my aching pussy.

"Oh, fuck *yes*," he cursed as he pushed inside me. "I was hoping, Addison. *God,* I was hoping. I can't stop thinking about you. About this, even if it's wrong."

I wrapped my legs around his waist and ran my hand through his hair, holding it away from his angular face. "How can *this* be wrong?"

He closed his eyes as if it would help before nuzzling in against my neck. His teeth found my skin, and as he bit my shoulder gently, he pushed his hips to mine, thrusting his cock deeper inside me as I cried out.

He had no answers, and as he began to move over me, neither did I.

She was picture-perfect.

As she lay there in the grass with her hair spread out all around her, Addison seemed untouchable—but I was touching her, and I knew I'd eventually pay the price.

When I was chasing her, I'd had one thing in mind—catch her and make her mine. Now here she was underneath me—*mine for this moment in time.*

I rose up over her, placing my forearms by her head and touched the strands of hair tangled in the flowers and grass.

She resembled a goddess, but as her body tightened around my cock and her mouth parted on a sob, I knew how human she was.

Curling my fingers into the grass and soil beneath us, I continued to move inside her. My cock slid deep as I rolled my hips and then slowly pulled away, drawing out the pleasure before she begged and pleaded for me to do it *again*.

Her fingers were digging into my ass, her nails no doubt leaving marks in my cheeks as she pulled me closer between her firm thighs.

"*Oh*, God," she moaned. Her lips were on my jaw, kissing and licking their way to my ear, where she sucked my lobe and told me, "*Harder*. I want it harder."

I cupped her ass, and when her hips pushed up, I squeezed and held her in place.

The second I braced my other hand over her head and began the steady rock of my hips, she was moving. Over and over she rubbed herself against me, brushing against my pelvis with every hard thrust of her hips, and that was it. Anything polite left in me was gone.

Addison was mine, and I was going to fucking have her.

Grayson let go of my ass and planted both hands by my head. That was all the warning I got. After that, he took me—and he fucked me hard.

His hair fell down around us as he bit my bottom lip. His hips began to pump his cock deeper inside me, and the sound that came from him when he pulled out sounded as if he was in pain.

He was beautiful. Like a caged animal finally set free.

The sweat that started to drip down his face and fall from his nose landed on my tongue. When the salty flavor hit my taste buds, I couldn't help the soft hum it elicited. He growled in response and shoved his tongue into my mouth, and as his hips hammered me into the ground, I knew that I'd never forget this moment.

The afternoon sun was shining, the soft, crushed grass was beneath us, and we were surrounded by pink and white wild-flowers. It was primal, it was earthy, and as he threw his head back and shouted, he came inside of me.

Grayson had *always* seen me, but this was the first time that I'd *ever* really seen him.

CHAPTER 18

 resent...

Right and wrong.

Two words, each made up of five letters, with two very different meanings and *very* different outcomes.

"What do you think is going to happen if you talk to me?"

"Nothing good."

I turn to see Doc looking at the black-and-white photo taped to my wall.

Psyche Revived by Cupid's Kiss.

It's the only thing I allow myself to imagine as I lie here night after night. I pretend that I have escaped my marble prison and that *he* will come and find me. But as I look to the door of my confinement and see my name below Doc's, I know *that* can never be.

Doc nods in agreement before he speaks again.

"What did you think would happen if you confided and trusted in *him*?"

I reach for the watch around my wrist and trace it with my finger. "Exactly what *did* happen."

"And what was that?"

Raising my eyes, I give a tight smile and repeat, "Nothing good."

"Okay," Doc chuckles. "I'll give you that."

"How kind of you."

"Well, no one could call you being in this place *good*, could they? Come on, Addison. Work with me. Let me help you, or at least tell me…why did you *do* what you did?"

Ahh, Doc is smart—trying to make me admit to what's on paper without saying what *that* is. The problem is, I'm onto him. I know his game.

We always have a choice. The real decision is—do we pick right, or do we pick wrong? Or do we float around in the grey area, somewhere in between?

"Addison?"

"Yes?"

"This empty room is lonely. So is an empty heart."

I take in the small space that's been allotted to me, *my* marble palace, and when my eyes come back to the photo on the wall, I find I have nothing at all to say.

He's right. I am lonely, and I have no one to blame but myself.

∾

Past...

"Hey, talk to me."

Scooting in against Grayson's side, I laid my ear over his heart. *Thump, thump, thump.*

"Addison?"

I rested my chin on his chest and looked up at him. "Okay, let's talk."

He pulled a pink flower loose from my hair, twirling it slowly before bringing it down to brush against my nose. Grinning, I sat up and kneeled beside him, tugging on my shirt. He rolled toward me and propped his elbow up, placing his head in his hand.

"I'm waiting."

"Not so patiently, it should be noted," I pointed out.

He pretended to zip his mouth shut, and I couldn't help my laugh as I plucked some grass from *his* hair. "I love how you see me."

The expression on his face was intensely sexual, but also tinged with a hint of self-admonishment. "Do you? Sometimes I don't even know what I see when I look at you."

"You see *more*."

"More?"

I sighed as he stretched his arm out and stroked warm fingers along my cheek. In that moment, I could have sworn every sound around me disappeared, as if we were in a world of our own.

"You see under all of *this*," I said, gesturing up and down my body before laughing when I realized I was kneeling in just a shirt. "Well, you know what I mean."

Grayson ran his fingers along the line of my neck, and I closed my eyes as he traced a path down my arm before taking my hand.

"How could anyone look at you and not see everything I do?"

Bringing our fingers to his bare chest, he moved them until we were tapping out the beats of his heart. *One, two three. One, two three.*

So steady. So safe.

I shuffled closer to his side so that my knees were touching his skin, and that was when he stilled our hands and sat up so his lips were by my ear.

"It's time to stop counting, Addison. Just let it go and relax with me. I'll keep you safe."

I swallowed and felt a tear roll down my cheek as he dipped his head and pressed his lips to the side of my neck. His fingers tightened around my own and held them still as I let the silence be just that—silent.

"I'm scared by how much I need you already," I admitted.

His mouth brushed over the shell of my ear, and he confessed, "So am I."

Wanting to get even closer, I crawled up onto his lap and straddled him, wrapping my free arm around his neck. He circled my waist, pulling me in tight.

"What happened the day of Daniel's accident?"

I pressed my forehead against his and felt the warmth and security that only came when he was near.

"Time stood still," I whispered.

"Tell me."

We were so close that our noses were touching. "You already know. Miss Shrieve told you."

"I went to her because I want to understand. Help me to see. Show me all of you, Addison. The parts that no one else sees—show *me*."

I shut my eyes, needing the anonymity it afforded so I could retell the memory that broke me.

"I was late. My dad had been talking to me about joining the track team. He'd said it was something we would have in common, like a father and daughter kind of thing."

"So you chose hurdles with Helene?" Grayson questioned as he stroked a hand up my back.

"Helene? Oh, Miss Shrieve? Yes." I gave a self-deprecating laugh. "He's never once been to a track meet."

I took a deep breath and tentatively touched his chest. When he nodded, I placed both of my palms against him and continued.

"I'm pretty sure I shouldn't care about that in the scheme of things…but I do. I signed up for him, and now he can't even find the time to come and see me."

"Why do you still do it then?"

I could feel my anxiety rising as his question echoed in my head. No one ever understood why I continued. They all thought it was for the glory. No one knew it was to try and stop the all-consuming guilt.

"Because if I quit, it means it was all for nothing. Doesn't it?"

Grayson gave a small shrug, and I could tell he was trying to understand, but could he? Could anyone?

"So instead you became the best on the team?"

"No, that was luck."

"Luck *and* talent. You forget, I've seen you fly down that track and over those hurdles like you were born to do it. That's not luck."

"It doesn't *matter* what it is. None of it does. I put all of my spare time into training and making sure I'm the best because if I'm anything less…"

"Then what? Daniel died for nothing? Who told you that?"

Defensive, I shook my head. "No one."

"Bullshit," Grayson fired back as he frowned at me.

I could feel myself wavering. He knew I was lying. He'd met my mom and dad. It was obvious to anyone that we weren't one big, happy family, but to someone as smart as Grayson? It wouldn't take long to work out that the only thing keeping the Lancaster's functioning were lies and unrealistic expectations.

"We're not done with *that*, okay?"

I'd seen him in this mode before. It was teacher mode, and I knew he wouldn't let it go, but right now he was after the…*more.*

So I gave it to him.

"Daniel looked right at me that day. I ran down to the

crosswalk between the high school and the elementary school. There were other kids around, laughing and talking as we waited for the light to change. For some reason, I looked over the road at him, and it was like time stopped. I couldn't even hear the crosswalk signal as it beeped and then he was just— gone."

"Jesus," Grayson cursed as his fingers tightened on my waist.

"Maybe if I'd been on time?" I suggested, not really expecting an answer.

"It could have still happened. You don't know, and you never will."

I lowered my eyes to my hands and fidgeted as tears began to fall. Trying to get a hold of myself and failing, I looked back at the man studying me with concern.

How do you explain to someone that you not only let yourself down, but everyone who ever believed in you? And how do you trust them with that secret without offering up what is left of your broken heart?

The answer is simple, *you can't*. So instead, I gave Grayson the shattered pieces that remained.

"He was my baby *brother*. I couldn't get to him...I couldn't save him. I just stood there with everyone else, as the truck..."

"Oh, Addison. Hey, it's okay. You don't have to say any more."

Grayson pulled me into his arms so our chests were flush against each other. Heart to heart.

I ran my hands around behind his neck and hugged him to me, discovering that once I'd started talking, I couldn't seem to stop. It was kind of like the tears that I couldn't seem to get under control.

"One minute Daniel was standing there, and the next...the next, he was on the ground...just lying on the road. He wouldn't open his eyes...wouldn't look at me, and there was blood...so much blood around him. I just needed him to say something, *anything*...but he never did and then she took me away."

"Who did?" Grayson asked as my tears fell down onto his shoulder and back.

"Miss Shrieve. She took me away from him...forced me to let him go."

I pressed my face into his hair and took a deep breath, trying to calm myself.

"*One, two three. One, two, three.* The crosswalk signal beeping was all I could hear after that, over and over. I started counting, trying to focus on anything but what was in front of me."

Grayson pulled back slightly, and his eyes held mine, steady and serious. "So the counting is a new habit? Since the accident?"

It was time to trust and offer up the final pieces of me.

"Yes. It helps calm me when I get nervous or anxious...like a safety blanket, I suppose."

He reached for my left wrist and circled the watch there. "The same with the constant time check?"

"Yes and no."

I looked down and touched the timepiece.

"Doc tells me it's an obsession...it's something I *need* to do without even realizing it, probably because I was running late that day. See, that's what was so funny the first day in your class. I couldn't believe I was late. I'm obsessed with time. Everyone knows that. I always need to see it or hear it...and now I sound like a crazy person." I laughed, but it sounded out of place in light of the current topic—hell, maybe I was crazy. "*Shit.*"

"No, no. Don't do that."

"Don't do what? Be embarrassed that I'm so fucked up? I don't even know what it's *like* to be normal anymore. I don't even know who I *was* before that day."

Grayson took my shoulders in a tight hold and shook me gently—trying to get me out of my own head.

"Addison, no one could go through all of that and come out the same. Who's asking you to be that girl? Child or adult, that doesn't make you crazy. It makes you human."

"Yeah?" I mocked, feeling my *crazy* morphing into misplaced anger. "Tell that the to the rest of them. Tell it to my father, who avoids me unless he needs someone to slap around, or my mom, who comes to every track meet *just* to make sure I win. Because if I don't…what was the point of me being late that day? The *only* way I made it through these last two years was to be someone else. If I am the best and the most popular, how can anyone pity me?"

Grayson took my hands and gently squeezed them. "I think for most, it's the easiest emotion to feel when someone is—"

"Damaged?"

"I was going to say suffering." Grayson ran a hand up through his own hair and cupped the back of his neck. "That's why you're attracted to me, am I right? Because I didn't know you back then?"

"Honestly?"

"Yes, Addison. I want you to be honest, please. Always."

"At first, yes. But not now."

"Why, what's changed?"

"I told you. When you look at me, you see more." I cradled his face in my hands and let my eyes roam over him. "And when I look at you, I see for the first time the possibility of everything."

"*Fuck,*" he swore under his breath. "How do I fight against someone like you?"

"You don't. I can be good, Grayson. I can behave. Just say you want me. That you want to be with me always."

"How?" he asked, circling my wrists. "How could this ever work? We'd have to sneak around. We'd barely see each other outside of school." He shook his head like he couldn't believe he was even contemplating it and touched me under the chin. "Do you want that? Can you *live* like that? Always watching what you say and when you say it? Not *ever* being able to tell anyone anything?"

"I just want to be with you, is that so wrong?"

"No. But the law says otherwise. My position as your teacher makes this impossible. Right or wrong? I don't know which is which anymore."

"*This* is right. Right here. Just you and me. Anywhere else and it wouldn't even matter."

"Yes, but we aren't anywhere else, Addison. It is what it is."

Grayson caressed my hair and then repeated the gesture several times without saying anything.

How could something so simple be so comforting?

"I wish it were that easy. There'd be no problems if you were out of school."

Sitting back slightly, I placed a hand against his chest. I was starting to feel frustrated. I couldn't help my age any more than he could help his occupation. "But I'm not, and you're here anyway."

His eyes latched onto mine, and the beating of his heart sped up as if I'd just reminded him of whom he was with.

"Yes. I'm still here. That should show you how much I'm willing to risk."

I traced one of his brows and promised, "I will never betray you. Not *ever*."

Grayson closed his eyes and tipped his head back to face the sun, and I couldn't help but lean in and place my lips against his throat, trying to soothe his obvious agitation.

"I never knew." He took my lips in a kiss that was as tender as it was passionate before he spoke again in a state of astonishment. "I never knew that I'd risk everything, even my freedom, just to touch someone. Just to touch you."

"And now that you know?"

"Now I have a choice to make."

~

One year.

If I'd met her only one year later or *waited* a fucking year— none of this would be an issue. But that wasn't the case.

As I held the girl sitting in my lap, I knew I'd crossed lines and broken laws. The shocking thing was, I didn't care anymore.

"What are you thinking? Tell me," she encouraged as she fingered my hair gently.

"I'm trying to decide what we should do."

Addison frowned. "We? I can make my own decisions, Grayson. I don't need you to make them for me."

"Yes, but they may not be the right ones."

"And yours are?" she accused as she moved off my lap and away from me. "You're not doing anything differently than I am."

Lunging forward, determined to make her listen, I pushed her back on the grass and hovered over her.

"*No.* I'm not. I'm naked in the middle of a field with a student. *My student.* I need to think for a fucking minute. I feel like I'm three steps behind because I never thought I'd be standing here to begin with. *God*, when did this become my life?"

"Let me ask you something," Addison posed, her blue eyes full of sincerity. "If I *wasn't* your student, what would you want?"

After the story she'd just told, my answer was easy and honest. "To take you away from here and start over somewhere new."

A beautiful smile, one that I'd never seen, appeared on her lips. She seemed like a completely different person. "I'd go with you."

"For a day?" I asked skeptically as I played with her hair.

She covered my heart and vowed earnestly, "Forever."

I blinked down at Addison and was reminded that by law she was still a girl and ultimately...

"You *are* my student, Addison."

As she nodded, I wondered where we would go from here.

"So, what do you want?"

Before I knew what I was saying, "I want Brandon gone" was out of my mouth and hovering between us.

She lifted up and kissed the corner of my mouth. "That's easy."

"I want you to graduate."

Kissing the other corner, she promised, "That I can do."

I tangled my fingers through the back of her hair and held her in place as I looked her in the eye and made it very clear. "I want to *help* you."

"I want that too."

She touched my cheek, and as her eyes fluttered closed and her black lashes swept her creamy skin, I couldn't help but kiss it and confess, "I never want you to stop needing me."

When her eyes opened, she softly kissed my mouth and asked, "Then what choice do you have left to make?"

She was right, what choice was there?

Right or wrong, it had already been made.

CHAPTER 19

 ast...

"Addy! Hey! Wait up, would you?"

Brandon.

He'd been calling out and running after me in the parking lot, and I'd been pretending not to hear. With my earbuds in and my iPod off, I was safe. When we reached the west corridor, however, he grabbed my arm, and I was out of options.

"*Hello!*" he shouted, waving his hand in my face.

I pulled the white cord of my earbuds so they popped out and flashed my failsafe sweet smile.

"Brandon? I'm sorry. I didn't hear you."

"Obviously," he sneered and pulled his bag strap up over his shoulder. "Where the hell have you been?"

How to answer that? Hmm...with Grayson, you know, *Mr. McKendrick?*

"I've been slammed with homework and then training for state. Plus Mom—"

"Shut up."

My eyebrows rose in surprise, and I put my hands on my hips. "Excuse me?"

"Stop lying."

He's right. But he didn't know that, and he had no proof. I didn't like his mood, so when he took a step forward, I backed up.

"You've been avoiding me," he accused. "Ever since the weekend."

I raised my chin and fired back. "That's not true. I text you last night."

"*We need to talk?* That doesn't count!"

"Well I'm sorry you don't think so. I've been *busy*."

"Too busy for me?"

"Too busy for anyone!" I yelled back, drawing the attention of the other students. One who just happened to be a smirking Jessica.

Scoffing, Brandon replied, "Yeah, right."

"What did you say?" I demanded, and then he slammed a fist into the locker by my head, causing me to jump.

He leaned in close, his tone menacing as he whispered, "I said *yeah, right.* Are you fucking someone else?"

I swallowed and made sure to keep my eyes on the pissed off guy in front of me. Never one to back down, I lied. "No. But I won't be fucking *you* anymore."

Brandon rammed his other hand beside my head and hissed out, "You're a liar. Do you think I'm fucking stupid?"

"I'm not lying."

Brandon laughed, and the sound was mean. "I followed you."

Oh *shit.* Immediately, I thought of Grayson.

"What do you mean you followed me? Do you know how creepy that sounds?"

Act calm, I told myself. *Don't say anything incriminating.*

"Creepy? I'd rather be creepy than a fucking idiot because my girlfriend is screwing around. So who is he?"

Shaking my head, I tried to imagine what he might have seen yesterday, but I couldn't ask without sounding guilty. So instead, I feigned ignorance. Maybe if he was annoyed enough, he'd tell me.

"I don't know what you're talking about."

"Yesterday, Addy!"

Again, he slammed his hands by my head. A few people stopped, but when they saw us together, they mustn't have wanted to get involved because no one bothered approaching.

That was nice to know if I was in danger.

"I didn't do anything yesterday. I went home."

"No, you didn't. I told you, I *followed* you all the way to the highway."

Fuck, this was not good.

One, two three. One, two three.

This was not good at all.

"But I had to turn around and go to practice. I sent you *ten* messages, and all I fucking got was, *we need to talk!*" He punctuated his angry words with another punch to the locker door.

"*Brandon!*"

The voice that boomed down the hall was so familiar to me that I would have known it anywhere.

"What the hell do you think you're doing? Back up! *Now!*"

Brandon looked me up and down with contempt. "We're *done.* This is over, slut."

That was when Mr. McKendrick stepped between us. He didn't even bother acknowledging me as he pointed to the opposite wall and ordered, "Shut your mouth and back off. Move it!"

Brandon's eyes never left mine as he walked backward to the other side of the hall, where his ass hit the lockers.

"You stay there and be quiet, we're going to have a little talk in a minute. Everyone else, get to class! This is not your morning entertainment program."

Seeing his broad shoulders in front of me made me feel at

ease. As always, with Mr. McKendrick I felt safe, as if nothing could hurt me.

"Are you okay?"

I focused on his face when he turned and walked closer to me. I touched the strap of my bag, needing something tangible to anchor me as I bit my lip.

"Yes, I'm fine," I managed.

"Okay." His eyes silently inspected me, and I could tell he wanted to say more but couldn't. "Do you want to tell me what happened here?"

"She's a liar. That's what happened."

I saw my teacher's jaw flex as he gritted his teeth. Looking over his shoulder, he said in a voice that was hushed, yet still one hundred percent effective, "I thought I told you to be quiet. I will get to *you* in a minute."

My eyes locked with Brandon's as he crossed his arms, clearly pissed off that I was getting to talk first.

He thought I'd been sneaking around with one of his buddies, which would make him a fool, or worse, bad in bed. I wondered how he'd feel to know it was this *man* who'd come between us.

"What happened here?" Mr. McKendrick asked as he looked down at me.

I wanted to tell him that Brandon was now gone, but I didn't want to risk the boy in question overhearing and speculating, so I shrugged nonchalantly.

"We broke up, he got angry."

For a minute, his eyes softened and Grayson slipped through, before he was quickly pushed aside and my history teacher resurfaced.

"Anything else?"

"Like?"

"Did he hurt you?"

I shook my head and shifted uncomfortably on my feet. No, Brandon hadn't hurt me, but he'd scared the hell out of me. It wasn't the rough handling but the thought that he may have caught *us*, and more importantly—would he continue following me?

"No. I'm fine."

I could tell he didn't believe that for a second, and just as he was about to say more, he was interrupted.

"Addison? What's going on here?"

Turning my head to the sound of the voice, I saw Miss Shrieve hurrying down the hall in our direction. She was dressed in a black pencil skirt and a pastel blue blouse, not her usual sweatpants—and suddenly, I felt like the student I was.

I was saved from having to answer because Mr. McKendrick did instead.

"Could you walk her to her next class, please? I'm going to have a little chat with Brandon over here."

I knew there was nothing to worry about with him talking to Brandon, but that didn't stop my anxiety and automatically I raised my arm to look at my watch.

Without missing a beat, *his* voice cut through my nerves as he promised in a soothing voice, "You're fine. You have plenty of time. Go with Miss Shrieve, okay?"

I did as I was told and dropped my arm before walking toward my coach. She reached out to touch my arm as Grayson turned and stepped in front of Brandon.

"Come on, Addison. Mr. McKendrick will get to the bottom of it."

Yes, I thought, but the problem was *he* was the "it" in that particular statement.

～

It was wrong that I wanted to challenge a teenage boy, but I was honest enough to admit that I was in the mood to work this out with my fists.

That wouldn't be happening though. Right now, I needed to

reign in my baser instincts and act like the mature adult I was supposed to be.

"So," I started out, crossing my arms over my chest and mimicking Brandon's stance. "Want to tell me what that was all about?"

"Not really."

The answer was surly, and as Brandon looked at his feet, I tried to forget the image of him slamming his hands beside Addison's head.

"It wasn't really a question. Stand up straight, and start talking, *now*."

Brandon pushed off the lockers and stood up to his full height, which was a couple of inches shorter than my 6'4 frame. It was obvious he wanted to tell me to fuck off, but he was out of luck.

"We had a fight, okay?"

"Clearly, but why would you ever think it's okay to treat a girl like that?"

"Like what? She likes it rough, just ask whoever she's been fucking around with."

"That's quite *enough*, Mr. Williams."

Brandon's pride was wounded. I could see it in the slump of his shoulders and the way he wouldn't look at me, and that right there was as effective as any punch in the mouth.

"Look, I don't care what happened between you two." *That's a fucking lie.* I was more than happy they were over. "What I do care about is the safety of my students. You will not treat anyone that way. Do you hear me? And you especially will not slam a young lady up against a wall and yell at her, *ever*. That's not how a man acts. You should be ashamed of yourself."

Brandon rolled his eyes, and I had the urge to slam *him* against a locker.

"You're going to be suspended. Was it worth it? Get your stuff. We're going to pay Principal Thomas a visit."

I waited as he bent down to pick up his bag and heard him mumble, "Whatever."

"What was that?" I demanded.

"I said whatever. She's hot but totally fucked up in the head."

I'd never considered myself a violent man, but as Brandon's words penetrated my brain, a red haze clouded my judgment.

I strode forward two steps until he was back against the lockers. In a voice I barely recognized, I grated out, "You need to shut your mouth, right now. I don't want to hear another word until we are in the main office, and when your suspension is over, you are to stay *away* from Addison Lancaster."

Brandon's eyes widened as he swallowed and nodded. I was out of line but not so far that it seemed unusual as far as I was concerned.

"Do I make myself clear?" I asked in a cool, calculated, and in my own mind, *deadly* fucking serious tone.

"Yes. *Sir*."

"Good."

Stepping aside, I watched Brandon march away in front of me, and I hoped like hell he understood to keep quiet, because I didn't think I could listen to anything more without physically reacting.

Luckily for Brandon, he seemed to get the message.

Unfortunately for me, it fueled the fire to his kindling suspicion.

∾

Present...

"Can I watch the news tonight?" I ask, making my way past Doc and into the common area.

"You can, but you won't find what you're looking for."

I stop just inside the room and see several other residents of the Pine Groves establishment milling around and sitting on the couches.

"And what is that?"

Doc studies me in quiet contemplation.

"You forget how well I know you, Addison. You're after answers, but they still don't know anything."

I push a stray piece of hair behind my ear as he asks, "Do you?"

"Do I what?"

"Do *you* know anything?"

I walk farther into the room, but before I'm out of hearing distance, I look back at the man I spend most of my days circling. I give him the hollow smile I've perfected while being in here. It's my *new* failsafe and it gives nothing away as I finally give him the truth.

"No, I know nothing."

Except, I think as I take a seat, *that he's gone.*

CHAPTER 20

 resent...

Fifteen days.

As I stand outside the library door, I take a moment to think. Doc had been right. Last night's news told me nothing. Not one damn thing. Except how long I'd been here.

Funny, it feels more like fifteen years.

I grip the door handle in front of me as I press my forehead against the wood and close my eyes. I can hear the blood rushing around my ears and I try not to give in to the urge but there it is—*one, two, three.*

"I know you're out there, Addison," Doc's voice calls to me from the other side of the door.

How? How does he know that I'm out here?

"I can hear you counting."

Shit, I'm doing it out loud?

I turn the handle and push the door open to find Doc sitting at the table I'd been seated at the other day. I close the door behind me and look at the clock on the wall—3 p.m., our usual meeting time.

"Come in, come in." He waves me forward.

I have no idea why he asked to meet me here today, but as I get closer, I see two large books open in front of him, and my curiosity is peaked. I move to the vacant seat and sit down.

"What are we doing here?" I ask when it's clear he doesn't plan to say much else.

Doc sits back in his seat, plants his fingers on the first book and spins it around until it's facing me. I glance down and see a beautifully illustrated picture of the purple hooded flower, and I know immediately what it is. So does he.

We had this discussion the day he showed me the photo in his office.

"Aconite."

My eyes flick up to connect with his, and I make sure they are devoid of any kind of emotion—after all, that's what he's trying to draw from me, a response.

"The Queen of Poisons."

I sit silently, waiting for him to get to his point. It's obvious he has one since he's bringing it up again.

"But you already know this. What was it you told me it means?"

My heart is thundering inside my chest. Clicking his fingers as if he "got it," he states, " 'Without struggle,' that was it. As in, whoever ingests it wouldn't be able to put up much of a fight before they die."

He knows what he's doing. He's pushing.

He's prodding at me, waiting for me to react, and *fuck*…it's close to working.

"Did you know that hunters used it to paralyze wolves? That was how it came by the name wolf's bane. It's fast, almost immediate, depending on the dose." He quietly considers me as he pushes the book my way. "But sometimes it can take a couple of hours, as you already know."

He sits back and waits as I look down at the page in front of me. I can feel the tears forming as I try to blink them back.

He wants me to talk. He's trying to break me.

I wipe away a tear that escapes, and I place my hand on the page. I touch the image of the flower and then seek out Doc's steady gaze. He slides the second book over to me.

"*Psyche Revived by Cupid's Kiss*. That's the photo on your wall. The only thing you brought with you, other than your watch."

My eyes drop to the second image, and I can hear the ever present—*tick, tick, tock*—as I stare at the black-and-white sculpture in the art history book.

Memories flood through me and threaten to overwhelm the tenuous hold I have on myself. A look, a kiss, a whisper in a voice that soothes…

"Addison?"

I blink at Doc. His expression is intense, his focus unwavering, and when he points to Psyche, he says, "There wasn't poison on her lips when Cupid revived her."

Snatching both hands back, I clasp them in my lap. I want to tell him, to unburden myself, but how can I?

Then in a voice that feels detached from me, I reply, "No, but she brought it to him just the same."

Past…

Three thirty and the final bell of the day had rung. I picked up my bag and walked out to my car. I needed to speak to Grayson and I hadn't gotten a chance all day.

Every time I'd seen him, he'd either been with a student or a teacher. There was no way I could approach him about this at school.

Brandon had been suspended because of me. I was trying

not to feel guilty, but it was hard when he'd been right about everything.

"So how's it feel? Being dumped in front of everyone?"

At the acidic voice, I stopped in front of my car and turned to see Jessica hot on my heels. I wasn't really in the mood to deal with her, but she'd been extra bitchy lately, and I had no idea why. Maybe it was time I found out.

"What is your problem with me?" I demanded.

She had both of her thumbs tucked into her backpack straps as she gave me a derisive once over.

"Oh, nothing at all, *Addy*."

"Yeah, that's obvious." I snorted, and the sound was ugly even to my own ears. "If you want Brandon, he's all yours. I don't care."

Teenage girls can be cruel. I should know because over the last year I hadn't always been the kindest.

"Gee, thanks for the permission. You know, it's about time you were brought back down to earth. Apparently, you *aren't* Little Miss Perfect. That's nice to know."

"I never said I was."

Jessica's mouth twisted into an ugly snarl. "No, but you sure do act that way."

This day just wasn't letting up. It continued to get shittier with every passing second.

"What. Do. You. Want?"

"I want everyone to see the shy little loser you really are. The same old Addison Lancaster as *before*."

Tick, tick, tock.

She was not going there, was she?

My bag slid down my arm as my anger bubbled up inside of me.

"Before what, Jessica? If you're going to be a bitch, then just let it all out."

She raised an eyebrow and gave a scathing laugh. "Everyone

tiptoes around you since Daniel died. We all know it was your fault. But it was two years ago, time to—"

That was *it*. I lunged at her, grabbing a fistful of her hair, and yanked her in close. When I was only inches from her, I shouted, "Shut up! Don't *ever* say his name."

She clawed at my arm, her nails digging into my skin, but I refused to let go.

How dare she even *think* his name?

"You *are* fucking crazy!"

She was right. At that moment, I felt insane. But I needed to know what was going on behind my back.

"Who said that?" I asked, pulling her hair harder.

"Let go of my fucking hair!"

"Answer me," I hissed, spitting like an angry cat.

"*Brandon*. He said you're a freak! That you count when he fucks you."

Shocked and embarrassed, I pushed her away and slumped back against the car.

I counted out loud? *Fuck*, I always thought it was in my head.

"It must have been nice for him to finally screw someone *normal*."

That final jab from her was perfectly timed, and before I knew it, my hand flew up and cracked against her cheek.

Instead of being shocked or upset, Jessica's mouth pulled into a distorted smile. "*Time's up*, Addy. Move along."

With that, Jessica marched off to her car. As she disappeared, my eyes caught on the man leaning back against his truck with one hell of a serious frown on his face.

How long had he been standing there?

Knowing I was about to get suspended right along with Brandon, I sighed and bent down to pick up my bag. I didn't even want to look at Grayson right now. I felt defeated and was starting to believe I really was the crazy lunatic they all thought I was.

Did I do this on purpose *to* be suspended? Because I felt guilty about Brandon? Who knew at this point.

I unlocked my car and threw my bag in just as I felt him approach. We weren't standing close, but it felt as if he was touching me.

"Want to tell me what that was about?"

As always, his voice soothed me, but I still couldn't bring myself to face him. I felt like a child, like his *student*.

"Just report me, and be done with it. I'll be suspended, and this whole fucked up day can be over with."

I was about to slide into my car when his hand moved to the roof and my name fell from his lips.

"Addison, look at me."

I could feel the wetness on my face as I shifted and did as I was told.

"What happened?"

I swiped the tears away and shook my head. "Nothing, I just need to go. My mom is going to kill me when she finds out."

"Hey, talk to me. That was the deal, right?"

I laughed then and looked around us. No one was in sight.

"Meet me later, if you still want to. Then I'll talk."

"I can't. I need to go and see my father."

"Please?"

He sighed, frustrated. "Where?"

"I'll be with Daniel."

He stepped back and asked, "Is this over? What happened here with Jessica?"

"Yes."

"Are you sure?"

"I'm pretty sure she said what she wanted to say."

"I should take you back inside to see Principal Thomas, you know that, don't you?"

"Yes."

He rubbed his weary face. "Get in your car, and go home. If she reports it, then…"

It went unsaid that he would have to back the claim, but I doubted Jessica would say anything. I had the scratches on my arm to prove she was just as involved.

"I understand."

"Good. Now go."

I got inside my car and watched him disappear in my rearview mirror as I pulled away. We'd have a chance later to talk about what really needed to be said.

∾

Fuck. Today just wasn't getting any better.

As Addison's car left the lot, I had to wonder where my priorities were.

This morning I'd had Brandon suspended for threatening a student and this afternoon—right now? I'd let Addison leave after a fight in the parking lot.

Fuck.

I was almost at my truck when Helene stepped out from around the front.

I'd always wondered how criminals felt when they were caught, and with each step she took, bringing herself closer and closer to me, I could feel my chest tightening and my palms sweating. This was it—*I was caught.*

"Grayson."

I tried for a smile, even though it felt more like a grimace, and when she beamed back at me, I felt the fist around my heart slowly loosening.

"I'm glad I caught you."

Nice choice of words. Were they on purpose?

"You are?" I asked, feeling nervous and hating it. Where the fuck had my confidence gone? I shoved my clammy hands into my pockets and tried to appear relaxed.

"Yes. After this morning, my day just got out of control."

That was an understatement if ever I'd heard one.

"So…I was wondering if you'd like to maybe go out and get dinner? Unwind a little."

Oh shit, she was asking me on a date. *Think, Grayson.*

"Just as friends, if you like."

Think fucking fast.

She shrugged her purse strap up her arm, and all I could think about was the way Addison did the same thing with her backpack.

"I was actually just about to go and visit my father."

That wasn't a lie. I *was* about to go and visit him until Addison had asked me to meet her instead.

"Oh," Helene replied, and I could tell she thought I was lying.

Well, maybe I could go and see dad today before I drove over to Oakwood.

"I didn't know you had family here."

"Yeah," was my brilliant response. *God, snap the fuck out of it.* "He's the reason I moved back. He's not very well."

"I'm really sorry to hear that," she offered and stepped closer, reaching out to comfort me. Why did I feel nothing with her? Life would be so much easier if I did. I looked down at her hand on my arm and then back to her face.

"If you need someone to talk to…"

"Okay."

She gave a tight grin. "Because you're *so* talkative."

I chuckled. "I'm sorry. I guess my mind's somewhere else."

She moved past me but at the last moment stopped and asked, "Oh, do you need me to come with you in the morning to report Addy?"

Just like that, the tight fist around my heart returned. I turned to face her and wondered what she was thinking, but it was clear—she'd seen everything.

The fight, me talking with Addison, and finally, *me* letting Addison leave without repercussion—so why the pretense? Why the invite to dinner?

"Sure. I figured it would be easier for everyone to deal with in the morning." When did I turn into such a fucking liar? "Especially after the incident with Brandon. I let Addison know we'd be dealing with it tomorrow."

There was a moment of silence, and I swore it felt more like ten minutes than ten seconds.

"How'd she take it?" Helene asked.

"Not well."

"That's going to mess with her track practice."

"Yeah. I bet."

She shrugged. "Oh well. She knows the rules. Doesn't mean I don't wish I could bend them. You know?"

I couldn't even formulate an answer. I was too busy thinking back to my conversation with Addison and trying to remember if I'd done anything inappropriate. No, I didn't think so.

I hadn't touched her like I wanted. I'd made sure to touch the car.

"It's such a shame, she's really let me down. Not to mention her parents. They'll be terribly upset if she can't compete at State."

She seemed to reflect on that thought for a moment, and I wondered if she was also disappointed because Addison hadn't lived up to whatever expectations she had placed on her. "Well, I'll let you go so you can visit your father."

"Thanks. I appreciate it."

Helene made her way to the car, and as she opened the door and looked back to where I was standing, she called out, "I'll see you in the morning at Principal Thomas's office. How's seven forty-five?"

Faking a smile, I returned, "Perfect!"

As she shut the door, I let out my first real breath since she'd approached and thought of how to tell Addison she was getting suspended. I knew what would happen when her parents found out and the hell she would pay.

Perfect? Not even close. No, try a fucking disaster waiting to happen.

CHAPTER 21

 ast...

I pulled into the parking lot of the hospice facility and sat silently, watching as a nurse wheeled an older lady through the front door.

People came here for one thing: to leave the world behind. Is that why I was here now? To leave *my* current world behind?

To lose myself in *this* emotional crisis where I had no control, so I wouldn't have to face the horrible choices I was otherwise making?

Resting my head back on the seat, I closed my eyes. I told myself that an hour here wouldn't make a difference in when I could see her, and then I remembered the way Addison had looked at me before she'd got into her car.

For the first time, she'd appeared defeated.

Climbing out of the truck, I slammed the door shut and stormed toward the entrance with misdirected anger. I was furious, and as I walked through the front doors, I felt my annoyance brewing.

If it hadn't been for my father getting sick, I wouldn't be back here in the first place. If he'd bothered to tell me earlier, I could have gotten to him sooner, had him cared for, and never… never *what?* Moved back to Denver? Gotten a job at the local high school?

Met Addison?

Stopping outside his room, I leaned against the wall and scrubbed a hand over my face.

Look at me, trying to find someone to blame. Way to man up.

It wasn't my father's fault I'd decided to fuck up my life. That was mine and mine alone. It was about time I owned it.

"Oh, Mr. McKendrick. Someone finally got ahold of you."

Pushing off the wall, I turned to see my father's nurse. I shook my head, uncomfortable that I'd been caught in a moment of disgusted self-reflection.

"No, I'm sorry. I just came by after work."

"Oh," she acknowledged.

As she touched my arm, her eyes conveyed a sympathy that was only ever borne from death. My stomach knotted, and I knew—he was gone.

"When?"

"Around ten minutes ago. We tried to reach you, but…"

But…I'd been lingering at the school, watching over Addison.

I'd missed him by minutes…mere minutes.

"Okay," I mumbled, not able to say anything else.

"I'm sorry. I realize this must be a shock when you thought you were coming here to visit."

It *was* a shock. I'd been furious at my father only seconds ago and now? Now he was dead.

"Yes," I managed to utter. I still couldn't wrap my brain around what she was telling me.

"It was peaceful. He was sleeping when he passed."

Peaceful.

He was at peace, and me—I was in some kind of hell.

"Can I see him? Have you moved——?"

"No," she interrupted gently. "He's still in there."

She turned the door handle to his room and pushed it open a crack.

"Is there someone I can call for you?"

Brushing past her, I saw the lone bed over by the window.

"No. There's no one."

"Okay. Then take your time and let me know when you're ready."

Without looking back, I walked over to where my father lay. The room was suffocating in its silence, and as I got closer, I noticed that someone had opened the window. I knew some believed that by opening the window, you freed the soul. I wondered if it had freed his.

I sat down beside the bed and took his hand. It was cool to the touch and when I leaned down over it, I felt a tear escape.

I'd come home to Denver to say good-bye and somehow managed to fuck that up too. *Jesus*, my sense of purpose had gone to shit.

"I'm sorry," I apologized as my body shook. "God. I'm so fucking sorry."

I'd let this man down in every way. Not only did I manage to break every moral rule he'd instilled in me, I'd let him down when he needed me the most.

Fuck, I don't deserve any kind of happiness.

I raised my head to look out the window, searching for my own escape, but there was no escaping my terrible choices. They'd been made.

The only thing I could do was...*unmake* them? Was that even possible?

The sun had shifted and was slowly beginning to set. The rays now streaming into the room were hitting something shiny on the set of drawers by my father's bed.

Releasing his hand, I stood and made my way over to see what it was. There, sitting on the flat surface, was a pen resting on a single sheet of paper. Scrawled across the middle was a quote.

Nietzsche.

My father had always been a fan of his work and passed the love of his writing on to me. I picked up the note and touched the words he'd written.

Gray,
 'What is done out of love always takes place beyond good and evil.'
 I understand.
 Dad

I clenched the note in my fist and brought it to my mouth, trying to hold myself together.

He was *still* teaching me, and here I was, still trying to learn from his lessons.

As tears blurred my vision, I shoved the paper in my pocket and once again, the pen lying on the drawers caught my eye. Picking it up, I noticed it was his old faithful.

As a teacher, he'd always prided himself on having something nice to write with, and this was the pen I'd given him for his 50th birthday.

It was black with a beautiful gold finish, and along the side his initials were engraved—*G.M.*—just like my own.

He'd never gone anywhere without it, and from now on, neither would I.

～

Present...

. . .

Tick, tick, tock.

I've been sitting in Doc's office for the last thirty minutes, but he hasn't said one word. Usually I'd enjoy the silence, but today it's starting to worry me.

What is this? A new tactic?

If so, I'm surprised to admit that I enjoyed the old ones better. This silence is nerve-racking. After yesterday in the library, I was almost certain we'd be discussing the flora and fauna in Colorado, but so far—nothing.

Well, nothing except for the new habit of tapping his pen and my new preoccupation of focusing on it.

It was irritating. It was intrusive. It was...*familiar.*

"Can I see your pen?"

I'm the first to break the silence, and Doc's smile is slow as it appears.

"Why? It's just a pen."

My eyes find his, and I call him out. "You're lying."

"Am I?"

"Yes."

Shrugging, Doc holds the pen out and looks it over. I too let my eyes move over the black and gold casing. If only I could see the other side.

Tick, tick, tock.

"How do you know I'm lying?"

"Isn't it unethical for you to lie to a patient?"

"How do you *know* I'm lying?"

Beginning to get annoyed, I roll my eyes at him and stand. "I just do."

"How?"

I cross my arms and refuse to talk.

"Addison?"

"What?" I snap, anxious to know if this is what I think it is and more importantly, why Doc has it.

"You *need* to trust me."

I watch Doc as he stands and holds the pen out to me. I reach for it, and it's almost like *he's* here in the room with me.

For the first time since I've been here, the loud ticking of the clock stops. Cautiously, I lift the pen and turn it to see *G.M.* engraved along the side—suddenly, the loudest thing in the room is my heart.

∾

Past...

The sun had finally set when I made my way through the gates of the cemetery and stepped down onto the green grass. In one day, everything had become extremely complicated.

I walked briskly between the tombstones, careful not to tread on the flowers sprouting out around the edges.

Brandon had followed me...followed *us*. What if he hadn't gone back for practice?

Not only were my actions reckless, they were putting Grayson's freedom in jeopardy. One wrong move and his career would be over, not to mention he'd end up in jail. He could lose everything, all because of me.

What made me think I had the right to ask that of him?

Doc was always telling me, *one choice can change the entire path you were once on.* Is this the kind of thing he'd been talking about?

Maybe it was time for me to make the right choice—the one to say good-bye.

I could choose to be unselfish and allow Grayson to move on from what he surely now felt was an obligation.

"Addison?"

The deep voice that drifted through the night didn't belong to the man I'd told to meet me here. No, the man standing in front of me was family.

"Dad...what are you doing here?" *And when are you leaving?*

"Why do you think I'm here?" he asked, his voice full of disgust as he looked away and faced the stone that marked his son's resting place.

"I'm sorry. That was a stupid question."

"Yes, it was," he agreed and lifted his arm, bringing up the bottle.

Whiskey. His go-to when he needed to numb the pain. They sent me to a shrink, but he swore he didn't need one.

Why see a doctor when liquor is cheaper?

"I'll just leave then."

"No," he discouraged. "Stay. You *should* apologize every day."

My head jerked back as if he'd slapped me. "I didn't come here to apologize."

He turned with a sway and spat at me with loathing. "Well you should."

Those three little words shouldn't have been able to cause such damage, but after Brandon and Jessica, they cut wide the wound that I usually held somewhat stitched together.

"I don't have *anything* to apologize for," I stressed, reminding myself what Doc always told me.

I turned to leave and had taken only two steps when I was pulled to a stop by a hand grabbing my wrist. He spun me around and yanked me in close before shoving his face close to mine.

I could smell the stench of alcohol on his breath as he assured me, "You have *everything* to be sorry for. It's your fault he's even in the ground."

I tried to pull my arm free, but my father's grip was stronger. I knew I'd have bruises tomorrow.

"Yes, *Addison.* Because of you."

I shook my head in denial. "Let me go!"

"It's hard to hear the truth, isn't it?"

"You're hurting me!"

"No. *Noooo.* I'm hurting!" he shouted and the torment in his voice was evident. That was quickly forgotten when his palm met my cheek, and the back of his hand caught my lip on the upswing. The reverberating crack that echoed through the night seemed to keep beat with the painful throbbing of my newly bloodied lip.

He'd hit me before but never where anyone could see it.

He hated me for what happened to Daniel, and I hated him for what he'd become.

Sobbing uncontrollably, I looked up into the face I once worshipped and managed to tell him, "I'm hurting too."

I stumbled back as he released me with a hard shove and heard him hiss under his breath. "Leave me alone. You're as poisonous as the fucking flowers that grow here."

∾

Present...

"My father," I manage as I drag my eyes away from the engraving on the pen.

"What's your father got to do with this? I don't understand."

Of course he doesn't. It's obvious he knows who this belongs to, and it's *not* my father.

I take a step back and sit down in the chair, still clutching what's in my hand tight—as if it will heal me.

Like the man who'd owned it had.

"The first night I saw this," I hold up the object under discussion, "was because of my father. Remember the way he liked to drink?"

"Yes, I do," Doc acknowledges and sits back down. "What happened? Tell me, Addy."

I feel a small smile tug at my mouth. "You haven't called me Addy for a long time."

"Addy hasn't *been* here for a long time."

He's right. I thought she was long gone. Turns out, she was just hiding.

"Right after what happened to Daniel, Dad started drinking. You know that, I told you in our sessions together."

"Yes, I remember. He was never home. Stayed out late, would drink, and come back the next morning after you and your mother left. Easy way to avoid his issues and the people in his life."

Pulling the pen to my chest, I hold it against my heart.

"He's a monster."

"He's grieving."

I can feel the anger inside of me as I spit the words "I don't care" from my mouth as if they're vile.

"Yes, you do," Doc patiently points out. "Otherwise, you wouldn't be so angry. It's okay to admit that."

"'*Whoever fights monsters should see to it that in the process he does not become a monster*'—I guess I missed the point of that lesson."

Doc places an elbow on the chair and rubs his chin as if thinking over the statement.

"Nietzsche, that's an interesting choice. You say you missed the point of the lesson. A lesson Grayson was teaching you?"

"How about a life lesson?"

"How about the truth?"

I lower the pen to my lap and twist the top between my fingers before answering.

"I fought with my father that night, and now *I'm* locked up in a fucking cage—guess I became the monster after all."

∾

Past...

Running as fast as I could, I made my way across the grass and up on to the road. I sprinted through the parking lot and was just about to make it past the gates when a truck pulled off the road. The headlights lit me up like the star of my own fucked up reality show.

Grayson.

I dashed to the side, out of the spotlight, and searched for a place to hide. I waited for him to pass, but he must have seen me because the engine rumbled to a stop, and the headlights switched off.

The next thing I heard was the truck door opening and then his booted feet hit the ground.

"Addison?"

I slipped into the small alcove in the stone pillars of the entry gates and tried to hold myself together. I was shaking and could feel my lip trembling, so I bit down on the cut, wincing at the pain as I tried to fight back the tears.

"*Addison?*" he called out into the night, much like the first time we were here.

He couldn't see me like this, *crushed*—not again.

I wrapped an arm around my waist and pressed the other to my mouth. I couldn't keep doing this to him. I couldn't pull him into this disaster that was my life and expect him to heal me.

Doc couldn't even do that, so to ask it of Grayson wasn't fair.

It was time to stop being so selfish.

"We need to talk," he whispered into the night. "Where did you go?"

I agreed, we did need to talk, but not now. As I stood there, hidden, I hoped for the first time that he would leave.

He must have understood my need because the next thing I heard was a curse and then his feet began moving. I heard the truck door open, and I waited until he backed out of the drive and pulled away before stepping out from where I'd been hiding.

I walked through the gates to make my way home when I saw something on the road.

Huh, it was a fancy-looking pen.

I picked it up and saw *Mont Blanc* written around the gold trimming of the cap. Down the side, engraved in cursive, were the letters *G.M.*—it must have fallen from his truck.

I stood up and tucked it into my jeans pocket, feeling a sense of calm wash over me. Even without him there and my lip pounding, the thought that I had a part of him with me soothed the pain.

I'd take comfort in that tonight and free him tomorrow— when I'd return this to him.

CHAPTER 22

 ast...

Standing in front of the mirror the next morning was a sorry excuse of my usual self. My hair was a mess, and my lip was split, swollen and bruised.

This cover was now worn. Ragged around the edges.

Grabbing the concealer, I opened it and started to apply what I hoped would be a decent cover-up job, but ten minutes later, it looked no better. I arranged my hair in a messy tangle, trying to hide the obvious flaw, but nothing could hide it. My bottom lip was an obvious eyesore.

Mom would not be happy.

Maybe if I was extra quiet I could avoid her and get by without having to lie about what really happened. She wouldn't believe the truth anyway; denial was a powerful emotion.

I picked up my school jacket as I left my bedroom and spotted Grayson's pen. I snatched it up and slipped it into my skirt pocket.

I needed to talk to him today, and this was the perfect excuse.

～

Present...

Standing outside Doc's office the next morning, I notice I'm early for my scheduled session.

I didn't sleep at all last night. My mind had been too busy. Too distracted.

You need to trust me.

Why? Why did I need to trust him?

I keep thinking back to those final days with Grayson and my current sessions with Doc.

Did they ever meet? How did Doc get the pen?

Last night I'd done nothing but think about it.

What did it all mean?

Well, I wasn't going to get any answers standing out in the hall.

I knock—*one, two, three*—but this time, I make sure not to count out loud. I'm aware of my actions.

"Yes? Come in."

Doc's voice filters through the wood, and I feel apprehension take hold.

Do I really want the answers I'm searching for?

I push open the door and look inside.

Unlike in our sessions, Doc isn't facing me. He's hunched over his desk, which is up against the back wall, writing in a journal. It doesn't surprise me that he keeps one. He seems the kind—old-fashioned.

"Addy?"

I close the door and step farther into the room.

"How'd you know it was me?"

He places his pen down then spins his leather chair in my direction. "How could you stay away?"

Frowning, I step closer.

"What do you mean?"

Doc gestures to the pen in my hand. "How long did you think about that last night?"

"I didn't stop."

"Exactly."

Confused, I raise my hands as if to say—*so?*

Doc stands and moves around his desk to stop in front of me. "Are you ready to talk?"

I look up at the man who'd stepped in and filled my father's place a few years ago. He is the only other person in my life, I'm discovering, that I really do trust.

I shrug, still not one hundred percent sold on divulging information.

"What do you need from me, Addy?"

"I need to know how you got this."

"That's easy," he answers. "Grayson gave it to me."

Past...

I made it to school in record time. I was early.

After I parked my car, I climbed out and scanned the lot. He wasn't here yet. That was good.

I smoothed my denim skirt down and rushed inside, making my way to the main building. With my head down to avoid eye contact, I walked quickly to my first class, hoping to make it without any kind of—

"Addison, can I please see you for a minute?"

Interruption.

Miss Shrieve. Great. Just what I didn't need this morning.

I came to a stop in the hall and pivoted to look at her. Her eyes narrowed as she caught sight of my face. I wished I could disappear, but I was trapped, and when she lifted her arm, I automatically flinched away.

"Who did this to you?" she asked softly, then stepped to the side of the hall, waiting for me to follow.

"It's nothing," I assured, not wanting to get into it.

I wanted to go to my history class and wait for Mr. McKendrick. I may have been ending things, but right now I was feeling anxious, and he was the only person who could calm me.

"It certainly is *not* nothing." Miss Shrieve took a deep breath and then let it out on a sigh. "What exactly happened yesterday with Jessica?"

Holy shit, she knew about yesterday?

Did Grayson tell her?

"Nothing," I replied hurriedly, thinking to myself, *please let this go.*

"Addison? You need to start talking. Your behavior lately… you know you're going to be suspended this morning, don't you?"

My stomach knotted at the thought of my mom's reaction to *that* news. She may not use her hands, but when it came to showing her disappointment, she could be as vicious as my father.

"Well, if you won't tell me, maybe you'll talk to Principal Thomas. Come on, Mr. McKendrick will meet us there."

Betrayal.

The second she said his name, I felt it.

It didn't matter that he'd told me it could come to this. The emotion was there just the same. Following silently, I came to a standstill when we entered the main office, and it was empty. He wasn't there.

I followed Miss Shrieve's gaze as she looked at the clock on the wall—8 a.m.

"Wait here," she instructed and made her way over to Mrs. Howard, Principal Thomas's secretary.

Angry, I reached into my pocket and gripped his pen like I wanted to snap it in half. The pounding in my head was from my anxiety kicking in, as any calm I usually got from *him* morphed to fury.

His betrayal cut deeper than the gash on my lip.

"Looks like it's you and me, Addison. Mr. McKendrick won't be here today."

Seething, I stood and made my way over to where Miss Shrieve was standing.

Why he would do this to me? Why would he leave me to face this alone?

I took a seat in front of the Principal's large desk and faced the balding man behind it. The clock in the hall became louder, drowning out the ringing in my ears.

Tick, tick, tock.

All sense of calm was gone.

He'd left me here, and that was when I realized I truly was *alone*.

Present...

"What do you mean Grayson *gave* it to you?"

"Why don't you sit down, Addy," Doc suggests as he sits.

"I don't want to sit down!"

I can feel the beginning of hysteria starting to grip me but what did he expect? All along he'd...what?

"Did you know Grayson?"

"Sit down, please."

Planting my ass in the usual seat, I sputter the only thing that makes any sense. "Did you and he...talk about me?"

"No."

Not able to sit still, I bounce back up to my feet as I point the pen at him.

"Stop being so fucking cryptic."

"I'm being *honest*. You're the one who has been cryptic," Doc points out and glances at the wall calendar. "For sixteen days now."

"I know how long it's been."

"Do you?"

"Yes!" I shout, frustrated at not getting the answers I think he holds.

"Are you ready to start talking to me like an adult? Trusting me?"

Pacing back and forth, I shake my head.

I'd once promised never to talk about this with anyone. Knowing that if I did, it could ruin the one person that I loved.

But does it count as a broken promise when that person is gone, and I'm all alone?

Past...

Suspended for five days.

Mom had been called at work, and I had been ordered to get myself right home. She would deal with me tonight.

I ran out to my car, and as I neared it, I noticed there was a note on my windshield under the wiper blade. Picking it up, I unfolded the paper to see the words: ONE, TWO, THREE, FREAK written in bold letters. *Jessica.*

I scrunched it up and unlocked the car, climbing inside. I

looked out at the kids running around the track and angrily slammed the door shut.

There went my track year at school and my perfect run of being the star everyone expected. Principal Thomas had told me I could make it up and still compete if I worked extra hard, but at this point, all I wanted to do was give up.

Starting the car, I pulled out of the lot with every intention of driving home.

That, however, was not where I ended up.

Work just wasn't in the cards today.

All night I'd lain in bed, staring at the ceiling and trying to decide where exactly everything had gone wrong. When was the moment that I'd truly lost my direction and not been able to turn back? Managing in the process to let down the man closest to me.

All I kept coming back to was the moment I first saw her.

That was when.

Dad had written, *I understand,* but somehow I doubted this was what he had in mind when he wrote it. He'd probably been thinking love on a grand scale, not on a scale that could potentially put his son behind bars.

Something needed to change. *I* needed to change.

So instead of going to school this morning, I'd gone somewhere else entirely.

I'd just gotten out of the shower after returning home when there was a loud knock on my front door. I pulled on a pair of jeans and slicked my hands through my wet hair. I really didn't want to deal with people today.

I didn't bother with the peephole before I opened the door.

Although I shouldn't have been shocked to see her, I *was* surprised by how she looked as she stood scowling in front of me. Her hair was tangled all around her face, and her bottom lip was puffy and split open. She didn't look anything like the girl who'd driven away from me yesterday afternoon.

White-knuckling the door, I tried to imagine telling her to leave. I tried to picture a time in my future where I wouldn't think about her and wonder where she was, or how she was doing, or even worse, whom she loved. Instead, I stepped aside and Addison stormed into my house.

The tension in the air was palpable.

I'd gone to her last night with one goal in mind—to end this. We needed to stop the madness we'd gotten caught up in, but now as she stood in front of me, all I could think about was touching her one last time.

~

Driving home, I'd been determined to forget about Grayson, or *Mr. McKendrick* as I'd been thinking of him today.

Where the hell had he been?

Just calling in long enough to say—*sure, suspend her*—before disappearing was bullshit. It was the coward's way out, and halfway home, I found myself making a U-turn.

I parked in my usual spot and made my way to his front door. I knocked three times and tried to keep my anger at bay, deciding that I would just end things and get out of there.

However, that decision flew out the window when the front door opened, and standing in front of me was a virtual stranger. Sometime between last night and this morning, Grayson had transformed.

Gone was the long hair I'd grown accustomed to, and in its place was a clean-cut version of my teacher. The stubble along his jaw was still familiar, and as he moved aside and I barged in past him, I couldn't help but look him over a second time. The change was so unexpected it almost broke through my anger, but then his eyes dropped to my lip and I remembered my shitty morning. I steeled myself against any curiosity and instead, fired both guns.

"What the fuck was that this morning?"

"This morning?"

"Yes. You know? When I got suspended."

Grayson closed the door and latched it before stepping closer to me. Without answering my first question, he inspected me and asked, "What happened to your face?"

"What happened to *me*?" I questioned, my voice climbing higher with each note. "What the hell happened to *you*?"

He said nothing as he made his way past me and walked through the house to the kitchen. I followed silently, since that was what he was going with, and waited. He opened a top cabinet and pulled out a bottle of alcohol.

Reminded of my father, I backed up a step. He turned and asked again in a tone that was not to be argued with, "What *happened* to your face?"

I touched my lip, grimaced and answered, "My father."

"Your *father* did this? When? Last night?" He paused and placed the bottle on the counter. Walking over to me, he gently grazed my bottom lip with his thumb and said, "You need to report him, Addison. Or I will. What fucking irony."

"What do you mean?"

"My father died yesterday. That's why I wasn't at work."

His words were delivered with such a sense of detachment it was as if he were talking about a stranger. If it hadn't been for the dramatic change in him, I would have thought he didn't care.

That wasn't the case though, and as I started to put it all together...his lack of presence this morning, the physical change in his appearance, and the alcohol sitting on the counter —I could tell that Grayson was wanting to escape.

"Do you want to—?"

"No," he interrupted, and I knew exactly how he felt.

I'd never wanted to talk after Daniel had passed either.

"I'm sorry—"

"Stop talking," he said, walking me back until I hit the kitchen counter.

"Okay."

As the edge dug into my back, Grayson's hands came down beside me, caging me in. Pushing forward, he leaned me back slightly until his body was pressed flush against mine.

"I came to end things with you last night, but you ran away."

Even though I'd been planning the same, to hear the words from him hurt.

"Then *end* it," I taunted, pushing my chin out. I'd be damned if I showed him he could hurt me worse than even my father's blow.

Grayson lowered his head until his stubbled cheek rested against mine and his lips were at my ear.

"I..." he started and then stopped.

I slid my fingers into the short strands now covering his head.

"You?"

He scraped his teeth along a line from my jaw to my chin. Then he lifted his head and looked me right in the eye as he sucked my bottom lip between his.

The sharp bite of pain that came from the cut on my lip made me wince, until his tongue came out and soothed it in a gesture so incredibly intimate, I felt my entire body tremble. Then his anguished words met my ears.

"I *can't.*"

Breathing became difficult as he brought a hand to my chest and placed it over my heart. He held my full attention as he began to lightly tap—*one, two, three. One two three.*

"I need..."

I waited, wanting to hear it—*needing* to.

His other hand trailed a path around my waist, stopping at the top of my skirt. "I need to feel alive again."

The word alive was so foreign to me, especially since the last few years I'd felt anything but. However, here with this man, I'd never felt more so as he continued to count my beating heart just like I had done his.

"I need everything."

His eyes came back to rest on mine and as his fingers curled under my shirt, I replied, "Then take what you need."

CHAPTER 23

 resent...

Doc watches me unrelentingly as I sit down in my chair and finally speak.

"I pursued him."

It's the first time I've ever said the words out loud, and I feel the weight of them.

Doc nods silently, his way of saying *continue*, and I try to find the best way to explain the unexplainable.

"The first time I saw him was the first time in years that I felt...peace."

"I remember."

"You do?"

Doc smiles at me, and although it's small, I feel the warmth of it. It's as if he's truly proud of me for trusting him.

"Yes. You came to see me after the first week of school. Do you remember what you said?"

Racking my brain, I try to remember that session, but when I think back to my first week of school, all I see is *him*.

"No. I don't remember."

"That's okay. You said it in passing, probably not even realizing the relevance."

"You're doing it again."

"What's that?"

"Being all doctor-like and cryptic."

Laughing, Doc sits back. "Oh, so now I know where you got it."

"Maybe a little," I admit half-heartedly.

"Good to know." Doc's eyes narrow as he tells me, "You came into my office and you couldn't sit still. You seemed distracted but not in a bad way. So I asked what was different that day, and you told me for the first time in two years—'Nothing, I'm just happy.'"

Huh. It was something so simple.

It seems unbelievable that's what gave me away, when happy is the last thing I ever expect to feel again.

∾

Past...

I pushed Addison's shirt up to reveal the pink lace bra underneath and felt my knees threaten to give way. *Yeah,* fuck walking away. The best I could hope for was to step back for a moment and catch my breath.

Moving to the other side of the kitchen, I told her, "Stay right there."

Disheveled. That was how she looked as she leaned back against the counter with her shirt bunched up over her breasts and her hair in disarray, and I wanted more.

"Take it off."

"My shirt?"

Coming to a stop against the opposite counter, I picked up the scotch and unscrewed the lid.

"Yes, your shirt. Take it off."

Without hesitation, Addison reached up and removed her shirt, dropping it on the tiled floor.

"The skirt too," I ordered and lifted the bottle to my lips.

With her beguiling blue eyes following my every move, she unbuttoned the top of her skirt. She traced the tip of her tongue over the cut on her lip, and I knew she had to be remembering the way I'd sucked it because *fuck*, I was.

The warm burn of alcohol made its way down my throat as I continued to watch Addison remove her clothes, and when her skirt fell away from her hips, something slipped from the pocket and hit the floor.

We both looked down at the same time, and there between us was a shiny black pen. One just like my—

"Where did you get that?" I asked and moved to where the pen was lying on the ground. Bending down, I picked it up.

"You must have dropped it last night," she said, "when you came to see me."

I stood and ran my finger over the engraving.

He'd been right. *This*, what I felt right now, wasn't good or evil. It was beyond that. I placed the pen on the counter and stepped in front of her.

"Come closer," I invited with a crook of my finger.

Raising her chin, Addison took two steps with the intention of more until I halted her with my hand and shook my head.

"Turn around. Show me *everything*."

Her lashes lowered as she inspected my body, and I felt that silent perusal as sure as a touch. She slowly turned, and my cock throbbed in response.

The creamy skin of her back came into view, and I wanted to stroke my fingers over it. I knew that eventually I would, but right now…right now, I was just going to look.

When her back was to me, I let my gaze wander down to the pink panties covering her ass. I couldn't wait to feel that lace under my palms, but I wanted her to make me *feel* again, and what better way to do that than to take all the power.

Coming up behind her, I noticed she was about to look back at me so I made sure she knew exactly what was about to happen. I wrapped one arm around her naked waist and put my mouth to her ear.

"You're going to do everything I tell you to," I instructed. She let out a soft moan and my cock pulsed. "Nod if you understand."

Quickly, Addison nodded.

"Good girl. When I let go, I want your bra to hit the floor, and then I want your hands on the counter."

When I got no response, I felt a thrill skate up my spine. The high I was getting from ordering her around was making me feel alive. "Do you understand?"

Addison's body trembled. She was getting off on the orders as much as I was from giving them.

That was more than fine. I could play that game.

Releasing her, I took a step back and brought the bottle up to my mouth, taking a swig as she made quick work of the bra. The straps slid down her arms, and when she removed the lacy material and dangled it by her leg, she looked over her shoulder and gave a seductive wink. Instantly, the temperature inside my kitchen hit fever pitch.

As nonchalantly as possible, I took another drink as her brow rose and she dropped the bra by her feet. Then calm as you please, she bent over and placed her hands on my counter.

Fuck, nothing had ever been so tempting in all my life.

Her hair was flowing in tousled waves and her tight ass was angled out toward me, encased in the sexiest, most feminine piece of lace I'd ever seen.

But this game, this *tease* was making my blood pump. It was making my cock pound, and it had made me *feel*. Which is exactly what I wanted.

"You look untouchable."

She glanced back at me, and for the first time since we began, she spoke.

"I really hope that's not true."

~

Present...

"Have you dreamed of Daniel lately?"

The question is so far from what I'm expecting to hear that it stumps me for a second.

"No."

"Hmm."

Hating that response, I'm quick to ask, "What does that mean?"

"What?"

"The *hmm?*"

"Doesn't mean anything," Doc says. Then, in his tricky doctor way, he adds, "Should it?"

Feeling a laugh, an actual laugh, bubble inside me, my mouth twists into a tiny grin. "I don't think so."

"Well, when we first started seeing each other after the accident, you told me you used to dream of him in a field of purple flowers."

I remember and can see the field from my dreams just as clearly as if I'm standing there now. The only new piece of this puzzle is the flower. Doc knows what the purple represents to me—death.

"Your dreams stopped when Grayson arrived. Did you realize that? I noted it right here." He picks up the journal he'd been writing in. "*Second week of school and Addison seems preoccupied. No dreams this week. What's changed?*"

I don't know what I'm supposed to say, so I sit quietly, feeling there is more where that came from.

"The agitated counting, the clock watching—they stopped too. Why, do you think?"

I knew that when Grayson had been around, the madness seemed to stop, but why was I not hearing it now? Why was the clock on the wall suddenly just a clock on the wall?

"I don't know," I admit.

"Sure you do. Try me."

Shrugging, I offer up the one thing I'd always felt around Grayson. "He made me feel safe."

"Safe?"

"Yes."

"But you were always aware you could be caught. That you could get in trouble. Yet, you still felt safe?"

When he said it like that, it seemed ridiculous, but…"Yes. I always felt safe with him. From the first moment I saw him."

"Addy?"

"Yes?"

"Do you think that maybe you replaced one obsession for another?"

"As in?"

"As in Grayson."

God, just his name alone makes the hole inside me feel all-encompassing.

"Do you think he became your new obsession? One who made you happy?"

I touch the pen resting beside my leg and remember the way I felt whenever I'd followed him home. The rush I would get when he walked into the classroom and the high I got when his mouth met mine were still there. I'd just buried them beneath the surface.

"Maybe, yes. But I don't think I was ever *truly* happy."

"No?" Doc asks, and he seems genuinely surprised at my response.

"No."

"Then what were you?"

That is easy to answer. "Fascinated."

"Ahh...yes. Maybe at first, but what came after the fascination?"

Looking him right in the eye, I confess. "The forbidden."

CHAPTER 24

 ast...

As I stood with my hands on the counter in front of me, I closed my eyes and listened to the sound of clothes rustling. Grayson was taking off his jeans.

My nipples beaded tight in the cool air, and the ache between my legs had me close to begging. But he'd been very specific, and until I was told to do otherwise, I wasn't going to move an inch.

"Widen your legs," he instructed, and I heard the liquid in the bottle slosh. "No talking, and no turning around." He drew a line along my lower back, tracing the edge of my panties, before he added, "You're just going to *do*."

My breasts rose with every breath I took, and when I remained silent, he placed the bottle on the counter and bent down so his lips hovered beside my cheek.

"Nod if you agree."

Continuing to face forward, I nodded and then shivered as he shifted slightly and licked my shoulder.

"I won't hurt you," he promised. "But right now, I have this need to destroy you."

I didn't quite understand what he meant, but when he moved behind me and his fingers dug into my hips, I decided it didn't matter. His hard cock pressed between my ass cheeks, and when his fingers curled around the edge of my panties, I couldn't help the moisture that flooded them.

I was throbbing with anticipation and he'd barely begun.

Grayson slid the material down and I could feel him kneel behind my bare legs and ass. When the words "Step out," met my ears, I immediately obeyed.

From my view above, I could see him toss the lace aside, and when he straightened, I saw his hard cock jutting forward. He cupped my ass, and I closed my eyes as my pussy began to throb. I couldn't help the *ahh* that escaped me as his teeth sunk into my left ass cheek.

I gripped the counter and pushed back, and as one of his hands moved between my thighs, a whimper emerged in the form of a plea.

God, I wanted him to touch me. I needed him inside me now.

He must have understood because two of his fingers began sliding back and forth between my slick juices. Gritting my teeth and trying my hardest not to say a word, I waited until finally it came—my next instruction.

"Turn around."

On shaky legs, I turned until I was facing him, and he got back to his feet. Leaning against the counter, I waited as he looked me over, and I allowed myself the same pleasure.

Completely naked, Grayson made every schoolgirl fantasy of mine pale in comparison to the reality. He was tall, muscled, and nothing my girlish brain could have dreamed up.

He was so powerful as he stood there inspecting every inch of my body. His hands curled into tight fists by his strong thighs, and his was cock pointing right at me.

Stepping forward, Grayson lifted me until I was sitting on the counter. Placing his palms on my thighs, he slowly pushed them apart as his eyes held mine.

Without breaking our connection, he reached over to where he'd left the bottle of scotch and picked it up. Bringing it to his lips, he took a long swig of the amber liquid, and when he pulled it away, he ordered, "Lean back."

Following orders had never been one of my strong suits, but with the look in his eyes and the sound of his voice making me wetter with every word that came out of his mouth, I couldn't help but obey. So I leaned back until I was resting on my elbows.

He flattened his palm between my breasts and dragged it down my body until he reached my bare mound, where he pressed the heel of his hand against me. I arched up, my mouth parting as he again took another drink of scotch.

"So fucking perfect. You always look and act so fucking perfect—but you're not, are you?"

I knew he wasn't really talking to me, but more admitting to his own delusions. When his heated gaze found mine and he moved down over me, the noise that left my throat was loud and needy and made his lips twist in a way that seemed almost cruel.

Grayson was battling his own monster right now, and somehow I knew that monster was me. He took hold of my hair, and when he pulled my face to his, I did what I wasn't supposed to. I spoke.

"I never said I was perfect. But come on, then. Everyone else has taken a turn at it—destroy me."

His eyes narrowed as his hips pushed forward, and I wrapped my legs around his waist, wanting his brand of destruction.

"Your father already tried," he whispered, and then in direct contrast to his dark mood, he gently kissed the cut on my mouth. "He tried, and he failed. Even broken, you're perfect to me. The perfect enigma."

His mouth found mine in a scorching kiss that made my knees weak.

The man holding me was vibrating with need—a need to satiate the turmoil brewing inside of him. The turmoil I'd partially created.

While Grayson brought peace and calm to my life, I brought worry and chaos to his. I wanted him to use me in any way he needed. I wanted to give back to him what I *took*—peace.

He raised his head and shifted away from me as he trailed his fingers down to my ankle. Lifting my leg until my heel was flat on the counter, he stared down between my wide-open thighs. Without another word, he lifted the bottle of scotch and poured it onto my stomach, where it pooled in my navel and then ran down to slide in between my legs.

Placing the bottle back down, he said, "It's not illegal if *you* aren't drinking it."

He didn't bother mentioning it was illegal for him to be drinking it *from* me, but I wasn't going to point that out.

He leaned down and kissed my navel, sucking the liquid from me as he flicked the little indentation with his tongue. I could feel every intoxicating pulse between my thighs as his sinful tongue licked its way down my stomach and over my mound. I closed my eyes to anticipate his next move.

He didn't make me wait long as he touched my clit with the tip of his tongue. Without meaning to, I bit my bruised lip and cried out from the pain.

I looked down as he looked up, and instead of asking if I was okay, he moved in and did it again. This time he watched as he tongued me.

I reached out to grasp his hair when I heard a firm *no*, and just that easily, I was put in my place.

Then he moved his fingers down and pushed them up inside me, and I moaned in pure ecstasy.

∾

It shouldn't be fucking possible that she was this thrilling to watch.

As her breasts thrust forward and her nipples remained hard, she shoved her hips up, trying to get my fingers in deeper.

Unable to stop myself, I leaned in, and as I pulled my hand away, I sucked her soaked clit between my lips. She tasted like scotch and sex, and I couldn't get enough.

Addison's arousal caused her juices to drip down my fingers, coating my palm even more with every thrust I made inside her. She was so wet it made me want to grab my cock and jerk off until I came. Her eyes never left me, and as I dipped my tongue down to taste her again, she parted her lips and whimpered in a way that made me want to make her scream.

She had a grip on me so powerful that one glance from her and I would pick up a knife and destroy *myself* if she asked.

But she wasn't asking that of me. Her body was begging me to take it.

So that's what I would do.

Sliding my hand away from her body, I grabbed her ankle and pulled it forward, wrapping it around my waist.

"Hang on," I instructed, and as she leaned up and did as I asked, I hoisted her off the counter and her second leg wound its way around my waist.

I turned, intending to take her to my bedroom, but when she pulled herself up my body and rubbed against my erection, I lost direction and instead, ended up in my dining room.

I pushed a chair out of my way and laid her down on the table, then stood back to take in my ultimate undoing. With her hair spread across the dark wood, her flushed cheeks and creamy skin stood out in stark contrast, and all I could think was that she was the most delicious thing I'd ever seen.

Her eyes found mine as she bent her legs so her feet were flat on the wooden surface and then she parted them. She placed her hands behind her head and let a sigh slip free, and that was all I could take.

Temptation be damned. I'd given in long ago. She was now my very own personal sin.

I crawled up over her and she speared her fingers through my hair, pulling on it as her legs wrapped around me. There was nothing shy about her, and I knew it was on purpose when she rose up and bit my lip hard enough to draw blood.

"*There*, now you have a reason."

Grabbing her head, my fingers tightened in her hair.

"A reason to what?"

The cunning smile that twisted her lips made me more than aware of exactly which part of the *good and evil* we were now dealing with.

She placed her mouth by my ear and whispered, "A reason to make me scream."

What? How did she...?

"You said you wanted to. Now you have a reason. So *fuck* me, and make me scream."

I was losing my fucking mind.

I didn't even remember saying that out loud, and as she began to laugh, I felt my sanity snap and shoved my hips forward—entering her with one hard thrust.

"Stop it," I demanded as I hovered over her, my breathing harsh.

Her eyes met mine and she taunted, "Make me."

My mouth crashed down on hers, and I knew I had to be hurting her lip because mine was now throbbing as hard as my cock. It felt like the room was spinning as I began to move inside her. Her hands slid down my back as her fingers dug into my skin, and I was convinced she was drawing blood with every rake of her nails.

Was this what it was like to fall?

Fall from grace? Fall victim? Or fall in love with Addison?

I wasn't sure, but as I continued to move in and out, violating her and every ideal I held true, I knew something was happening to me.

Placing a palm beside her head, I pushed up and looked down at the cause of my life's upheaval. As she rolled her hips, she cupped her breasts, and I knew I wasn't the one doing the corrupting.

I pushed on her cheek, turning her face away so I no longer had to bear witness to my weakness. I found myself studying the long line of her neck, and for the first time—I felt the urge to really hurt her. To snap her in half.

Addison had come into my life and was single-handedly ruining it. *Wasn't she?*

I looked over her bruised face and swollen lip, and suddenly, all of the anger I was feeling drained away, and in its place came exactly what my father had predicted—love.

What the fuck was I doing?

As she turned her face back to me, I moved to cradle her cheek.

"Why would I ever want to destroy what's keeping me alive?" I asked as my mouth found hers and our bodies began to move as one.

My heart was pounding so hard I was certain Grayson could feel it as his body pressed against my own. With my legs wrapped tightly around him and my fingers clawing his back, I made him as much my prisoner as I was his.

Grayson's muscles flexed with every thrust of his hips, and each time he drove into me, I felt as though he was branding my body. His hands found their way into my hair, and as his mouth tasted mine, I reveled in the way he was losing himself.

For a brief moment, I'd witnessed the anger he'd kept at bay. Even though I knew he'd never hurt me, the second he'd pushed my face away, my heart had fluttered with fear.

Intoxicating or disturbing?

I couldn't decide. But not once did I question what would happen.

If anything, I almost welcomed the peace I would gain from this man's hand.

"What's happening to me?" His ragged voice broke through my thoughts and then he buried his face into my neck.

I stroked my hand over the back of his hair when he started to fall apart, and I could have sworn I felt tears on my shoulder. His hips picked up the pace, and as I held onto him, I let him slake his lust, need, and desire inside of me.

He pounded out a punishing rhythm and when I felt his body tense above me, my own responded—as did my heart.

Right there on his dining room table, I shattered around the man who had given to me his very being.

CHAPTER 25

 resent...

Today's session was draining.

Reliving memories from the past is not something I enjoy. It's actually the one thing I'll do anything to avoid under normal circumstances—but nothing about this situation can be called normal.

Sitting on my temporary bed, I pull the black-and-white photo from the wall and study Psyche.

Maybe it would have been easier to be taken by the monster in the long run.

Closing my eyes, I bring the picture to my chest and lie down, thinking of the man who'd given this to me. It's the first time I have given myself *permission* to remember. Every other memory has been a rude flash of what everyone is calling wrong.

But what we had wasn't wrong. *Was it?*

They are so busy trying to fix the *problem*, to calm the turbulent waters that we stirred—but what they don't realize is *he* was the calming force, and without him, the waters will always be rough.

How do I move on and accept that he is—no longer?

They want me to close the book and be done with this chapter in my life, and while I agree I need to forget…it is to protect, not to banish.

The hurt, it never goes away. I can tuck it into a part of myself, the part where Daniel hides and hope I don't ever lose it. But if I stay here, if I stay broken, I will eventually forget him. *They* will make me.

Sitting up in my bed, I reach for the nightstand beside me and touch the pen. Then I glance at the watch around my wrist.

Maybe? Just maybe…

I unfasten the timepiece and lay it on the stand before picking up the pen and tucking it into my nightgown pocket.

No counting, no ticking, no anxiety.

God. What I wouldn't give for a minute, just one more minute, with him.

He was always the one who grounded me, who made everything seem…*right.* How can it ever be again?

What gave him the right to escape this life and leave me behind?

Doc is trying to tell me something, and I'm trying to understand. He's prompting me to remember the good. He's encouraging acceptance of what we did.

But why?

Yes, there were moments of madness, but what is love without some madness?

It wasn't wrong.

No—it was just misunderstood.

≈

Past…

. . .

"What are you thinking about?" I asked as I studied the man lying beside me.

Grayson and I had moved from the dining room to his bedroom and were now stretched out on his stark white sheets. He had the arm closest to me bent back and angled behind his head and the other was resting so his palm was over his chest.

He shifted his head on the pillow, and instead of answering me, he asked, "What are we doing here?"

I sat up beside him, bringing the sheet with me and holding it over my chest. I didn't have an answer for him, not the one he wanted.

He seemed so unlike himself. Not only in appearance, but emotionally as well.

"I just don't know where you think this can go," he stated, seemingly surprised at his own words.

He was ending things. The tone of his voice felt final.

When he turned away, I heard myself ask softly, "Do you want me to leave?"

"I should."

His answer wasn't a yes, but it certainly wasn't a no. I knew he was conflicted, and at that moment, I would have done anything to ease him. I'd never known this need to reach out and unburden another. But how could I help him when he seemed so tormented?

Clutching the sheet to my chest, I stood and looked back to where he'd reached out an arm across the empty mattress.

"I don't know what you want, Grayson."

With a humorless laugh, he placed his other arm over his eyes. "Yes, you do. But you should walk through that door, put your clothes back on, and get the hell out of here. You should have done that the first time."

"Why would I do that when everything I've done has been to get closer to you?"

Dropping the sheet and proving my willingness to be there, I walked over to the large photo of Cupid and his love, and then I glanced back at Grayson.

Was he *my* love? Would I do anything to follow him like Psyche had?

"We both know that I never do what I *should*."

Grayson's eyes found me where I'd stopped and then he placed both of his hands behind his head. "That's true. You don't, do you?"

He wasn't giving away anything, only offering up what he needed to in order to act civil. Deciding it was up to me to keep him engaged, I pointed to the black-and-white image hanging on the wall.

"You really love this one, don't you?"

Nodding, he looked to the three on the opposite side of the room. "I like those too. But something about Psyche calls to me. Do you like it?"

"Yes," I replied wholeheartedly. "You're really good. Those are amazing, but this one…"

"Yes?"

I faced the photo once again. "It's the way he's looking at her, as if—"

"—there's nothing he wouldn't do to save her?" Grayson ended my thought.

"Yes. She's hanging onto him as if her life depends on it."

"It did. She just didn't know it…"

The final word trailed off to a whisper and had me returning naked and unashamed to the end of his bed. "Maybe that's why she's hanging on so tight, because she knows more than he thinks?"

"Maybe she needs to learn to let go," he suggested unflinchingly.

I wasn't going to make this easy for him. If he wanted to end this, he would have to be the one to do it. He'd have to say the words.

"So where's your camera, or are you just a lucky shot with a phone?"

"No, no phone. Old-school, Addison. It's in the cabinet behind my desk."

I walked around to the wooden cabinet, opened the doors, and saw the Nikon camera sitting there with a zoom lens beside it. Feeling a grin tug the corners of my mouth, I picked it up and looped the strap over my head so the camera was sitting between my breasts, then turned to face him.

Walking over to his side of the bed, I trailed my fingers along the sheets and watched as he brought one of his hands down from behind his head. I put my knee on the mattress and when it dipped, I shifted my other leg up and over his waist until I was straddled above him.

"How old are you, again?"

As his eyebrow winged up, I wondered if maybe I should have broached that question differently.

"Thirty-two, why?"

"Who doesn't have a digital camera?"

Grayson rolled his eyes and shook his head against the pillow. "I *do* own a digital camera. I just own a film camera too."

Kneeling up, I brought the Nikon in front of my face until I was looking through the viewfinder at him.

"Don't," he said in a voice that was soft but adamant. His troubled expression reminded me that I was *not* the calming force in his life.

I was the exact opposite.

Moving the bulky camera aside, I asked, "Don't..?"

"Don't look too close."

Lowering the Nikon, I touched the stubble on his jaw. "What are you afraid I'll see?"

Without touching any part of my naked body, he still managed to slay me.

"Everything I've become."

Present...

"So, Addy, what are we going to talk about today?"

I raise my brows and point to myself. "I get to choose?"

"Sure. I've asked a lot of questions the past few days."

"So have I," I remind him.

"How are your studies coming along?"

I shrug. "They're coming."

"So you think you'll be ready for the test?"

The minute I'd been dropped off here at Pine Groves like an unwanted *thing*, I swore I'd never let anyone dispose of me again. Plus, even though it feels like a lifetime ago now, I'd once made a promise to graduate. This was the closest I could come to fulfilling that promise.

"Yeah, I think so."

"I never asked, what made you want to complete your GED here? Why not just go back to school? They would have allowed it."

My mouth falls open with incredulity. "You're kidding, right? It's bad enough I have to see my parents again when it's pretty clear by the *zero* visits they've made that they don't give a shit about me. Why would I ever go back to that school?"

"Well, there are people there who clearly care about you."

Getting pissed off, I can see now that I should've taken advantage of his offer to ask the questions.

"Such as?"

I know who he's going to say. In all the time I've been seeing Doc, the one thing I've learned is—he isn't a pussy. I have to give him credit for that.

If he wants to know something, he asks, no matter how uncomfortable it might make you.

"Helene."

"Don't you mean, *Miss Shrieve*?" I ask him, reaching up to twirl my hair around my finger.

"What do you think of her?"

I give him a pointed look that tells him *exactly* what I think.

"Okay. Let's go back to the *polite* way to think of her."

"Why do I have to think about her at all?" I can hear my petulant, bratty tone, and I detest it instantly. Pulling myself together, I ask, "What about her?"

"You tell me."

Looking away from him, I bite my top lip and then answer honestly. "I don't ever want to see her again."

"But—"

"*But* nothing."

"You've been through so much together."

I feel the ugly curl of my lip as memories of my coach hit me. "No, she just always turns up when my life is falling apart."

"Is that how you see it?"

I stand up, done answering his questions. "That is how it was."

I turn, fully intending to leave when he says my name— bringing me to a stop. "What?"

"Where's your watch?"

I reach down to touch my wrist. "In my room."

"So there's hope?"

I step through the door and before I shut it, I tell him, "Yes. It's in my pocket."

～

Past...

After several tense moments of silence, I finally broke the ice.

"I'm sorry about your father."

He closed his eyes as if he couldn't stand to look at me. "So am I."

"Were you close?"

"Yes."

I slid off of him to kneel by his side and confided, "I was close to my father too."

Grayson sat up and touched my cheek. He brushed a thumb over my lip, and even though I knew he was conflicted about having me there, right then he couldn't deny his need to comfort me.

"Then why does he hit you?"

My eyes closed as I leaned into his palm. "Because I'm there."

"Have you told anyone?" Letting out a deep sigh, Grayson scooted back until he was sitting up against the headboard. "I can't just let it go, Addison."

"Doc knows."

"Doc?"

I laugh a little and then twist the curl hanging over my shoulder.

"Yeah, he's the therapist my parents have been making me see. His actual name is Dr. Wolinski, but I told him he looks more like a Doc."

Grayson's brows furrowed as if he was pondering my description. "As in *Back to the Future*, Doc?"

I beamed at him, and for a moment he seemed to forget his worries and smiled back. It was magical.

"Yes, exactly. Slightly balding on top with wild, grey hair on the sides. He's just like Doc. Kind of acts like him too."

Grayson's mouth returned to a serious line. I interlaced our fingers, not even caring that I was so extremely vulnerable when it came to this man.

"Why can't I do this for you?"

"Do what?"

"Chase the monsters away."

"Is that what I do?" he questioned, and I crawled on his lap.

Looping my arms around his neck, I kissed his cheek and whispered, "It's okay. I understand."

Pulling back slightly, he asked, "What's okay? What do you understand?"

"That I'm your monster."

He neither agreed nor disagreed with my words as he tumbled me back on the bed. We rolled over his sheets, and I quietly devoured my teacher, determined to have all of him—like any monster would.

CHAPTER 26

 ast...

I left Grayson's place an hour later, not feeling much better than when I'd arrived. Pushing through the front door, I expected to walk into an empty house. That was not what greeted me.

"Where the hell have you been?"

My mom was sitting in the living room with her foot tapping the floor impatiently.

"I walked—"

"Cut the crap, Addison. It's two o'clock. You left school at eight forty-five. Want to know how I know that? Miss Shrieve called to tell me."

She stood and made her way over to me. I looked at her perfectly styled hair and flawless face enhanced by touches of makeup and wondered if she would mention the fact that her daughter had a bruised and swollen lip.

"I walked home," I told her again, cool and calm.

She'd taught me over the last couple of years that the truth wasn't rewarded—it was ignored and used against you.

"You're lying."

"So what? Do you even care?"

Stopping only inches from me, her eyes flickered down to the cut on my mouth, and I purposefully tipped my chin up so she could see exactly what the monster in *this* house had done.

"Answer me," she demanded, not even acknowledging what she'd seen.

Knowing the best way to strike was at the heart. *I aimed—*

"I went to see Daniel."

—and I hit.

She visibly flinched at his name, and I wondered for the first time if half of the reason I couldn't move forward was because no one would let me.

No one except for Grayson.

"When was the last time *you* went to see him?" I asked, knowing full well the only time she'd ever visited her son's grave was to bury him in it.

"Get up to your room and don't expect to leave there until it's time to return to school."

Narrowing my eyes, I spoke in a voice that I hardly recognized. It was full of revulsion and malevolence. "Don't you want to know about my lip? Did Miss Shrieve ask you about *that*?"

Instead of answering, she pointed to the stairs and ordered, "Get out of my sight."

Turning away from her, I climbed the stairs and thought back to an hour earlier when I'd been somewhat content.

How could it be that the only semblance of peace for me was with someone I wasn't allowed to have?

Present...

. . .

"I thought I might find you here," Doc says, making his way into the quiet space that I feel is somewhat my own.

"I like the library."

"Because it reminds you of him?" he queries, moving into my domain.

Wondering, as always, what his angle is, I ask, "Why would you say that?"

"He was a history teacher. They usually like books."

"He liked art too," I make sure to mention.

"Did he?"

"Yes, and photography," I reminisce.

Doc walks around to stand behind me and places a hand on the back of my chair. "Anne Boleyn?"

"Yes."

"Didn't she lose her head over a guy?"

I lift my face so I can find Doc's eyes, and I can't stop the burst of laughter. "Is that your version of a joke?"

"It was kind of funny, right?"

"*No*," I tease. "He beheaded her."

"Yes, he did. But to be fair to him, he was upset."

"So? Divorce her, don't behead her," I suggest.

"Maybe that was the only way out he could see."

"Then he was blind. I'm sure there were other ways than death."

"Perhaps he was desperate…"

As those words left his mouth and hung in the air, my old anxiety started to creep up.

"You're annoying me. I'm trying to write my paper."

"Why did you pick Anne?"

I don't bother looking over my shoulder as I state matter-of-factly, "Because I think she's interesting."

"What about her appeals to you?"

Jesus, he's relentless today, not giving me an inch. He's making me talk, making me think and remember things I'd made myself forget.

"Her strength. Her ambition."

"That's appealing to you?"

"*Yes*," I tell him, exasperated.

Doc makes his way around to the other side of the table, but instead of sitting, he just stands there, appearing deep in thought. "You don't think that *too* much ambition is dangerous?"

"It can be, if used for evil."

"And did *she* use it for evil?"

"I don't believe so, not intentionally. She wanted to be the queen. I'm sure many others also desired that honor. She just happened to go after it and succeed."

"Hmm," Doc muses, and the sound grates on my nerves. "It's said, you know, that King Henry the Eighth moved heaven and earth to be with her, but his obsession, his lust, blinded him to the main reason he wanted her in the first place."

"Oh, and what's that?"

"Her intelligence. Her mind is what ensnared him and in the end, was also her undoing. You didn't pick her because of her ambition, Addison. You picked her because *he* was teaching you about her in school. Your mother told me. Somehow in your mind, she brings you closer to him."

Did I? Is my mind trying to tell me something subconsciously?

Instead of accepting that insane logic, I sputter out, "No...I just never got to finish it *before*."

Doc grins and it seems somewhat mischievous. "Then you better keep going. I'll see you at three."

Past...

"Addison! Come on!"

It was Monday afternoon, and I felt as if I'd been trapped in my house for a year. Mom watched me like a hawk every time I left my room, so I only came out for meals. Except for this time. Right now, I was coming out because it was time to—

"Hurry up, or we'll be late to Dr. Wolinski's!"

—visit my therapist.

The drive over to Doc's led us through the snooty neighborhoods in town. Each street was lined with big trees and even bigger houses. This was the first outing I'd had since I'd been out of school for three full days and wouldn't be returning until Thursday.

That's if I survived until then.

Mom pulled the car to a stop by the curb and turned to me. "I'll be back in an hour."

No shit, I thought as I pushed open the car door.

"Addison?"

Without answering, I waited for her to continue.

"Don't say anything you'll regret later."

Knowing exactly what she was referring to, I licked my lip that was slowly healing but still obvious to anyone looking at me.

"So now it's okay to lie?" I asked. "Make up your fucking mind."

Before she had a chance to reprimand me, I climbed out and slammed the door shut. I walked up the pebbled path to the side of Doc's house where he had a private office and turned to watch her drive away. For a moment, I wished she'd never come back.

I tried to shake off the thought and knocked on Doc's door. When he opened it, I couldn't help but laugh. His crazy hair was all over the place, and I had to admit that other than Grayson, this man was the only other positive force in my life. He was the one person I truly trusted and relied on.

"Addy, it's so good to see you."

Still laughing, I stepped through the door and made my way over to the comfy couch by the window. "Really?"

"Always. You know that."

I sat down and looked around his cozy office.

Doc had certificates hanging all over the walls, and photos of his wife and three daughters adorned his huge desk. As always, he made his way over to the chair across from me and sat down.

"Isn't that kind of an insult? If I'm here to see you, it means I'm crazy. Doesn't it?"

"Do you feel crazy?"

"Not lately."

Doc's eyes creased at the sides and the lines around them made me think he laughed a lot. This man was happy—truly happy.

"What do you feel lately?"

"Are you happy?" I asked out of the blue, curious to know if I was right.

Doc thought about it for a moment and then grinned. "Yes. I can honestly say that I *am* happy. Are you?"

My answer was easy. "No."

I couldn't remember the last time I was happy. I'm not sure that anyone cared enough to ask—except Doc, and he was being paid.

"Then how do you feel?"

I contemplated my answer before I spoke. How do you tell the man your parents have employed to fix you that what makes you happy and content is something that's crumbling apart in front of you?

"Trapped," I finally replied.

"Hmm."

I rolled my eyes and shook my head. "I hate that response."

"Why? It's neither positive nor negative."

"It's indifferent. I hate that."

"Well, what would you like me to say? You said you felt trapped. You already know my next question."

I began to twirl my hair around my finger, a habit I'd started while sitting here under Doc's close scrutiny.

"You're going to ask me why."

"Exactly."

Seeing no other way out, I sighed. "I got suspended for five days."

Doc brought his pen to his mouth and chewed on the cap. A habit of *his*, I'd discovered.

"I know."

"How do you know?"

"Your mother called and told me. She also mentioned you were late getting home that day."

"What else did she say?"

"She said you lied about where you'd been."

I let go of my hair and clasped my hands in my lap.

"Well, she's not wrong."

"So..." Doc paused, and I knew what was next. "Do you want to tell me where you went?"

I really wanted to, but I couldn't. So I didn't say a thing.

"Okay, I'll take that as a no."

Doc knows what my silence means. I'd been coming to him long enough that he knew now was not the time to push.

"Will you talk to me about how you got that split lip?"

My eyes connected with his, and I could hear my mom's voice in my mind, threatening me.

"Again, I'll take your silence as a no. Some other time, perhaps?"

Feeling agitated, I stood and walked over to the photos on his desk, picking up a silver frame of his wife and daughters.

They were sitting along the trunk of a fallen tree with their arms interlocked at the elbows. Each of them was laughing, and their eyes were lit up with pure happiness. I envied the ease they shared with one another and the love that was directed at the person taking the photo.

Her husband, their father—their rock.

I'd had that once, during the blind acceptance of youth, until one shattering moment ripped it all away to reveal it was

241

nothing but veiled innocence. It was a lie created to make me feel safe because *my* rock wasn't something I could hang onto— but something that inflicted pain.

Grayson also had photos, ones he'd taken himself. However, they were of places, not people, and now that his father was gone, I had a feeling he was as lonely as I was.

"I don't know what to say."

Doc seemed to process that before recommending, "Let's start with the basics."

"Okay."

"You said you're feeling trapped. Can you tell me what being trapped feels like or means to you? That's not hard, right?"

"I guess."

But the more I thought about it, I realized I wasn't the one who was trapped. *He* was.

I trapped him. Didn't I?

"Addy, what are you thinking? Tell me."

"Nothing."

"Don't lie to me, Addison," Doc stressed. "You can evade the question, you can choose not to answer, but don't lie. I can't help you if you don't tell me the truth."

I leaned back against the desk and whispered, "Someone I know is in trouble, and I feel like I can't do anything to help. So I feel trapped."

"Trouble how? At school? With their parents?"

I almost laughed at the ridiculousness of this conversation. It wasn't as if I could tell him who or what I was talking about, but maybe...*no.*

"In life."

I stopped and pleaded with my eyes not to push any further.

"Okay. They're in trouble with *life.*"

"Yes. This person is going through some issues and I want to help, but no matter what I do, it isn't going to be right. I can't talk to anyone. All I want to do is reach out and make them feel like they make me feel…"

"And how's that, Addy? How do they make you feel?"

I struggled to find the right word and settled on the one that I'd felt when I looked at Doc's photo. "Safe."

Doc took a moment and brought the pen down from his mouth, before asking, "Well, has this person ever hurt you?"

"No!" I'm adamant in my denial.

"Does this person make you do things you don't want to?"

I shook my head and could feel the furrow between my brows.

No, Grayson never pushed himself on me, but I couldn't say the same in return.

"Then I don't see the problem. In fact, I would go so far as to say whoever it is has changed you in a positive way. I've noticed it myself."

I tried to ignore the rapid pounding in my chest as my heart beat overtime.

"What do you mean?"

"Sit down, would you?"

Without questioning him, I did as I was told.

"Ever since the beginning of school, you've been less despondent and much more responsive. You've been social, engaged, and you haven't even noticed today that I took the clock off my wall. These are all clear indications to me that your behavior has changed."

I agreed with him but still. "That doesn't answer my question. How do I help them?"

Doc shrugged. "Maybe the thing that is bothering you and making you feel trapped is that you can't."

CHAPTER 27

 ast...

Six days.

It had been six days since I'd last seen Addison. I thought it would leave me feeling more centered, less off-balance, but I all I could think of was her.

I'd taken Friday off to go back to the facility my father had stayed in and finalize his estate. Then I'd had the dreadful task of arranging a funeral for one.

I still couldn't quite wrap my mind around the fact that he was gone—forever.

Helene had been the first to offer her condolences Monday morning, but while she'd been talking to me and extending her sympathy, I'd been picturing Addison. I'd memorized the way she'd looked as she knelt beside me with my camera in her hands, trying to see behind the walls I'd kept up around her.

Addison Lancaster. Ingénue or Siren?

The first time I heard her name, I knew I was in trouble.

Last Thursday when she'd shown up at my house, all

pretense of what was going on between us had fallen away. The excitement and lust that originally drew me to her had been replaced with emotions I was scrambling to get ahold of. Complex emotions were threatening to overwhelm me, but somewhere amongst the disorder, there was some part of it that made sense. She was the only thing that had brought me comfort in my darkest of days.

I walked into my classroom, and stopped by my desk, and immediately I knew she was there. My eyes searched out the seat that had sat vacant since Monday, and there she was, polished as ever.

Her lip had fully healed, and her hair was curled to perfection. Her blue eyes found mine, and I knew right away that something was different.

She resembled the girl I'd first met only weeks ago, except this time, her eyes weren't full of mischief or rebellion—they were flat and dispassionate.

"Good Morning, Addison," I managed, my voice sounding strained, even to me.

"Good morning, Mr. McKendrick."

Trying to get a read on her, I walked around to the front of my desk and leaned back against it.

"You're early."

"Am I?" she asked, but if anyone knew where they were at all times, it was Addison.

"Did you need to see me about something?" I prodded.

This version of her was terrifying in that I had absolutely no idea what she was thinking.

"Yes. Am I required to hand in the paper from last Friday?"

Is she serious?

Sitting right in front of me was a stranger. The girl who'd teased and provoked with the tilt of her lips and batting of her eyelashes was gone—just when I'd been coming to accept her.

"The Anne Boleyn paper? No. There's no catch up in my class for suspended students."

She shook her head as if disappointed. I wondered if she expected different treatment. But then I kicked my own ass because of course she did. I'd had her under me, naked and spread open as I lost myself inside her. Was a little leniency out of the question?

Not for her, but for Brandon, who also was unable to make up the credits, it would be completely unfair. She had to know that.

Pushing off my desk, I walked down between the tables and chairs until I came to a stop in front of her. As she tipped her face up to me, I had the urge to bend down and take her lips with mine.

Selfless didn't describe me or my prior actions, but now, right this second, I didn't care about the consequences I might suffer. I only cared about her.

"If I could give you the time to make it up, I would."

She placed her hands on top of the desk, interlocking her fingers. "It doesn't matter anyway."

Crouching down until I was eye level with her, I held onto the edge of the wood to prevent myself from reaching out and touching her. "Are you okay?"

"I'm fine," she replied. Her tone conveyed she was anything but. "Are you?"

"I'm feeling more myself today."

"Yourself, huh? As opposed to drinking a bottle of scotch and—"

"Yes," I cut her off, not needing a recap of my transgressions. "As opposed to that."

"Hmm."

"What's that supposed to mean?" I couldn't help but ask.

Before she had a chance to answer, the classroom door slammed open, jolting me back to reality.

I stood and turned to see Brandon making his way into the room, leading Jessica by the hand. They looked to where I was standing, and Jessica flashed me a smile. Her gaze then dropped to Addison and it disappeared—no love lost there.

"Good morning, Brandon, Jessica. Please go ahead and take a seat."

I strolled as calmly as I could back to the front of the room, trying not to reveal anything I didn't want known.

"*Sure,* Mr. M," Brandon agreed a little too readily.

I watched him walk to the seat beside Addison and then he glanced back over his shoulder at me. The move was confrontational, and when I sat down behind my desk, I realized he was sizing me up. *But why?*

As the other students began filing into the room, I reminded myself that Brandon knew nothing—there was no way he could. He was probably still pissed off from being suspended last week. As the final bell chimed, I watched him turn to Addison.

She didn't spare him a passing glance but merely sat silently as she had been a few minutes earlier.

But then he looked back to me.

His eyes were inquisitive. His stare, suspicious.

Right then I realized there were much more dangerous things in my life than Addison.

Present...

Doc told me to meet him out in the courtyard today.

Apparently, he has finally had it with his tiny office, not that I can blame him. Compared to the one at his home, this one must be a real drag.

"*Ahh,* isn't it beautiful today?"

I look behind me to see Doc making his way along the path surrounding the small fountain. He has one hand up to shade his eyes and the other is swinging a yellow envelope by his leg.

I scoot over on the bench and wait for him to sit. He takes the spot I've vacated and then bumps our shoulders together. "I *said*, isn't it beautiful today?"

I give a look that screams, *really?*

"Don't give me that look."

Feeling my lips twitch, I can't help from asking, "What look?"

Then in his best "girl" voice, Doc mimics who I can only assume is one of his daughters, "*Seriously?*"

Laughing out loud, I admit, "It really *is* a beautiful day."

"See?"

"So, what does it matter? I'm still in here."

My insolent response doesn't seem to faze Doc in the slightest. Instead, he shrugs.

"Technically you're *out* here, but that's neither here nor there. The point is, today we have a different result."

"As opposed to?"

"The last time we were out here. You cried that day, do you remember?"

I think back several days and remember standing here with Doc. The memory is clear. The sun was the same, but he was right—today I noticed it was a beautiful day, today…

"Today you smiled."

∾

Past…

History class went by fast enough, and as soon as the bell rang, I leaped to my feet to leave. I had a meeting today with Miss Shrieve at ten, and I didn't want to be late. I also didn't want to give Grayson a chance to ends things before I was ready.

After my session on Monday with Doc, I understood what needed to happen, it was just harder than I imagined. A few simple words and this would all be over. Life would return to normal—wouldn't it?

And what was normal? Life before *him?* That didn't sound like the ending I wanted either, but what other choice was there? Doc was making me realize I was not helping Grayson the way he helped me.

Wanting someone and needing them was entirely different than being good for them—and it was more than clear, that I was not *that* for him.

"Oh, Addison, come in."

Why my skin prickled at Miss Shrieve's invitation I couldn't have guessed, but the way she examined me as I stepped into her office and took a seat made me uncomfortable.

She held up her index finger and gave me a tight smile. "One second. Let me shut the door."

I placed my bag on my lap and clutched it tightly as I waited for her to make her way back around and take a seat. Again, her eyes shifted over me.

"How are you today?"

That was the question of the day, apparently.

"I'm fine."

"Are you?"

I nodded and tried to be more convincing. "Yes. I'm fine."

Even though the one person who shouldn't be running through my mind, is.

"I spoke with your mother the day you were suspended and released early to go home."

Why are we rehashing this? I knew it all already and so did she, so what was the—

"Your mother mentioned you came home last Wednesday with the bruised lip."

I remain silent, wondering exactly what she was getting at. That was when she dropped her bomb.

"I know that Jessica didn't strike your face on Wednesday in the parking lot. So, who did that to you?"

I wondered exactly who she thought did it. If she'd seen that Jessica hadn't slapped me, just how long did she stand there? Had she seen me talking to Grayson?

"It's okay, you know. You can tell me."

I thought about that and then, for first time in days, I heard the—*tick, tick, tock*—of her clock. That was when I asked with a little more malice than I expected, "And why would I do that?"

She didn't flinch, not even to blink, as she spoke in a tone that was clear and invited no deviation. "I'm your teacher. I'm here to help you, to guide you. I'm someone you can trust implicitly."

I didn't trust her—not at all.

"Are we done?"

She sat back in her chair and silently nodded, indicating that yes, for now we were done. I stood, and just as I got to the door, she called out my name. With a palm on the handle I looked back.

"Perhaps you should talk to Mr. McKendrick. It seems like you trust him."

Without saying a word, I opened the door and left Miss Shrieve's office.

∼

Present...

"What's in the envelope?"

Lifting the yellow rectangle, Doc hands it to me.

"It's for you."

I start to open it, but he puts his hand over mine. "Nope. Not yet."

"Not yet?"

"Nope."

He removed his hand, and I put the envelope on the bench between us and sighed. "Okay, O wise one."

"Ah! There's your sense of humor!" Bringing a hand to his chest, Doc admits, "That does very good things to this old heart."

"You aren't *that* old."

"Is that right?"

"Yep. You're only as old as you feel."

"And how old do you feel, Addy?"

"Nice one. How long did you think about that before you threw it in there?"

"Last night *and* this morning. But...back to the question. How old do you feel?"

I stretch my legs out in front of me and then shrug. "I feel like a child here. Someone is always telling me what to do."

"Well, you know why. They just want to—"

"I know. Make sure I don't hurt myself or anyone else," I finish for him. "I don't want to hurt *anyone*, not anymore."

"Why?"

"Look where it got me," I tell him, gesturing around us.

"Sitting on a bench with me on a nice sunny day? Could be worse."

"Locked up. I mean it got me locked up."

"Hmm..."

"There you go again."

Pointing to the envelope, he says, "Open it."

Picking it up, I unseal it and pull out what's inside. There in my hands is the smiling face of Brandon Williams.

Standing all around him are members of his new track team, and he is front and center, beaming at the camera. I can feel the anger I'd forgotten for days start to bubble up inside me. The picture had been featured in the Sunday newspaper and stated that Brandon Williams was now the National 100-meter dash champion.

My head snaps around to Doc, and fuming, I get to my feet.

"What the fuck is this?"

"Addy, please. Watch the language."

"*Explain*. Why would you give me this?" I demand, shoving the article back at him. He takes it from me as he stands, but before I can pull my hand back he takes ahold of it.

"He hurt people. Didn't he?"

"You *know* he did. They already told you when I was admitted here what happened."

I don't understand. Why is Doc throwing this in my face? I don't want to know about Brandon. I don't care about him. I don't care about—

"But he's happy. Just look at him."

"I thought I could *trust* you!" I shout. He's hurt me just when I thought I didn't have any feelings left *to* hurt.

"You can," he tells me. I shake my head, quite adamant he is lying.

"Listen to me. You *can't* let these people continue to have such a hold over you. Use your head, not your heart. Make yourself *want* it. Crave *it*, not some illusion, Addison."

The use of my proper name pulls me from my angry haze. "Make myself want what? You aren't making any sense."

Letting me go, Doc points to the paper in my hand. "What he has. Freedom."

CHAPTER 28

 ast...

"Addison!"

I stopped walking and saw Grayson at the far end of the hall. The bell for lunch had rung and I was planning to step out and take the hour in my car, by myself—where I could try and get my usual facade back in place.

Miss Shrieve had been insinuating too much and asking too many questions—too many potentially *damaging* questions. They weren't damaging for me but they would be for the man now striding down the hall in my direction.

I waited off to the side where my locker was and watched several students greet Mr. McKendrick as he passed them. It wasn't unusual for a teacher to need to see a student, but I knew from the look in his eyes that it had nothing to do with school.

When he stopped an acceptable distance from me, he asked, "Where are you going? We need to talk."

"We do? Why?"

Checking to make sure no one was within earshot, he asked in a hushed tone, "What is going on with you today?"

Not quite sure what to say, I couldn't bring myself to look at him. "Nothing."

"Bullshit," he hissed.

He was right. It *was* bullshit.

He gestured to the small alcove at the end of the lockers, and I obeyed without protest. After talking to Doc, I realized that I'd been using Grayson for my own selfish reasons and giving nothing but pain in return.

It was time to free him from my burdens.

"You've shut down. I want to know why."

Refusing to draw this out any longer but knowing this wasn't the time or the place to get into it, I said, "Maybe I've realized a few things."

It sounded ridiculous even to my own ears.

He must have thought so too because his mouth pulled into a grim line, and the emotions swirling in his eyes were oscillating between anger and concern.

"Oh yeah, like what?"

I swallowed, and gestured between us. "That this—"

"Yes?" he interrupted, his cutting tone and his expression making this much more difficult than I expected it to be.

"*This* is going to hurt you," I stressed on a whisper.

As if he'd forgotten where we were, Grayson stepped forward, forcing me back against the wall and demanded, "Is that so? And who finally made you understand this? Because it sure as hell wasn't me when I was telling you *no*."

"Doc," I supplied instantly.

Grayson's eyes widened as he rubbed his fingers over his lips. "You told him about us?"

"No," I answered, horrified he would think such a thing.

Unable to help himself, he lowered his face until it was close to mine. I was about to remind him where we were when he fumed, "Then what the fuck are you talking about, Addison?"

"You need to back up," I warned, looking from side to side. "Anyone could see us."

"*Shit*," he cursed and stood back up straight.

"I don't want to be something that you look at and *hate*. I can't be that to you, not when you are the opposite to me. I'm bad for you. Poison," I finally told him.

There, I couldn't get much more honest than that. He began pacing and then came back to stop in front of me. "No, you're not."

"Yes," I disagreed. "I am."

"So, what? That's *it*? You're just going to walk away?" he asked, his face showing his incredulity. "After finally getting what you want, you're done?"

"No," I denied, his fury making my heart hurt.

I didn't want to be doing this, but I was trying to do the right thing for a change, couldn't he see that?

"I'm going to finish school and hope you still—"

"That I still what, Addison? I've been telling myself how fucking wrong this is from the very beginning and I *still* haven't stayed away." Then he did the unthinkable. He touched my hair, stroking his fingers over the curls. "I can't stay away."

I could feel tears in my eyes as the full impact of that tiny gesture *here*, where it could hurt him most, showed the depth of his emotions.

"You need to try. Let me do this. It's the right thing. For both of us."

Pulling his hand back, he pushed it into his pocket.

"Too many people are watching. You'll only get hurt being connected to me."

He shook his head, clearly frustrated. "Like who?"

"Brandon."

"I don't give a fuck about him," he spat, and the venom in that statement showed just how far we'd come. In the beginning, Grayson had denied any jealousy, but right here in this moment, it was obvious he was feeling something.

"Miss Shrieve," I added, deciding to go a different route.

"What about her?"

"She had me in her office for a meeting this morning."

Something flashed in his eyes, almost as if he was suspicious of why she'd called me in. *Did he know something?*

"What for?"

"My lip. My mom told her I came home Wednesday after school with it. Miss Shrieve also saw us in the parking lot. Did you know that?"

"Yes."

I pushed away from the wall. "Were you going to tell me?"

"She didn't see anything she shouldn't have," he stated, defending his actions.

"How do you know? God, no wonder…" I trailed off as I thought back to the comment about him and trust.

This was *not* good.

I made a move to step around him when I saw Brandon walking down the hall, but Grayson reached out and grabbed my wrist, pulling me back to where he was standing behind the lockers.

"Where are you going?"

Yanking my arm away, I gritted out between clenched teeth, "Let me *go*. Brandon's coming."

Grayson released me instantly and stepped away, just as Brandon rounded the corner and found us.

"What the fuck is this?"

~

Present…

After knocking on Doc's door, I pace back and forth in the empty hall.

In my left hand, I'm holding the envelope with Brandon's

photo, and in my right, I have the pen he'd given me—Grayson's pen.

Both symbols in their own right of *distrust* and *trust*.

As his door opens, I stop pacing and thrust the envelope at him. He takes it from me without a word and then steps aside.

"Why?" I ask as I walk inside and he shuts the door. "I want to know why you gave me that?"

"I told you why."

"So I can break free?"

"*Yes*, break free of everything that keeps you trapped," he tells me, pointing with the envelope.

"This picture isn't important," he explains and throws it on the floor. He's more animated than I've ever seen him. "Yet, it gets more of a reaction out of you than I've seen in days. *You*, Addy! *You* are what's important. Not what happened back then. Yesterday is done. What are you going to do with today?"

My eyes focus on him, and I feel the urgency building. There's a craving he's ignited inside of me.

"I don't want to be in *here* anymore."

"I know. So what are you going to do about it?"

The answer is obvious. It's been there all along. "I'm going to fight."

A grin appears on Doc's face. "And?"

I grin back at him. "I'm going to win."

∾

Past...

"Dude, get your hands off her!"

Fuck, was the only word coming to mind as Brandon sized up the situation.

"Hey, he wasn't doing—"

"He was grabbing you, Addy," he accused.

Brandon was right, I had been grabbing her, and I wanted to grab her again. Instead, I fell into my self-righteous teacher mode. *What a fucking joke.*

"Don't you need to go to lunch?"

"No, I need to report your ass. Why the fuck are you touching her anyway?"

"*Brandon!*" Addison shouted, and I could tell by the way she had her arms wrapped around her waist that she was trying to hold herself together. I knew that, because I was scrambling to do the same.

"What? No teacher is supposed to lay a hand on a student. And they certainly shouldn't be grabbing one. Wasn't that why *I* was suspended?" he asked, getting up in my face.

I took a step back and reminded myself that this was a student, not someone I could punch in the jaw and demand he shut the fuck up.

"Mr. Williams, I think you're mistaken with what you saw."

What am I saying? I couldn't believe I was stooping this fucking low.

"Am I?"

"Yes, you are. What the hell is the matter with you?" I questioned.

Sure, compound the issue by being a dick—my father would be so proud.

"I think you know," he inferred, looking from me to Addison who, when I glanced over at her, seemed wounded and broken —once again damaged and this time by me.

There was nothing I could do about that now, I was in too deep and couldn't stop—not after what Brandon had seen.

"I'm getting sick of your mouth. I think you should start walking before you say something you'll regret."

"That I regret?" He mocked. "I don't think so."

"Brandon, just go. You're making this worse," Addison pleaded, drawing our eyes back to her.

"*What* am I making worse, Addy? Jess says she left you in the parking lot last week and you were fine, but she saw *him* talking to you before she drove away. Now there's a rumor you got your busted lip that same day. It wasn't Jess, so who was it, huh? Mr. McKendrick?"

That was not an accusation I'd expected, and it almost knocked me off my feet. I tried to wrap my mind around what he'd just hurled at me.

"Are you implying that *I* hit Addison? Because if you are, that is one hell of an allegation."

"Well, you have to admit, it doesn't look so good does it, *sir*? Do you like to touch all of your students?"

"What the fuck?" Addison sputtered, sounding as perplexed as I was.

"Shut up, Addy," Brandon ordered, pointing a finger at her. I wanted to hit him, just for that.

"Alright, that's it! I've had it."

"Oh, yeah?" he challenged, and I could feel my anger reaching its boiling point. I clenched my fists by my sides and willed myself to calm the fuck down.

"Yes. You need to leave or we're going to the front office right now, where you can kiss your track scholarship good-bye."

That's when Brandon pulled his arm back, balled his hand into a fist and launched it forward, punching me in the side of my face. I grabbed my jaw and pushed my tongue to the inside of my cheek, tasting blood.

"Brandon Williams!"

Oh fantastic, just what I fucking needed—Helene to join this circus.

Glaring at my attacker, my *student*, I warned, "I suggest you back up, before I really lose my temper."

He seemed to realize what he'd just done because he slowly backed away and shook out his fingers.

"You're about to visit with Principal Thomas and you can explain to him why I have a bleeding lip. You do know that's cause for expulsion, yes?"

"What on earth is going on here?" Helene demanded of the three of us, and after what Addison had been alluding to earlier, I had to wonder what my fellow employee was thinking.

Before Brandon had a chance to speak, I made sure to pin him with an unrelenting stare and invited, "Do you want to tell her, or should I?"

He didn't bother answering as he turned on Addison, who seemed to have shrunk into the wall. Her head was down, her shoulders were shaking, and her fingers were white as she dug them into her sides.

I wanted to reach out and comfort her, but that was what got us in this situation in the first place. Why I wanted to yell at Helene for doing what I couldn't made absolutely no sense at all.

She placed a hand on Addison's shoulder and I'd never seen such a violent reaction from her. Addison pulled away as if Helene would infect her and aimed an icy look her way.

"Addy? Are you okay?" Helene urged gently.

Addison pivoted toward me, and her eyes took on a look I hadn't seen since the night by her brother's grave.

My Addison was gone, and as she fell apart in front of me, she raised her arm and pressed her watch to her ear as a tear slipped free and rolled down her cheek.

The ticking was back.

We were over.

Time was no longer standing still.

CHAPTER 29

 ast...

God, how long would this take?

I'd just given my false recap of what happened between Brandon and me, and as predicted, he would be expelled. He'd have to finish the school year at a different high school.

"Mr. McKendrick, if that's all, you may leave. We'll take it from here."

I stood, pushing the chair back and then looked at the boy—and that's what he was, just a boy—slumped down in his seat. Brandon glared at me, and I felt the full weight of my negligence.

This boy had trusted me—I'd let him down.

"I hope things turn around for you, Mr. Williams."

I offered my hand to him, but instead of taking it, his eyes took on a hard glint—I'd put that there. *No*, he'd already had an edge. I'd just sharpened it.

Raising his gaze from my hand, his top lip curled as he told me, "You better go and find Anne."

Anne? What was he...? And then I remembered my lesson on King Henry's wives.

... Many believe he chased Anne and was drawn to her because she resisted his attempts...

He didn't know how wrong he was. I hadn't chased Addison, but I was about to. I needed to find her.

I left the office without saying another word. My lip was throbbing and my head was starting to pound but that didn't stop me from heading straight for the parking lot.

Addison couldn't leave because if she did, her parents would be called, and she wouldn't want that. I looked at my watch and knew I had the period free, so I headed across the track and through the gate. I spotted her car in the lot and made my way over.

I peered through the window and saw nothing. It was empty.

Straightening, I surveyed the lot. There was no one around. I was about to go and check inside, when I spotted something.

Over by my truck, I saw white material peeking out from underneath and knew immediately that it was her. I jogged over to where I'd parked and rounded the tail of my truck bed—and there she was. Sitting up against the huge tire on the driver's side, she seemed so small and fragile.

As the loose gravel crunched under my shoes, she turned to see me walking toward her. She had her knees bent and pulled into her chest with her arms wrapped around them.

"Addison," I whispered softly.

She looked like a trapped animal. Trapped inside her mind.

Her hair was a mess, probably from dragging her hands through it, and I could see her fingers tapping on her knee—*one, two, three. One, two, three.*

I kept my distance and crouched down until we were on the same level. "Addison."

She raised her head and I had to clasp my hands in my lap so I wouldn't follow my instinct to reach out and touch.

"Talk to me," I coaxed gently.

Nothing. I got nothing from her. She'd withdrawn inside herself.

Pulling my legs out from under me, I planted my ass firmly on the ground and placed a foot on either side of her, careful not to touch.

"What's going on? I thought—"

"What?" her voice was faint when she finally spoke up. Her eyes held me in place and for once, I felt at a loss for words. "What did you think?"

I shrugged. "I don't know. I guess I thought I could make you feel better."

She brought an arm up and wiped her nose on her sleeve.

"Yeah, let's make sure *I'm* better. God, now you're thinking just like them."

Before I knew what I was doing, I crawled over until I was kneeling by her side.

"No. I'm nothing like them," I told her emphatically. "I'm here with you, aren't I?"

How could I have ever thought she was what was wrong in my life? She was the only thing that made any sense, and when she was broken and hurting, so was I.

My dad was right—if I wanted her heart, I had to take it. If I was doing this out of love, it was beyond good and evil.

"Addison."

She continued staring past my shoulder, so I took her chin in my hand and *made* her look at me.

"Addison, look at me." As her eyes focused on mine, I repeated the same words she'd once told me. "Look at *all* of me."

Her hand cupped my throbbing cheek, and as her thumb

gently swept over the stubble and bruise I knew was forming, fresh tears welled in her eyes. I released her chin and brushed my hand over her hair, pushing it back from her face.

"What's going on in that head of yours, hmm?"

With a shaky breath, she finally admitted, "I'm broken."

I shook my head. "No, Addison. Just perfectly imperfect. None of us are perfect."

Her bottom lip jutted out, and as tears ran down her cheeks, I couldn't help myself, I leaned forward and put my lips to them. Her cheek was cool and the tears warm as I lifted my mouth. I brushed my nose with hers and whispered what I could no longer deny. "I love you."

She pressed her forehead to mine and replied so softly I almost missed it, "You shouldn't."

Her answer made my heart ache and my head swirl.

I knew she was right, it didn't make any sense. I shouldn't love her. It couldn't end well, and I'd already lost the only other person who meant anything to me. This was just setting myself up for heartbreak. But as I took this broken girl in my arms and she crawled up into my lap, there was no way I could deny she had my heart firmly in her hands.

Present...

"I thought I might find you here."

I turn to see Doc stepping into the library where I'm studying.

"Yeah, I needed to find a poet for the English portion of the test."

"Oh," Doc says as he pulls out the chair beside me and sits down. "Who did you decide on?"

I slide the book I'm reading over to him.

"Aleksandr Pushkin."

"He's Russian."

"I never would have guessed," Doc replies dryly. "Which poem? He has so many."

I wait until he looks up from the page before I tell him, "I chose 'Farewell.' It seemed fitting."

Doc returns his attention to the book and locates the poem. Before he has a chance to say anything, I clearly recite Pushkin's words. I'm finally at peace with the decision to fight, move on, and perhaps even let go.

"It's the last time, when I dare
To cradle your image in my mind…"

Doc closes the book as I continue the poem word for word, and when I finish, he says softly, "That's beautiful, Addy. I'm proud of you. It *is* time to say farewell to the past. I'm glad you recognize that. Keep up the good work here. The big test is just around the corner."

~

Past…

Crawling on to Grayson's lap, I touched his hair and felt the pain in my chest intensify. I knew this was good-bye. I had to break it off here.

"I shouldn't have started this. I didn't know," I confessed, and grazed his lips with my fingers. "I didn't know it would be like this. That you would love…that…you need to walk away now. Forget about me."

One of his hands smoothed down my back as he replied, "Probably."

I was relieved that he seemed to understand what I was trying to do—until his lips found the corner of mine and he whispered, "But I'm not going anywhere."

As a tear slipped between our lips, my tongue came out to taste it and found his mouth. Our lips connected and I lost myself in him.

I tangled my fingers into the shorter strands of his hair and held his head as I pushed my tongue deeper, hungry to find his. His hands moved to my hips, pulling me up against him, and as we disappeared into our own world, we recklessly forgot the one around us.

Until our two worlds collided.

"*Grayson?*"

As the voice penetrated the silence and I felt Grayson's body freeze, I knew I hadn't imagined the voice that was almost as familiar to me as his was.

"Addison? What...what are you doing?" the unbelieving voice asked, trying to make sense of what she was seeing. I scrambled away from Grayson and back to where I'd been sitting against the tire.

This wasn't going to end well, and as I looked at the slump of his shoulders, I knew he was aware of that too. But he'd known all along, hadn't he? I'd been naive to think it could have ended any other way.

Getting to his feet, Grayson turned and stepped in front of me. He was protecting me from the woman standing between the two cars we had been hiding behind. Once they were face to face he opened his mouth and spoke.

"Helene."

CHAPTER 30

 resent...

"Let's go back to the photo you have on your wall of Cupid and Psyche."

"Okay," I agree.

"Venus plays an important role in that tale, wouldn't you say?"

"I suppose so, yes." Curious where Doc's going with this, I nod.

"She's the reason Psyche is originally sent away *and* the reason she meets Cupid. Not to mention, the very person who ultimately brings them together in the end."

"Yes, but only because she tried to have Psyche killed."

Doc thinks about this a moment and then says, "But *because* of Venus, she is swept away by Cupid, who in the end, saves Psyche."

Why is Doc trying to make it sound like Venus had done these two a favor? It was fate, not Venus, that had brought them back together. I consider him carefully, trying to understand his logic.

"Okay, so?" I ask, truly stumped.

"So do you want to tell me why you hate Helene so much?"

My face scrunches up as I question, "Helene? What's she got to do with this?"

"Well, isn't she who you imagine when you think of Venus in this story? That photo *is* how you see yourself, am I right? As Psyche?"

"So what if it is?" I ask, feeling surly as hell. Helene had taken everything away from me. First Daniel and then *him*.

"So it makes sense that she's Venus in this story, and she set out to ruin you. Isn't that how you see it?"

I guess he was right, but as I remember what happened that day and the days that followed, I shake my head.

"She didn't set out to do it. She just did."

~

Past...

"*Grayson*? What are you doing?"

Miss Shrieve's voice cut through the quiet parking lot like a gunshot, and her aim was as accurate as a sharpshooter.

"Look—" Grayson started.

"*No.* What the hell do you think you're doing with her?"

She gestured at me with her eyes wide as I got to my feet. It was as though the entire world was closing in. I felt the air being sucked out from around us until all that remained were tense questions.

"Are you out of your *mind*?"

"Helene—" Grayson tried again, but he was quickly cut off as my furious coach stepped forward and pointed at him.

"You were *kissing* her!" she shouted, appalled.

I wrapped my arms around my waist and stepped up beside him to say something, *anything*, when Miss Shrieve turned to me.

"And *you*! Aren't you in enough trouble? This...this is just unacceptable!"

Spinning on her foot to storm away, I was surprised when Grayson reached out and took her wrist, pulling her back around to face us. The shock was evident on her face as she looked down to where he was holding her.

"*Let*. Me. Go," she demanded.

"Not until you let me explain," Grayson pushed, adamant that she listen.

Believing it was best if I stayed quiet, I shrank back and waited to see what would happen.

"Explain what? You were kissing a student!"

Shaking his head, he told her, "You don't understand."

"You're damn right I don't! Was that your way of comforting her?" She let out a scornful laugh and tried to yank her arm away. "Let me go, Grayson."

"No. Not until you listen to me. *Please?*"

"Why? Give me one good reason why I should?"

"Because it's my fault," I finally spoke up.

She cut her eyes to me, pinning me where I stood, before disagreeing. "No, Addison. *He* should know better." She tugged on her arm again. "Now let go of me."

Shaking my head in denial, I stressed to her, "But it was *me*, I was the one who—"

"Addison, *he* is your teacher. *You* are his student. I don't care what you think *you* did. He should have said no, end of story."

"*No!*" I cried out. She was making him sound like a monster. "That's not the end of the story!"

Grayson spoke up. "Addison, please."

"*What?*" I demanded, starting to feel my panic rise.

"She's right," he told me quietly, and it was as if someone had reached in and tore out my heart.

"Of course I am!" Miss Shrieve hissed, as if she felt she had to talk quietly or get in trouble for conspiracy.

"Not about everything," he clarified. "But she is right that you *are* my student, and I should have waited. I should have waited for you."

"Are you *listening* to yourself?" my coach asked in a way that implied he was insane. "Is this because of your father, Grayson? Were you…I don't know, looking for comfort?"

Both of us remained silent as she grappled for a plausible excuse.

"Oh, I see. This has been going on longer than that." She paused for a minute and then sucked in a quick breath. "Did you…" She trailed off and then tried again. "Addison…your lip…"

A murderous look crossed Grayson's face. "God no, Helene! I'm not a fucking monster."

Taken aback by Grayson's outburst, it took me a minute to react, but it was time Miss Shrieve knew the whole truth. Since she thought she knew everything, at least I could exonerate him of this.

"My father hit me. That wasn't the first time. It was just the first time he did it where you could see."

For a moment, she seemed to soften and in slipped the one emotion I never handled well—pity. "Oh, Addison, why didn't you tell someone?"

I turned to Grayson, who stood beside me looking utterly shell-shocked, and then I glanced back at her.

"I did."

This was not going well. *Fuck.*

I could feel both pairs of eyes on me, and all I could think was—*this is it, it's all over.*

"You told him? A man who's been taking advantage of you?"

"*No*. It's not like that," Addison tried to defend, but it was no use. Helene was only seeing this one way, and it was the way I should have seen it—black-and-white. For her, there was no immoral shade of grey.

"*Yes*, it is, Addison." Looking back to me, she informed me in a voice full of disgust, "You have to understand, I'm *going* to report this."

I rubbed my forehead, stressed, and then swallowed. *Yes, I understood but fuck…*

"One day."

"What?" she snapped, and I didn't dare look away as I begged for the first time in my life.

"Give me one day. I'll turn myself in tomorrow."

Her eyes darted to Addison, but I didn't dare.

"Why?"

Trying to think of a good excuse, I clung to my dead father once again, and lied—*that which is done out of love is always beyond good and evil. I understand.*

Would he understand *this*? Were my thoughts good or evil? I didn't know anymore.

"I need to finish clearing up some financial matters with my father's estate. Sign some paperwork, get it squared away before whatever happens, happens."

Relenting, she told me, "*One* day. That's it. If I don't see you here by 3 p.m. tomorrow, I'll report you myself. And stay away from her, you hear me?" She took a step away and said, "Addison, come with me."

I felt Addison's hand brush my arm and I nodded. *Yes…go with Helene. She'll protect you from me.*

Or was she protecting me from Addison? I didn't know anymore.

I was starting to think that as wrong as we were for one

another, we were also the only two people that were perfectly suited for the other.

"Don't do this, not to protect me. You did nothing wrong," she told me, her blue eyes full of tears.

That was the problem. I'd done everything wrong. As she moved farther away from me, I had nothing I could say to comfort her because no matter what she *wanted*, the wheels were in motion. Nothing could stop the inevitable from happening.

There was no escaping it—my crimes had finally caught up to my passion.

∽

Present...

"She wouldn't listen to me."

The silence is smothering as tears blur my eyes, just like they did that day.

"Who, Helene?"

"Yes," I whisper, remembering how I felt when she took me away from Grayson that afternoon. Helpless, heartbroken, and at the same time—furious.

"What would you have told her if you could?" Doc's question pulls me from my memories.

"That it was my fault. That he didn't want what happened."

Doc shakes his head from side to side in disagreement. "But that's a lie." Again, the silence stretches between us. "Isn't it Addy?"

I swallow and blink back my tears. "He didn't even know he wanted it until I…"

"What, made him see you?" Doc suggests.

"Yes."

"I'm pretty sure he'd tell you differently."

"And how would you know?" I snap, my sadness beginning to overwhelm me and alter my mood to one of anger.

"I don't. Not for certain. But why would a man—a sensible, seemingly good man—do what he did, unless he wanted to?"

"Stop talking in circles!" I yell, jumping up from my seat and balling my fists.

Sizing me up, Doc asks with infuriating calm. "Is that what I'm doing?"

"Yes!"

"No, Addy, I'm trying to make you see that it wasn't *your* fault."

"What?" I ask, this time laughing humorlessly.

"You once told me that you didn't want to be pitied because of what everyone else thinks, but I've never been overly concerned with what everyone else thinks. Maybe...you should be pitied for what *you* think."

I close my eyes, trying to block him out, but he continues.

"You think you're alone because of what you did. No. Uh-uh. You're alone because of what you *didn't* do."

Opening my eyes, I wait for whatever he is going to say.

"You didn't walk away."

CHAPTER 31

 ast...

Tick, tick, tock.

One day. The more I thought about his words, the more disturbed I became.

One day and then what?

After Miss Shrieve walked me back to her office, she asked me a ton of questions, none of which I answered. Instead, I sat there thinking about Grayson.

Numb—I felt numb.

"When did this start, Addison?"

"How did he approach you?"

"What he did was wrong. He should never have gotten involved with you. Did he ever hurt you?"

"I need to call your parents."

The last comment had my head snapping up and my eyes meeting hers.

"No, not yet," I begged.

"Addy, I can't—"

"You told him you'd give him a day," I reminded her.

"Yes...*him*."

"If you call my parents, they will go—"

"Crazy? As they should, Addison. I still can't believe it."

Lowering my gaze to avoid her judgment, I started to fidget with my nails.

Tick, tick, tock.

Her clock was loud in my mind as I sat there trying to think, trying to work out what he'd meant by asking for more time.

One day. One more day to do what?

"Addison? You can *never* see him again. Do you know what is going to happen to him tomorrow?"

Gritting my teeth, I could feel the tears coming back and I wanted to yell at her, *Shut up! Shut up and let me think!*

Where was Grayson? Did he go home? What must he be thinking?

I needed to get to him before...before what? I didn't even know.

One day.

"He'll be suspended and unable to work, followed by felony charges and jail time."

"*No!*" I shouted at her. "He did nothing wrong. You can't do this to him!"

"Addy, I haven't done anything. He did."

I glowered at her, angry that she would dare threaten this man. This remarkably *good* man. Was I angry with her or myself? Who had really done this to him?

Me.

I felt sick as everything I'd done leading up to this moment flashed through my mind, and all I could see was him saying no and me—*not listening.*

"Addison, I have to call your parents," Miss Shrieve repeated, almost as if she were sorry. Not sorry enough, though, because she still reached for the phone.

"I thought you liked him."

My voice was barely a whisper in the room, but it made her pause for a moment and then she placed the phone back down. "I do...*did* like him, Addy. Before I knew—"

"Before you knew *what*? You don't know anything. He *helped* me..." My voice faded, and I wiped away a tear. "Is that so bad?"

"No, Addison. Helping you isn't the problem, and I think you know that. He should never have been kissing you the way he was or touching you." She stopped for a minute and then asked bluntly, "Was there more to it? Were you two intimate?"

I knew this was the moment she expected me to open up and trust her, but she was in for a big disappointment. Instead, I stared at the woman who was trying to ruin the man I loved— and shut all the way down.

"Addison?"

With my face an inscrutable mask, I remained silent.

"You didn't do anything wrong, Addison. He..."

As she kept talking, I made the decision to flip the switch. To forget everything that Grayson and I had done.

I concentrated on the—*tick, tick, tock*—and let the madness come and devour me once again.

Fuck! I slammed my palm against the steering wheel as I sped home.

The entire way I kept checking over my shoulder, expecting cop cars to pull in behind me with flashing lights.

Guilty.

Yes, I was fucking guilty. Guilty of loving the wrong person at the wrong time.

Pulling into my drive, I jumped out of my truck and made my way into the house. Everywhere I looked I was reminded of what I'd done with Addison here.

Jesus, I'd deluded myself. How'd it come to this?

How did I convince myself that somehow we wouldn't get caught, that I wasn't throwing my life away? But tomorrow...tomorrow I'd be fired. Worse, I'd be charged like some kind of fucking sexual predator. All because of a quick...

No.

This wasn't about sex. It wasn't even about a kiss.

I needed to get fucking real. I'd done it and would do everything all over again just for a moment with her. For her smile, her laughter, and the way she looked at me with absolute trust in her eyes.

Addison had been hungry for guidance, acceptance, and love—and I'd reveled in having the power to give it all to her.

I marched to the kitchen, grabbed the scotch and a glass and saw my father's pen sitting on the counter.

Picking it up, I studied the engraving and remembered getting it made for him. I ran my finger over the letters and felt as though they were mocking me.

Son, if you want her heart—go and take it.

Somehow, I didn't think he'd be too happy I took his advice. I poured more than I should have of the scotch and raised it.

"Cheers, old man."

I raised the glass to him and then slammed it back before closing my eyes.

I pictured Addison with tears on her cheeks and fear in her eyes as she'd walked away with Helene earlier—scared. Then I remembered the day in the field with the sun shining over her when I'd stupidly promised to keep her safe.

Who am I kidding? I can't even keep myself safe.

Lifting the bottle, I poured another glass and swirled the contents around.

What the fuck was I going to do now? Tomorrow by three, everyone would know what I'd done and that would be it.

Over. Finished.

I'd never see her again. Never touch her. And I would never know what would become of her.

I downed the contents of my glass. The prospect of never knowing was a worse punishment than the public or any judge could give me.

I dropped my head into my hands, remembering Addison's words, *I'm your monster.* She was so very wrong. I was honest enough to admit I was fighting myself.

I'd become my own monster.

~

Present...

"You have a big day tomorrow," Doc says with a smile.

We're back in the library, where I spend all my days now, studying for the test that is almost here.

"Yep. It's such a long test."

"How long, again?"

"Seven or so hours," I tell him, turning the page in my textbook.

"That *is* long. Are you taking it here?" he asks and I raise a brow.

"No, I was going to break out and do it at the public library."

Doc's smile is warm and slightly...smug.

"Okay, Miss Smarty Pants. I *meant* are you going to take it here in the library?"

Grinning at him, I nod. "Yep. At 9 a.m."

"Do you have everything you need?" he asks as he clasps his hands on top of the table. I look at the face I now consider to be friendly.

"Yeah, I think so," I tell him before going back to the book in front of me.

"Addy?"

"Hmm?" I respond, figuring Doc will just keep talking as

usual. When he doesn't, I stop reading the paragraph I'm on and glance up. "Yes?"

"Make sure you have pencils tomorrow. You can't use a pen."

I look at the pen sitting beside the textbook on the table and reach out to touch the shiny gold trim. I'll just take it with me then.

It's my good luck and my hope, and I'm hanging on to it.

Just as that thought enters my mind, Doc's voice filters through. "You should always have one or two, just in case. Here," he says, sliding three pencils over to me.

I reach forward to take them, and he places a warm, calming hand over mine.

"Addy?"

"Yeah?"

"I'm proud of you."

I can't help but smile as he gives me a gentle squeeze before lifting his hand.

"I just wanted you to know that."

Gripping the pencils, I hold them to me as if they are worth as much as the *Mont Blanc*. Now I have two good luck charms.

Doc has always been on my side, even when I was fighting him every step of the way. My parents may have lost their direction and turned into pitiful examples of what a role model should be, but they did one thing right.

They gave me Doc.

∼

Past...

I sat with Miss Shrieve as she dialed my mom's number and pressed the phone to her ear, and before I even thought about it, I was up and reaching for the door.

I could hear her shouting my name as I sprinted down the hall toward the exit. I didn't stop as I pulled my bag around and yanked out my keys.

I had no idea what I was doing as I jumped inside the car and started the engine. As I left the parking lot, I saw my coach come to a stop at the gate in my rearview mirror.

My blood was pumping with adrenaline as I weaved through the traffic in front of me.

I couldn't let this happen. Not to him.

I had to tell him how sorry I was and tell him to go, to run. He needed to leave—now.

Making it to his house in record time, I got out of the car and ran to the front door, my breath coming fast as I pounded on it and waited.

I knew we didn't have much time.

Miss Shrieve would've already called my parents by now— and possibly the principal at this point.

I rapped my knuckles on his door again, and heard the locks click and the handle turn. Standing back, I waited as he pulled the door open, and when he came into view, I couldn't help but launch myself at him, wrapping my arms around his neck. I didn't realize I'd been holding my breath until his arms embraced me, and I exhaled in relief.

I touched his face, running the back of my hand down his jaw. "We need to leave."

"What?" he asked, pulling away. "No, Addison. I can't leave."

"Yes, we both can. We can drive away. I can dye my hair. You could shave yours. Then we can ditch the truck somewhere and—"

"Addison. *Addison*," he cut in, smoothing a hand down over my hair. "I can't do that. Then what? We live on the run? No, I've done enough. I can't do that to you."

Loosening his hold, he stepped back and asked in a gentle, but firm tone, "What are you doing here? You heard Helene.

You're supposed to stay away from me and tomorrow I'm going to—"

"What? Turn yourself in? Go to *jail?* Do you know how ridiculous that is? I *wanted* this!"

Running his hands through his hair, Grayson spun away from me and cursed. "*Fuck*, Addison! It doesn't matter! No one will care. It's over! *This*…this is over!"

I bit down on my lip to keep back the cry that was threatening to break free. His words were harsh and cut deeper than any knife ever could.

"Turn around," I implored.

"No."

My eyes roamed over his powerful body and rested on his shoulders, as broad as ever. But this time, instead of offering strength and safety, they looked formidable, as if he was blocking me out. And he was.

"You should go."

I grabbed his arm and jerked him around to face me. "Look at me!"

His eyes were glassy as he did what I asked, and seeing the emotion in them triggered my own tears to flow freely down my face.

"I'm sorry," I sobbed, not knowing what else to say. "I'm so sorry."

I did this. I destroyed this man.

His fingers trailed over my cheek and down under my chin. Tipping my face up to his, he pressed his mouth to mine and whispered, "I'm not."

Sweet, she was so damn sweet as I touched my lips to hers, savoring the taste.

I cupped her cheeks and then slid my hands back into her soft hair as I deepened the kiss. She placed a palm on my chest, feeling the beat of my heart, and then she dug her fingers in.

I lifted my head, and she spoke the words I'd heard for the first time several weeks ago. "Meet me?"

Searching her eyes, I shook my head and she brought a finger to my lips.

"Please don't let this be it. It can't be. Meet me at Daniel's. I'll wait, Grayson—I'll wait for you."

I knew there was no way I could deny her—I nodded.

Somehow, some way, I would get to her.

CHAPTER 32

 ast...

That afternoon proved to be a lesson in torture.

After returning home, my parents sat me down and pretended to care, and they did that by asking a lot of uncomfortable and demeaning questions. They'd also done the one thing I wished they hadn't—they had called Doc to be a part of their charade.

"Addison..." my mother began as she sat back on the couch. She smoothed out the non-existent wrinkles from her cream skirt and folded her hands in her lap. "Addison, we are trying to understand what happened with this...this teacher, Mr. McKendrick."

Just hearing her say his name in a way that said she was repulsed made me want to spit nasty, ugly words at her. Instead, I lowered my eyes and refused to answer.

If they wanted answers, they'd get nothing from me.

As far as they were concerned, Mr. McKendrick existed only as my teacher.

"Addison—" my father started.

"*Don't,*" I snapped. I had no problem cutting him off. How dare my *loving* father question me and my motives or Grayson's for that matter?

Realizing that they were getting nowhere, Doc scooted to the edge of the couch and in a gentle voice said, "Addy?"

My eyes flicked to his and, again, I said nothing.

"It's okay, Addy. You've done nothing wrong."

I wish that were true, but the fact was, I'd done everything wrong.

Why couldn't anyone see that?

Blame belonged to no one except me. This was entirely my fault.

Present...

Tomorrow is the day of my exam.

Sitting on my bed, I look around the small room that's become my home these past thirty days and wonder how I will feel when I step outside the front doors.

No one has come to visit me while I've been here at Pine Groves—no one except Doc.

My mother signed me over and then left me here to heal, or more likely, to disappear. Either way, she'd made it more than clear she didn't want to see me until I would no longer be an embarrassment to the family.

That won't be a problem because I have no desire to *ever* see her again. I wonder how she feels in that big house all on her own since my father was booked and sent away for his abuse.

All of this stemmed from decisions she failed to make, like protecting her daughter from a father with a drinking problem and a strong arm.

I look at the photo on the wall and notice the edges beginning to curl. Every day it's becoming a little more worn and broken, even as I'm getting stronger.

Soon, I'll be strong enough to face whatever comes my way because in two days I will be free to start over.

∾

Past...

I pulled the truck into the parking lot of the cemetery and looked at the time. In ten minutes it would be midnight.

Turning off the headlights, I took the keys from the ignition and bent down to rest my forehead on the steering wheel. I clutched it so tight I thought it would break, but all it did was provide something for me to hang onto as I started to fall apart.

The thought of them questioning me tomorrow over the nature of my relationship with Addison made me feel sick to my stomach. Yet, I knew it wasn't the relationship but the lie I would tell them to cover it up that made me feel that way.

The disappointment I felt was only superseded by the fact that I believed my actions were justified.

Was this what love was supposed to be like? An emotion that made you want to willingly give up everything for another—and how much was I willing to give?

I was in all kinds of trouble. My career was over, my reputation would be ruined, and my life...my life was still to be decided.

I squeezed my eyes shut and smashed my hand onto the wheel. My shoulders shook as the enormity of the mess I was in finally hit me.

Where did you go, and who did you turn to, when you had no one?

"Dad," I whispered out into the darkness. "I could really use your help right about now. What do I do?"

I looked down to the center console, spotting his pen. I picked it up, tracing my finger over his initials, and thought of how disappointed he'd be.

I uncapped the pen and opened the glove compartment to find what I needed.

Nothing could be changed, not now. It was done.

I wanted Addison, and she wanted me.

But sometimes, you just don't get what you want.

My mother continued trying to justify why I did what I did. I must have been seduced, coerced, talked into falling for this older man—this sexual predator.

As I sat there, I remained silent, knowing that anything I said would only make the situation worse. Doc was watching me carefully, almost as if he was trying to read my thoughts.

All the while, my father sat pouring glass after glass of bourbon, looking more drunk as the night went on.

"You are grounded indefinitely, except to visit with Dr. Wolinski," my mother told me as she stood to shake Doc's hand.

I was close to begging Doc to stay, when I heard him suggest to my father, "I don't think that will help the situation tonight, do you?"

"I don't feel like *you* help the situation at all," my father slurred, standing to make his way upstairs, no doubt to pass out. I knew he'd checked out the day he'd picked up a bottle of alcohol and began drinking it like water.

My father was gone. There was no doubt about it.

Several hours later, I sat in my room watching the clock as I waited for my parents to go to sleep.

Dressed in jeans and a black sweater, I pulled my hair back and secured it in a ponytail and then snuck out my bedroom.

Walking to the front door, I opened it and made my way to the side alley. I followed my usual route until I reached the main road opposite the cemetery.

I sprinted across the empty road and through the old gates before following the drive to the parking lot. The empty parking lot.

He wasn't there.

I searched the shadows frantically, trying to see if I was missing him standing anywhere. Maybe he walked? But he lived too far from here, so why would he?

I sat down on the edge of the curb, brought my legs up to my chest, and waited.

I nervously rubbed my sweaty hands over my jeans and placed my chin on my knees.

He'd be here.

If I waited, he would come. He said he would.

I would sit here on my own and wait.

I could do that.

For as long as it took.

~

Present...

Today is the day.

I stand outside of the small library and take several calming breaths.

I can do this. I just have to walk inside, sit down, and take the test.

Sliding my hand inside my pocket, I take comfort in feeling the pen in there. My good luck charm.

Ever since Doc gave it to me, things here have been better. I feel stronger, as if I can really move forward, even knowing the truth of my past.

I may not ever know *his* truth, but I know mine, and I'm starting to believe I can accept and live with it. I am a survivor and he wouldn't want me to be anything but that.

I turn the handle and step inside to see Doc standing by the table with a smile.

"Good Morning, Addy."

"Good Morning."

"Are you ready?" he asks me.

Nodding, I walk farther into the room and pull out my seat. He slides the papers over to me and points to the clock.

Nine o'clock.

"It's time."

~

Past...

I checked my watch again, just as I had every fifteen minutes for what seemed like forever.

5:45 a.m.

I'd been waiting for over three-and-a-half hours, and he wasn't here.

Maybe he was just waiting for the right time. Or maybe something happened to him, and he was already being held at the police station.

I wasn't sure, but there had to be a good explanation for why he wasn't waiting for me.

Grayson wouldn't just leave me here.

I got to my feet and brushed off my jeans.

Maybe he was down *at* Daniel's gravesite. I did say to meet me at Daniel's. Maybe he'd misunderstood.

Stepping off the concrete curb, I made my way through the rows of rectangular stone.

As I came up to Daniel's in the far back corner—I saw it.

There, lying on the bottom of the headstone, was a folded piece of paper with *Addison* across the front.

I bit my nail nervously and kneeled down to snatch up the letter. I knew it was from him. It had to be.

But why? Why didn't he wait for me?

With a shaky hand, I unfolded the paper and a black-and-white photograph fell into my lap. *Psyche Revived by Cupid's Kiss.*

When I saw his writing, that same cursive writing he'd first scrawled his name across the chalkboard in, I knew.

This is all he'd left me with.

Addison,

I don't even know how to start this.

Honesty seems the best option right now since you're the only other person who knows what happened between us.

I'm sorry for so many things. Most of all, for not being with you right now. I'm sorry I broke my promise to you and let you down.

You know why I didn't stay and why this can't work. Still, as I sit here writing this, I know I would do it all again for just one more kiss from you.

No one ever told me that loving someone would feel like you were giving up every last part of yourself, but that's how I feel, Addison. From the second I saw you, I was done. I gave it all to you.

Something about you called to me, and I have never regretted you, even as I questioned us.

But, Addison, I'm going away, and I won't be coming back—not ever.

You need to move on. Find a way to be free of your monsters because remember, they will devour you. Just like mine has devoured me.

I ask one thing of you before I go. Please understand that you were never my monster.

You, Addison, will always be my Psyche.

Love G.M

Gone...

He was gone.

Balling up the paper, I lay down with my cheek pressed to the grass covering Daniel and felt what was left of my heart shatter.

Everyone who truly loved me was gone, and as I gazed at the beautiful purple flowers surrounding his headstone, I made a decision.

I would go too.

CHAPTER 33

 resent...

Tick, tick, tock.

The clock is loud in here, not because I'm anxious, but because the silence is deafening. It's been a little over seven hours. In fact, as I look at the clock, I realize it's been seven hours and fifteen minutes since I began.

Studying my final answer, I mark the page and sit back.

I did it.

I feel a smile cross my lips as I realize I've kept my promise, providing of course I pass, which I'm certain I did. The answers had seemed to come easy as I'd been writing them.

I reach into my pocket and pull the pen out.

It *was* good luck—just like I knew it would be.

As I sit there waiting for Doc to arrive, I think about all of the things I want to do when I leave here tomorrow.

Feeling impulsive for the first time in a long while, I reach out and grab the scrap paper beside me. I remove the lid of the pen and write, *Things I want to do,* across the top.

But nothing happens. My good luck pen doesn't work.

I scratch it across the paper several times and still nothing.

I shake it, trying to get ink down into the tip and then realize this type of pen takes cartridges. Gripping the black plastic beneath the golden nib, I twist it open to see if the cartridge is empty. As it comes apart, I tilt it into my hand and watch the contents slip free.

Suddenly, the clock on the wall goes silent, and time once again stops as I stare at what is now in the palm of my hand.

Past...

Lights.

Bright white lights were all I could see as my eyelids fluttered open.

One, two three. One, two three—it's back.

I tried to raise my right arm but it felt heavy, as if it were made of lead, and when I looked down to see why, I saw an IV needle protruding from my skin.

Squinting against the brightness, I looked around the quiet, sterile room, taking in my surroundings.

"Hello, Addison."

Doc.

My throat burned as I swallowed and tried to speak, but nothing came out.

Doc walked over to me and shook his head. "No, don't push yourself. There will be plenty of time to talk later."

Later?

There wasn't supposed to be a later. I was supposed to be...
wait—a hospital? I was in a hospital.

One, two three.

How did I get here? How did they know where to find me?

I had so many questions, but I didn't ask any of them. Instead, I closed my eyes.

None of it mattered.

I was still here, and he was still gone.

Nothing had changed.

～

"Addison…Addison?"

I could hear my mother's voice as I once again opened my eyes. When I saw her standing by my bed, I wondered how much time had passed since I last woke.

"Addison? You need to wake up, young lady. These men want to ask you some questions."

I looked at the door where the two men were standing. One was dressed in a drab grey suit and tie and the other wore a police uniform.

What were the police doing here?

"Good morning, Addison."

I really wished people would stop calling me that. *He* used to call me that.

"I'm Detective Lawson, and this is Officer Davidson. We have a few questions for you."

I wondered if I wished hard enough, if they would disappear. But then the Detective said something that captured my full attention.

"When was the last time you saw or had any contact with Grayson McKendrick?"

Why were they asking me this? How long had I been in the hospital?

"I know you've been a patient for a little over a week, but we need to talk to him, and he's nowhere to be found. I'm sure you can understand why we are here, Miss Lancaster."

One, two three. One, two three.

Couldn't find him? What did they mean?

My mind felt foggy as I tried to remember—*tried* to catch up.

"We've had no luck reaching him on his phone, at the school, or at his home. His truck is gone, and his neighbors haven't seen him for days."

I didn't know what he was talking about.

"When we searched his house, we found something you may understand better than us. Do you feel well enough to look at it?"

I didn't, but I was too curious not to, so I nodded. He passed me a plastic baggie with a piece of paper inside, and when I read the words, I felt my stomach turn.

I went without struggle as I tasted the Queen of Poisons.

"So? Does that mean anything to you?"

Maybe...but nothing I wanted to talk to them about.

What did Grayson mean when he wrote that? What had he done?

"Addison?" My mother's sharp voice cut through my thoughts.

I'd forgotten she was even in the room.

"If you know something, you need to tell these men."

I didn't need to tell them shit, and I knew she could sense my contempt. She looked away from me and refocused her attention on the police in an attempt to explain away my behavior.

"Addison's been through quite an ordeal. She hasn't spoken since she woke. Maybe it's best if you give her some time to think about it?"

Think about it?

I didn't want time to think.

What did he mean, he'd tasted the Queen of Poisons?

The flower or...me?

In the end, it didn't even matter.

He was gone, and I would never see him again.

I couldn't fathom the thought and didn't want to think at all.

One, two, three.

❧

Present...

Sitting in the small library, all I can hear is ringing in my ears as the blood rushes to my head. There in the palm of my hand is a small, square negative.

An old-school *film* negative.

I close my fingers into a loose fist, knowing that whatever this is...whatever secrets were inside this pen—*his pen*—they are meant for me.

What is the picture?

I have to get the print. I need to know.

There is one thing I'm now sure of. He didn't leave me that day.

He freed me.

❧

Past...

"I know you're awake, Addison."

Doc.

I shifted my head on the pillow and saw him walk into my hospital room.

"They're going to transfer you to the Pine Groves Psychiatric Facility in the morning, did you know that?"

Choosing to keep my mouth shut, I watched as he walked farther into my room and pulled a chair beside my bed.

One, two three. One, two, three.

"Your mother had them admit you for thirty days."

Fucking great.

Maybe I'd feel better about it if she were doing it because

she was worried—but she wasn't. She was worried about what her high society friends thought of *her*.

Oh, there goes Mrs. Lancaster. Did you hear her daughter slept with that teacher and then tried to kill herself? No wonder they put her away.

"I agree with this decision," Doc said, breaking through my thoughts.

My eyes widened in surprise at the betrayal of a man I once believed was my ally. As he reached out to me, I snatched my hand away.

"Come on, Addison."

I wished he would stop calling me that.

Doc *never* called me Addison. I was always Addy.

"We were lucky we found you the other morning. I think this is for the best right now."

I had nothing to say.

Apparently, I was the only one left to protect me, so I would retreat.

I would hide until it was safe again for me to come out—no matter how long that took.

∽

Present...

"All done?"

I turn to see Doc walking through the door of the library. After sliding the negative back into the pen, I slip it into my pocket and stand.

"Yes. All done."

Doc's smile is contagious as he beams proudly and places his hands behind his back. "Good, Addy. That's terrific. How do you feel?"

Right now I feel anxious, excited and full of adrenaline, and none of it has to do with the papers on the table behind me but rather the secret in my pocket.

A secret that came from *him*, which had been given to me by…

"Doc?" I ask as I make my way over to him.

"Yes, Addy?"

"When you ask me questions, you always ask me not to lie."

"Yes, that's true."

"If I ask you something, will you tell me the truth?"

He regards me for a moment before he replies. "I will. If I'm able."

Holding up Grayson's pen, I watch Doc's eyes move to it.

"You said Grayson gave this to you."

He says nothing as he continues looking from the pen to me.

"When?"

"The day I gave it to you," he says, and my mind begins to race.

He gave this to me only recently, a little over a *week* ago.

I throw caution out the window as I stare up at the man who'd told me I *needed* to trust him. I do trust him, and I just hope this isn't a mistake because I have to know.

"How do you know it's from Grayson?"

"Well, with the initials on the pen, it wasn't that much of a leap, Addy."

I step back and begin pacing.

"Why…" I start and then stop, rethinking my question. "How did you know it was for me?"

Doc walks over to me and takes my arm, stopping me in my tracks. "It came with something else."

I wonder for a moment if he knows about the negative.

"It was addressed to my home office, Addy. I didn't recognize the name of the sender, and when I opened it, I found the pen and a note that read, *'It wasn't good, and it wasn't evil—it was just love. She deserves love. Make her understand. Take care of her, Doc.'*

That first part is a play on a quote from Nietzsche, did you know that?"

I try to take it all in, but my heart is thundering so hard in my chest I'm surprised Doc can't hear it.

"You quoted Nietzsche to me, also. That's not a coincidence, is it?"

There's no use denying anything anymore, and I am beyond being evasive. I just want to know…"Where did it come from? The envelope, was there a return address?"

"*Addison*," Doc warns. "Whatever you're thinking, *really* think it through. He sent the pen to you later, I'm assuming when he thought you were ready, and that's when I gave it to you. To encourage you. To give you strength."

I grin up at Doc.

He doesn't know it, but he has given me much more than that and so has Grayson.

Grayson doesn't just want me happy. He wants to tell me something, and I am more than ready to listen.

CHAPTER 34

The Here & Now...

Release day. It is finally here.

It feels like I've been at Pine Groves for thirty years, not days. A knock sounds on my door and I see Doc step inside. I know that it's thanks to this man that it has *only* been thirty days.

"Good Morning, Addy."

"Hey, Doc," I tell him as I start to fold my clothes.

"Big day for you today."

Nodding, I walk past him to pick up a sweater that's sitting on the small set of drawers in here.

"Yes. I'm ready."

"Are you?" he asks, making me turn to face him.

"Another test?" I joke with a grin.

"No, a legitimate question. Are you ready, Addy?"

"Yes," I assure him and pick up my sweater. I walk back to where he's standing and place a hand on his arm. "I feel good."

"Okay. So you have your prescriptions and my number if you need anything?"

I squeeze his arm and smile, feeling happy tears spring to my eyes.

Doc is the one person in my life I can count on, and I know he'll always be there for me. Somewhere along the way, he'd reached me. Just as he is with his family, he's also my rock—the one person that grounds me.

"I've got it," I promise and step around him to finish packing.

"Your mom sent a cab."

Glancing over my shoulder, I raise a brow. "Why am I not surprised?"

"I can give you a lift home, Addy."

I stretch across the bed to take down the photograph on my wall, and as my fingers graze Cupids wings, I suddenly have an idea.

"I need to stop somewhere on the way."

I turn back to face Doc and hold up the photo. "I want to get a new copy of this. Would you mind if we stop at the camera store?"

Doc reaches out and takes the crinkled photo from me.

"Psyche."

"Yes," I murmur. My love for this photo and the memories that go with it are some of my most treasured.

Doc slips his hand into one of his pockets and pulls out an envelope, handing it to me. I feel my heart almost stop as I recognize what he's giving me—my letter.

Grayson's letter.

I take it from him with a trembling hand and look up at him, my mind full of questions. I'd thought this letter was lost when all I'd woken up here with was the photo…but *no*.

Doc knew all along about Grayson. About me. About *us*.

"The morning I found you, you were clutching this as if your life depended on it, and Addy…it did."

Confused, I bring the letter closer to me and feel my heart start to beat again.

"I got a call early that morning. The person didn't say who they were, just that they saw you going into the Oakwood Cemetery. It was obvious they were worried about you, and you shouldn't have been out at that time."

I stare at Doc, disbelieving. *Is he telling me what I think he is?*

"I knew that was where Daniel was buried, Addy. I knew the call was about you, and when I got there and found you on the ground..."

Doc shakes his head and brings his hand up to rub his face.

"It was like seeing one of my daughters lying there. You were so still...I thought I was too late. But then I saw your hands move with your chest as you took a breath, and...that was when I called the ambulance."

I sit down on the bed with the letter tight in my hands.

"You had that"—he points to the envelope—"in your hands. I picked you up and carried you out of those flowers and then took the note from you. I read it, Addy, because God, I thought maybe you had written a suicide note. I soon realized it was from your "friend," the one you had spoken to me about. Grayson."

I open the envelope and pull the crumpled letter free. A second piece of paper falls out with it—the note Doc said came with the pen. Both letters are in the same cursive writing. That's how Doc had known for sure whom it had come from.

All of Doc's questions, all of the clues, are like one giant puzzle.

I run my fingers over Grayson's words and wonder what it all means. Another thought then comes to me.

"Why didn't you give it to the police?"

Doc walks over and sits on the bed beside me. He doesn't look my way as I turn to him.

"We all have choices to make in our life, Addy. Right or wrong."

Yes, I remember those parts of our sessions.

"Well, I had a choice to make when I found that. Could I

use it to help you? Or did I give it to people who would eventually use it in a way that would set you back?"

What Doc is telling me is unbelievable. No one has ever done something so selfless for me.

"You needed the pen and the letter to heal. Just as Cupid revived Psyche with a kiss, *he* revived you with words. Every single word he wrote in that letter helped *me* to help *you*. He reached you, even though he wasn't here."

I tremble as I touch the paper in my lap, remembering how broken I'd felt when I first read those words, but now...now it felt like—

"He saved you after all," Doc spoke softly, finishing my thought.

I put my head on Doc's shoulder and whisper the only words I can manage. "Thank you."

I sit in the front of Doc's black SUV and buckle my seat belt as we pull away from Pine Groves. I feel a sense of freedom washing over me as the air rushes in through the windows.

Finally, I'm free.

Doc is driving me to the camera store and then we will head to my house. On his back seat is the one bag I'd had dropped off for the past thirty days, and in my hand I hold the letters he'd given me in my room. The only mystery left is inside the pen in my pocket.

He pulls the car up to the front of the store, and I jump out. "I'll just be a few minutes."

"Take your time. I have my book."

He nods at me, trusting me, and though I hate deceiving him, I need to know what's on that negative. I pull open the door and make my way to the front desk. A woman with jet-black hair and eyeliner to match approaches me and smiles.

"Hi. How can I help you?"

I take the pen from my pocket and unscrew it. Looking over my shoulder, I check to see that no one's around before tipping it upside down on the counter.

"Oh cool!" she says as the negative falls out.

"Right?"

"Yeah, very double agent." She laughs, and I see the flash of a tongue ring.

"Can you develop it?" I ask.

I want to know what's on the negative, but I'm also terrified to find out.

"I can. It'll take a few minutes."

"That's fine. Oh, and can I also get a copy of this?"

I place the old photo I've had on my wall down on the counter.

She picks up both objects and tells me yes and then walks out to a back room.

I go and sit on one of the chairs against the wall and start to bite my nail.

Nervous habit?

Oh God. I can hear him in my head, see him in my mind, and with the negative and his letter in my possession, I have more hope than I've ever had before. I pull out the small note he'd sent to Doc with the pen.

It wasn't good, and it wasn't evil—it was just love. She deserves love. Make her understand. Take care of her, Doc.

Where was he when he wrote this? I need to know.

Grayson's right.

What we had was as simple and as complicated as love could be. We were two people who were perfectly suited and met at exactly the wrong time.

"Hey there."

I look over to where the girl has come back out behind the counter. Jumping to my feet, I rush over and notice she is frowning at me.

"Here's your copy," she tells me and hands me the reproduced photograph of Cupid and Psyche. She then pushes the second photo over to me—the photo from the negative.

"This is what appeared from the negative. It's a photo of the same sculpture you have there, but whoever took it didn't get out of the light. There's a shadow on the side and there are also some numbers scratched into the film. If you ask me, this other copy is so much better. The quality and so on."

I pick up the photo and hold it up.

There, right in front of me, is Grayson.

Oh, he'd been clever. All you could see was his shadow on the wall behind the sculpture, but I knew it was him. He was okay. Then I saw the numbers down in the corner, but they were tiny.

"Can I have this one blown up?"

The girl shrugs.

"Sure."

When she comes back with the enlarged copy, I grab it with eager hands. I study the numbers this time; there are six of them. I read them over and over. *What are they?*

"Okay, that's nineteen dollars and sixty-two cents."

I give her the only credit card I own and then begin to fold the photo so I can push it into my pocket. The look of horror on her face almost makes me laugh. I didn't want to frame this picture, I wanted to work it out.

This is yet another clue in this puzzle.

I run back out to the car and hop inside.

"Get it?"

I nod and pull out the copy to show him. All the while the six numbers are running through my head.

Doc pulls out of the lot and begins the drive to my house. When we pull up, I notice my mom's car is gone.

Nice, she isn't even here to welcome me home.

I unbuckle my seat belt and reach back to grab my bag. I push open the door and look back at Doc, realizing that he is the only person that knows the answer to the one question that remains.

"Doc?"

"Yes, Addy?"

"Where did the pen and note come from?"

He gives me a slight smile and finally tells me.

"France. The return address was a nonexistent one in France. I checked it out."

France?

I guess I shouldn't be surprised. Grayson loves Europe. It makes sense that he would go back. Why did I think that photo had been taken anywhere else?

But where in France? Where is that sculpture on display?

Now I have a new direction to look in.

"So, will I see you on Wednesday for our session?" Doc asks.

I purposely evade the question and give him a bright smile. "Thanks, Doc. For everything."

He knows me though, and even as his eyes narrow, I see the side of his mouth twitch.

"Of course, Addy. Keep my number, you hear me?"

I feel an ache in my heart as I think about what I want. If I do this, I don't know when I'll see Doc again.

Unable to find the words to tell this man what he means to me, I lean across the car and kiss his cheek. "Stay happy."

He brushes a hand over my hair and replies, "You too."

Once I'm back inside my home, I sprint up to my room and boot up my laptop. As I wait, I pull out the photo and run my fingers over the shadow—Grayson.

His arms are bent and it's clear he's holding the camera. I wish I could see him. But at least I have this, which is more than I had yesterday, or the day before that. I also have these numbers...

My computer beeps, indicating it's ready, and when I look up, I see it. At the top of the monitor is the date—made up of six numbers.

Snatching up the photo, I read the digits again and feel my pulse speed up.

It's a date! That's what's on the photo he's given me...a *future* date.

I open the Internet and the first thing I type in is, *Psyche Revived by Cupid's Kiss*. I hit enter and sit back, waiting.

I can barely breathe as I wait for the page to load the results, and then...there it is. The first entry is exactly what I've been hoping for.

A closer look at *Psyche Revived by Cupid's Kiss* at the *Musée du Louvre.*

The Louvre—Paris, France.

I look back at the photo beside my keyboard, and instantly I know. *This* is exactly what Grayson is telling me.

I can't believe I'm standing here.

People brush by me from every direction, and I grab the handle of my suitcase with shaky hands. My eyes seek out the information I'm looking for and then it flashes on the screen.

United Airlines, Denver to Paris – 7:10 a.m. Gate B52.

I roll my luggage to the check-in line. As I wait, I close my eyes and think about the photo and letters in my carry-on.

Am I doing the right thing? I'm not sure, but as I get closer to the desk, all I can think about is the date on the bottom of the photo. It's for two days from now.

"Miss?"

The brunette behind the counter is calling my name, and I blush as I step forward.

"Yes? I'm sorry," I apologize, feeling slightly scattered.

"No problem. How can I help you?"

I look at the board again and can't help the smile I give.

"I'd like a one-way ticket on the seven ten flight to Paris, please."

"Sure thing. Can I please see your passport?"

I nod and take out the passport my mother made me get last year when she'd decided we should have a *family* vacation. I've still never used it.

The lady behind the desk swipes it, and as she starts to type in my information, she asks, "A one-way ticket, huh? Leaving it up to fate? I like that."

I swallow, feeling nervous. "Yeah, something like that."

She chuckles as she passes me back my documents.

"You'll love it. It's such a beautiful city and so romantic. Maybe you'll have an epic love affair!"

I feel my heart skip at her words and wonder if I'll get my happy ending.

After everything I've been through, it feels as if my dreams are right there…almost within my reach.

"Okay, the ticket is $789.00. How would you like to pay for that?"

Oh, I know exactly how I'd like to pay for that.

I open my wallet and pull out the cash my mother kept hidden in her drawer. Now she'll really have something to miss, because I know for a fact she sure as hell won't miss me.

"Cash, please."

I give her the money, and several moments later, she hands me the ticket.

"Have a fantastic trip. I hope you find what you're looking for."

"Thanks," I say, and all I can think as I make my way to my gate is—*so do I.*

EPILOGUE

*T*he Louvre—Paris, France...

Thirty-seven days.

That's how long it's been since I've seen her.

I wait at the back of the loud exhibit hall and watch as people shuffle through to look at the sculpture in the center. All I can hear is the—*tick, tick, tock*—of the watch fastened around my wrist.

I glance down at it and see that it's been nearly three hours.

Three hours since the front doors have opened, and three hours that I've been waiting.

I'll wait all day and all night, if that's what it takes.

Raising a hand, I push my fingers through my hair which is finally starting to grow out, and that's when I see her.

She steps into the room I'm standing in, and all of the noise surrounding me disappears.

All I can see—is *her*.

She looks as perfect as the first day I ever saw her.

Her hair is curled in soft waves flowing down over her black coat, and she's clutching what looks like a photograph—*my* photograph.

My instinct is to call out to her, but I wait.

I wait and watch as she looks around, her eyes moving over the people near her and when she stops, I know she's seen it. Psyche and Cupid in their lover's embrace.

She seems drawn to the marble couple in the center of the room, and I see her raise a hand to her chest and place it over her heart as she approaches.

I can hardly believe my own eyes—she's here.

I step out from behind the sculpture and all I can manage is her name. "Addison."

Her stunning blue eyes find me, and as she looks my way, all I can think is...

There she is, staring at me—my salvation, and my new beginning.

ACKNOWLEDGMENTS

Thank you to Donna and Jen for working around my crazy schedule and beta reading over several days. It was much appreciated.

I would also like to thank Kristin, whose professional insight only added to what it was I was trying to say.

Xx Ella

ALSO BY ELLA FRANK

The Exquisite Series

Exquisite

Entice

Edible

The Temptation Series

Try

Take

Trust

Tease

Tate

True

Confessions Series

Confessions: Robbie

Confessions: Julien

Confessions: Priest

Confessions: The Princess, The Prick & The Priest

Confessions: Henri

Confessions: Bailey

Confessions: Ethan

Confessions: Zayne

Confessions: Chloé

Prime Time Series

Inside Affair

Breaking News

Headlines

Intentions Duet

Bad Intentions

Good Intentions

Chicago Heat Duet

Wicked Heat

Wicked Flame

Sunset Cove Series

Finley

Devil's Kiss

Masters Among Monsters Series

Alasdair

Isadora

Thanos

Standalones

Blind Obsession

Veiled Innocence

PresLocke Series
Co-Authored with Brooke Blaine

Aced

Locked

Wedlocked

Fallen Angel Series
Co-Authored with Brooke Blaine

Halo

Viper

Angel

An Affair In Paris

Lust. Hate. Love

Elite Series

Co-Authored with Brooke Blaine

Danger Zone

Need For Speed

Classified

Dare To Try Series

Co-Authored with Brooke Blaine

Dare You

Dare Me

Truth Or Dare

Malvagio Series

Co-Authored with Brooke Blaine

Forbidden Mafia Prince

Sinful Mafia Prince

Park Avenue Princes

Co-Authored with Brooke Blaine

Infamous Park Avenue Prince

Insatiable Park Avenue Prince

Scandalous Park Avenue Prince

Possessive Park Avenue Prince

Salacious Park Avenue Prince

www.ingramcontent.com/pod-product-compliance
Lightning Source LLC
LaVergne TN
LVHW092321060425
807897LV00008B/91